T0193830

MORE PRAISE FOR *MEETING THE OTHER CROWD*

"Eddie Lenihan's book offers wonderful glimpses of a world we need to re-cover and reimagine."

—JOHN O' DONOHUE, author of *Anam Cara*

"Read these stories, not at your peril but to your delight, whether young or old."

—DAN R. BARBER, *The Dallas Morning News*

"Lenihan presents his tales with gusto, respect, and conviction. His stories are bite-sized but memorable morsels. His voice fairly breathes authenticity arising from three decades of collection and cherishing legends and lore."

—JOSEPH P. MCMENAMIN, *Richmond Times-Dispatch*

"Endearing."

—PIPER JONES CASTILLO, *St. Petersburg Times*

"Intriguing . . . This fairy folklore is in danger of passing away, as are the storytellers, says Lenihan, who is determined to capture this 'hidden Ireland' before it's gone."

—VIRGINIA ROHAN, *The Record* (Bergen County, NJ)

"This is a book that will make you think twice the next time someone asks you if you believe in the wee folk."

—TRISHA PING, *The Sun* (Gainesville, FL)

Eddie Lenihan

WITH *Carolyn Eve Green*

The Fairy Stories of Hidden Ireland

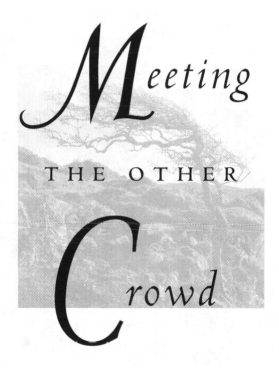

Meeting

THE OTHER

Crowd

JEREMY P. TARCHER / PENGUIN

a member of Penguin Group (USA) Inc.

New York

Jeremy P. Tarcher/Penguin
a member of
Penguin Group (USA) Inc.
375 Hudson Street
New York, NY 10014
www.penguin.com

The Library of Congress catalogued the hardcover edition as follows:

Meeting the other crowd : the fairy stories of hidden Ireland / [collected
and edited] by Eddie Lenihan with Carolyn Eve Green.
p.   cm.
ISBN 1-58542-206-1
1. Fairies—Ireland.   2. Fairy tales—Ireland.   3. Tales—Ireland.
I. Lenihan, Edmund.   II. Green, Carolyn Eve.
GR153.5.M44   2003   2002031985
398.2'09417—dc21

ISBN 1-58542-307-6 (Paperback edition)

Book design by Jennifer Ann Daddio

To all those tellers now gone

WHOSE VOICES ARE NOT FORGOTTEN,

and to those still with us

WHOSE KNOWLEDGE IS MORE

INDISPENSABLE THAN EVER

Contents

PART ONE

"The Queerest Thing I Ever Saw"

WHO THEY ARE AND WHAT THEY WANT

PART TWO

"There Since the Start o' the World"

FAIRY PLACES AND SIGNS
OF THEIR PRESENCE

PART THREE

"Their Own Way of Collecting"

GIFTS, PUNISHMENT, AND OTHER
OUTCOMES OF FAIRY ENCOUNTERS

Author's Note

The stories here have been gathered from oral sources. In capturing the words of Irish elders, we have tried as much as possible to preserve the tone, style, and syntax of the speaker. Where changes have been made, they are only to clarify the speaker's intent or occasionally substitute an English term for an Irish one. While the locales are real, some people's names have been omitted or changed to protect the privacy of the sources.

Editor's Preface

BY CAROLYN EVE GREEN

MEETING EDDIE LENIHAN cannot be entirely unlike en-
countering one of Them. Certainly our finding each other had
a touch of magical coincidence. And, like an unaware citizen
stumbling upon a fairy place, I carried with me that uncertainty, anxiety, and curiosity that keeps us transfixed even as our
instincts of self-preservation tell us to flee to safer ground. Just
as you may, in reading this remarkable collection of stories,
come to understand a few of the basic codes of conduct for ap-
proaching Them, I came to realize that Eddie would not with-
stand any of my simpleminded American assumptions about
the fascination of Irish fairy lore. Perhaps as the humans are
to the fairies, so is a youthful American woman of media to
an Irishman standing watchfully at the threshold of an old and
new world.

One fine summer morning, over our usual infusion of Chi-
nese tea, my husband, Ken, and I were discussing our ongoing
search for authentic storytellers and the purchase of a tree for
our front entrance. The search for storytellers arose from our
production of an audio series for children, *Secrets of the World,*
which had been our full-time obsession for nearly two years.
As for the tree, well, what kind of tree would both invite guests
and protect boundaries, produce flowers in spring and display

autumn color, and survive the Colorado climate? Ken, meanwhile, had opened the *New York Times* to an article titled "If You Believe in Fairies, Don't Bulldoze Their Lair." Beneath this appeared a picture of Eddie Lenihan standing in front of a rather modest looking hawthorn tree—soon to be the solution to both of our current conundrums.

Inspired by the article and an unexpected plethora of hawthorn trees at the nursery, we did purchase a hawthorn tree that very day. A few days later, while recording tales from the Black Sea with Laura Simms (a storyteller extraordinaire), we asked Laura if she knew of an Irishman named Eddie Lenihan.

"Eddie! He would be wonderful for this series. I have his phone number right here," she said, without a moment's hesitation. "Let's give him a call." And so we did. He answered the telephone right off and a tentative meeting of minds began.

In the months before his scheduled arrival for recording in Colorado, my anxiety grew. We exchanged a few letters in preparation for the recording project. I quickly saw that he had many worthy battles to fight and the mere hint of compromise, of reshaping the tales he had so meticulously collected over twenty-seven years to cater to American notions about what is suitable for children, turned his responses to ice. Hopefully it is now clear that I was never interested in compromise, but in providing enough cultural translation for that project so that the truths of the stories could reach the ears of American children and so that their value might not be overlooked by cautious or literal-minded parents. In many ways, we were both three steps ahead of each other. Only through Ken's reassurances to me and his conviction in the great value of the project was I able to keep a steady course until Eddie's arrival.

The morning before he was scheduled to fly in, the phone rang. Ken answered to Eddie's voice, agitated and cursing under his breath about a ten-hour flight delay out of Ireland—and who could blame him for being frustrated, this man who can't possibly find enough hours in the year to complete the work he sets for himself? For my part, I had created a rather imposing, macho figure of this man, which Ken's well-humored account of the morning phone call only heightened. I was near literally holding my breath until we should meet.

The moment we met, beside the baggage claim carousel at Denver International Airport, my conviction in my own powers of projection dissolved. Here he stood, only a few inches taller than me, compact, intense, tentative and firm at once.

If you have never been to this airport, it is worth going sometime just to witness the scale and strangeness of this massive tentlike structure that has been erected as a model for future hubs of air travel. With its white peaked rooftop, glass walls, multicultural murals with hidden symbols, gargoyles guarding automated doorways, and computerized voices announcing stops on the underground train that transports you from the gates to the terminal, DIA is designed to future shock. (It certainly overwhelmed me when I arrived in Colorado from our previous home in Nova Scotia a few years ago.) Picture a lone hawthorn bush with a venerable history of sheltering armies of fairies that somehow refuses to be felled in a field ransacked by developers and you might have some idea of what it was like to encounter Eddie Lenihan in the middle of DIA. He stood there, just like the tree he had recently protected from developers in his homeland, small and sturdy, holding back the tide of modernity, and utterly refusing to be intimidated.

We three exchanged some words about the absurdity of the mechanized world and the mounting obstacles we all face in the name of convenience, establishing a baseline of camaraderie. He checked us both, head to toe, gave a strong handshake, and the work began.

The Irish have learned to use many indirect names for the Good People, so as not to offend them by being too forward. Just so, I learned in the recording studio to approach Eddie with both delicacy and honesty—careful not to jar his intense concentration on the stories, but waiting for those in-between moments, whenever they might suddenly arise, where a question could be asked and its inevitably candid answer brought back into the fold.

It was soon evident that the few tales he shared for children in those three days of recording were merely a hint of what resides in his treasury. Soon after he returned to Ireland, I phoned and asked him if he might be willing to collaborate on a project for adults that would allow us to unearth far more of his collection and bring it to a large audience. To my delight, he agreed, and this book is the result.

One never knows how much is safe or appropriate to reveal in a writing that will go to press. And so it must be with each one of the storytellers whose accounts appear in this book. At what point is too much said? One must find the means of transmitting the essence of the story without violating what is, by nature of the encounter, secret and delicate. So it is with writing about Eddie. Suffice it to say that after three days in the studio together there was no doubt in my mind that he is more than a memorizer of great tales. He is a transmitter of that other world—fearless, respectful and, I daresay, choicelessly chosen to be so. We never had a recording session like that, before or since. Perhaps, if the time and circumstances are right, the details could be written elsewhere. Do not think for a moment, though, that Eddie himself will abide these words without argument. Deeply modest and devoted to his tradition, when I first asked Eddie whether or not he believed in the fairies he simply looked at me and said, "Well, all I can tell you is that I know of many things that cannot be explained." That, again, appears to be part of the code of conduct. So, as you read these ordinary and outrageous tales, leave aside the mind that is merely interested in dissecting cultural anomalies and, by all means, do not rush headlong hoping to find some gimmick for accessing another dimension. Go wakefully, cautiously. Steady yourself, and the magic will happen by itself in the most subtle and ordinary way.

Introduction

ONE MIGHT SENSIBLY ASK, "Is another book on Irish fairies really necessary?" since there are many already in circulation. My answer would have to be that, firstly, there are not really as many as might seem, and secondly, that most of those in existence are merely rehashes ad nauseam of the same old ingredients. And also, as often as not, the tales are presented in an unorganized fashion and as entertainment, mainly for children.

At first I, like many another, enjoyed these stories and the often grotesque idiosyncratic illustrations that accompanied them. But there came a time when I grew tired of the same old thing, particularly once I had, in the mid-1970s, begun to go out and talk to aged Irish people throughout the Irish countryside.

What I found astonished me. For here, still alive, was a world I knew next to nothing about, a hidden Ireland, a land of mysterious taboos, dangers, otherworldly abductions, enchantments, and much more. I was immediately hooked, and ever since, I have been busy following up every lead, trying to discover ever more about this parallel Ireland which most Irish people acknowledge exists, but which few of them, except the very oldest or professional folklorists, know much about.

The astonishing thing is that it does still exist, into the twenty-first century, in spite of attacks from all sides. The Catholic Church has not approved of belief in it since its own doctrine clashes with fairy belief on many important points. The state, mainly in the form of the National School system, until very recently has done its best to convince its charges that such "superstitious nonsense" was a throwback to an age of ignorance, that what was needed today was facts, numbers, enlightenment. And, more recently still, the IT revolution has made a sincere belief in such a world seem almost simpleminded.

Yet an undeniable fact is that genuine fairy stories still exert a fascination over young and old alike when told. Not read. Told. In my travels all over Europe and the U.S.A., telling these tales that I have collected personally over the years, I have time and time again been amazed by the reaction of people who could have no connection to—hardly even knowledge of—the places I was referring to: Corbally fort, Rathclooney Lake, The Hand, Tulla old graveyard, places that in themselves were insignificant—except for one thing: They all have a story attached to them, a story that sets them apart always and forever from every other place in the much-storied Irish landscape.

"Forever"? I, though no sociologist or anthropologist, could see, as I continued my collecting, that there was a looming problem. For as Ireland's modernization gained pace from the 1980s on, and as the old people were listened to with less and less attention and appreciation, this ancient lore began to wither. The death in 1983 of Jack "Donaleen" Leahy, my first great teacher/teller, at the age of ninety-three, shocked me into the realization that even the toughest fall at last. His death gave me the title for my third book, *Even Iron Men Die,* and he is still a landmark in my collecting career. I can never forget him, for he provided me with the sine qua non of folklore collecting: a sense of wonder, a doorway into a different world, a different way of seeing things. And it is this gift, if I may call it that, that has kept me collecting ever since, even when common sense and economics dictated that I spend my time and money on more profitable pursuits.

Yet profit can sometimes be measured in terms other than the economic, and time is something that does not come our way twice, so I have made a very conscious choice: to follow old Irish stories to wherever they are to be found, particularly stories of the fairy world—and this for practical reasons. For I have found by experience that wherever fairy stories are to be discovered one will inevitably find more besides, whereas if there is no knowledge of the fairies one may be reasonably sure that there is little else of old lore of other kinds, either. It is one of those things the years of collecting have taught me, a sort of yardstick I use now almost automatically.

But fairy stories, what are they? Fictions for children? Entertainment to pass long winters' nights? Or something more?

It can be said at once that they are mainly not for children. They are far too serious, too complicated for that.

Certainly they were to pass long, dark nights when electricity was either not there or a novelty, and they did so admirably. And in the process they provided something else, too—a sense of continuity with an immemorial past, as well as giving due respect to those present who could contribute something venerable, exciting, interesting to the occasion.

But that intimate Ireland has all but passed away. Within a single lifetime Ireland has changed from a predominantly rural to a mainly urban society. This fact underlies all. Old people, the tradition-bearers, have become virtual exiles in their own land, disregarded, unvalued. Old lore is no longer passed on, this for a complex of reasons. Partly it is a belief among older people themselves that they are ignorant in comparison to the new "schooled" generation. And yet those same old people have a fierce pride in their specialized knowledge from times past. But so much of it is now seen as useless in practical terms, a museum piece only, a subject for nostalgia—"the good old days," e.g., horse lore, hay making, hand turf cutting, house dances, stations, blessed-well pilgrimages, American wakes, so many trades (smith, shoemaker, tailor, harness maker, weaver, cooper, basket maker, thatcher).

There are no tinkers traveling in the old way any more. Their trade (tinsmith) is no longer needed because of the prevalence of plastic. They've moved to towns, where their presence is much resented.

There are no traveling beggar men or women now, either. These were the people who brought stories and ballads from place to place and entertained in return for their overnight keep. Traveling gangs of railway linesmen did the same. But many of the railway lines, especially those in the west, have been closed.

Cattle fairs are no more, replaced by large, bureaucratic cattle marts. These street fairs attracted all kinds of performers, e.g., ballad singers, reciters, musicians, fortune-tellers, etc. All gone!

Local race meetings and hare-coursing meets are few and far between now, with the same result.

Poteen making is almost extinct: There's no need for it when everyone can afford whiskey.

Religious beliefs of the older, formal kind have loosened, declined, with a consequent near disappearance of their outward manifestations, e.g., benediction, sodalities, processions, the rosary, holy pictures, statues, etc.

Fairy belief has declined almost in tandem with these.

Education and means of travel and roads have improved enormously, therefore people's attentions aren't confined to their own localities anymore. Also, education, down the years, tended to frown on *real* fairy lore and belief, since most education was church controlled. Nowadays, education merely ignores the matter.

Media pressures have grown vastly, especially in the last decade or so. Advertising is now inescapable, all-pervasive.

The factual has become ever more pressing (rules, regulations of all kinds) at the expense of the imaginative. That it has had an enervating effect is odd, since our parents and grandparents had to be very factual to survive, yet they retained a vivid faculty for the nonfactual, too.

The fields, the roads, aren't being walked nearly as much anymore. One might travel fifty miles at night now in rural Ireland and never meet a single pedestrian. The younger generation knows practically nothing about the *personal* landscape around them, despite plenty of "environmental education" in school.

Cuaird (night visiting) is gone and, with it, storytelling.

Meitheal (communal farmwork) is gone, with the growth of the money economy and the consequent ability to buy services and machinery.

The coming of electricity (including free phones for old-age pensioners) pushed back the frontiers of night, of the dark. This has had a huge effect on people's attitudes towards night-time (when most supernatural occurrences were felt to happen).

Most things have become immediate—light, heat, communication, food. This has changed people's perspectives on time. Yet, ironically, today people constantly complain of never having enough time.

The invasion of quiet, personal time and places by technology (mobile phones, Walkmans, and especially television) has been relentless.

Practically no one grows food for personal use now, or keeps pigs for bacon, so *piseógs* have declined—and *piseógs* were very related to the otherworldly—as well as closeness to the land.

Place names and their attached lore are practically gone (field names, river-pool names, etc.).

Calendar custom is very much attenuated.

Local loyalties have been largely (though by no means wholly) superseded by the international (e.g., Manchester United), maybe because the local hasn't the glamour, the profile, that wealth can bring—as well as the media attention!

The retreat of local democracy and services (e.g., court-houses, shops, police stations, post offices) brings decline and a sense of despair to small, rural communities, while fast-growing urban areas absorb more than their share of what the public purse can provide. The huge and relentless expansion of towns has become more and more pronounced, drawing the younger generation from rural areas.

There has been a precipitate decline in family size, first with contraception, latterly because of the expense of child rearing. Now we have the irony of huge, hotel-sized private houses springing up all over Ireland, lived in by only parents plus one or two children, whereas previously it was mainly the opposite: small houses, huge family. Once, it was children that demonstrated status; now it's house, car, holiday.

It is against this background that I have worked at the urgent task of collecting (on audiotape and, in more recent years, on video) what remains. And it has been a rich harvest, though one diminishing at an alarming and steady rate, since in the Ireland of today, inhospitable to most of what fairy belief represents, no new tellers of the tales are emerging and the older ones are inevitably dying off.

This collection is different from most existing books on the fairies, in that it is based entirely on oral sources, and I have collected all the stories myself. I do not claim that my compilation is exhaustive, but it gives a fair indication of what is still available today, or was until very recently. I do not attempt to cover all of Ireland, and this is deliberate. First, I did not have the resources. Second, in confining myself largely to the southwest (i.e., Clare, Limerick, Kerry, parts of south Galway), I am in the part of Ireland I know best. Yet, it still gives a fair indication of what might be available if a thorough search of all of Ireland were conducted. It is vital that this work should be presented now, for though there has never been an era without change, the present one has seen unimaginable shifts in all kinds of attitudes and within an unprecedentedly short time. A sure sign of this is when those living in a society thus changing are vividly aware of it—and not by any means just its oldest members.

If there are distortions in this book I hope they will be confined mainly to this introduction, since in the body of it I have let my informants speak for themselves, something they are remarkably well able to do, in all their variety. But who are these people? Rural for the most part, farmers, fishermen, tradespeople, laborers. Some of them did not necessarily believe what they were telling me, whereas others' belief was unshakable (not that I tried to shake it, but by the questions I asked I was able to ascertain clearly enough their frame of mind).

Which brings me to the matter of skepticism. I am constantly surprised how few *convinced* skeptics there are in Ireland (rural Ireland, at least, though I suspect the same is true in towns and cities). I make a habit of telling at least some fairy stories every time I have a telling session nowadays, in order to get reaction from members of the audience afterwards—and I never cease to be amazed at how willing most of them are to discuss the subject, often mockingly (in a friendly way) at first, but almost inevitably this soon develops into a litany of personal experiences, or heard ones, of the supernatural/otherworldly/ "strange." I can categorically say that never have I encountered a hostile group on this subject, though I have actively searched out such people. It is a subject that fascinates Irish people of most ages and shades of opinion—so long as they are approached on the matter with a sense of urgency, frankness, and conviction, and with no hint of jocularity or concession to levity (because, paradoxically, this is what they expect, sooner or later—"You're only joking, aren't you!").

In strange pubs, after sessions, I usually go and mix with the audience, get their immediate reactions, opinions. In nearly every case they *want* to listen, are delighted to be reminded (if they are middle-aged or old) of material familiar from their younger days, which they haven't heard much of in recent times, and if they're younger (say, eighteen to thirty) fascinated by something they have never been told much about at all. And many of these younger people I meet are angry that they have been deprived of these stories, and want to know why.

I enjoy very much seeing such people beginning to question what they have always taken for granted; i.e., that these things were only for children, that they were old-fashioned, "stupid," out-of-date, and all the other epithets that apply to the scarcely known.

In February of this year I was at Dublin Airport in freezing conditions, with only the driver in an otherwise empty bus, waiting for air passengers who never showed up because all flights had been canceled due to the bad weather. Rather than just sit there, we made small talk for a while. Then he asked me, almost apologetically, "Haven't I seen your face before, someplace?"

"Probably," I said. "Maybe telling stories somewhere."

"That's it!" He was excited now.

"I knew it! You're the lad that do be talking about the fairies." Then he became serious.

"But do you believe all that ol' stuff, huh?"

"I do," I replied directly. No point in beating about the bush on a subject like this, as I've found through long experience.

"An' d'you think They're there?"

I could sense he was between laughter and indecision.

"I do. In fact I have no doubt at all about it."

He drummed his fingers on the steering wheel, stared blankly out onto the snowy bus park, thinking. It was obvious that he was trying to make up his mind whether he should tell me something or not. To help him, I briefly told him several of my own experiences with old people I had spoken to over the years. He listened to what I had to say of fairy forts,* paths, bushes. And, as soon as I mentioned these fairy bushes, *sceachs,* he interrupted me.

"Did you ever see the tree near the mart in Claremorris?" And for the next five minutes he told me all about it, how on several occasions attempts had been made to cut it down, all ending in misfortune. He finished by advising me to go see it for myself if I didn't believe him.

I said I would, and I probably will. I have no reason to disbelieve that the bush is there, though I reserve judgment on its "fairyness" until I inquire further into it.

*A circular enclosure surrounded by an earthen bank on which whitethorn (hawthorn) bushes often grow. Often also called a "lios" or "rath" and giving its name to very many Irish places (e.g., Listowel, Rathmore). To archaeologists it is known as a "ringfort" because of its shape. Such forts vary in size from circa a quarter to circa an acre in extent. There are over 45,000 of them throughout Ireland.

But this is not the main point here. The point is that there I was, with this stranger, and because I replied firmly to what might otherwise have been merely a matter for joking, I found out something new, something most likely interesting about Them.

And it has been thus over the years, and there is a lesson here: You will rarely be turned away if you have a sympathetic ear and a definite approach. And you will discover something else: Most Irish people have some instinctive belief in the world of the fairies, even if sometimes it has to be excavated carefully from under a veneer of busy modernity.

I cannot claim to be an apostle or prophet of anything—a disciple, rather, of great, though very often "uneducated," teachers. Yet it gives me much personal satisfaction to be able to put forward with ever-growing confidence my certainty about the reality of fairy belief, a belief that is as old as the Irish people. Fads, fancies, and fashions have and will pass, but this strange conglomeration of respect, doubt, fear, hesitation, and conviction I have discovered in the swirl of modern Irish life, all focused on Them, is something, firstly, to be wondered at, then eagerly grasped. For I am sure that it will not, cannot, survive under the immense pressures and distractions I have already mentioned. Under a different guise, maybe, but not as fairy belief. And what a tragedy that will be, for if the human need for things above and beyond the mundane, the merely explainable (by science or whatever), is to continue to thrive—as no doubt it will—how much more fitting that it should do so as part of an Irish culture, one that is immeasurably old and instinctively recognizable, rather than as a belief in aliens or extra-terrestrials merely from other parts of our galaxy or beyond.

Yet I am not so sentimental as to imagine that people can be other than creatures of their time and place. And our time and place is a world, a society that emphasizes the technological rather than the personal (despite what advertisers might have us believe), the superficial and fleeting rather than the profound, the commercial at the expense of the communal. All these changes have their price, and the casualties we can see all around us.

My mission, if *mission* is the correct word, has been and is to attempt, as much as one person with no more than modest private resources can do, to show that the older beliefs, in one of the shapes in which they presented themselves (fairy lore), are not yet dead; rather, gone underground for want of a suitably sympathetic framing context. The episode of the fairy bush (*sceach*) at Latoon, County Clare, in 1999 was a graphic reminder of the power of these older beliefs to reassert themselves given the assistance, even briefly, of the media to which we have become accustomed (radio, TV, newspapers), rather than the older, almost vanished methods of dispersal—storytelling around the fire at night, or conversation at fair, market, and pub.

Briefly, what happened was this: Over seventeen years ago I was told by an old man (since dead) at Latoon, near Newmarket-on-Fergus, of a lone whitethorn bush in a field called Lynch's Crag. He said that the fairies of Munster would gather round it on their frequent journeys northwards to fight the fairies of Connaught. On their way back from these battles they would again collect there, to assess their losses and wait for stragglers, before traveling back across the river Shannon and scattering to their homes.

On several occasions, very early in the morning, while collecting cattle to drive to local fairs, he had noted lumps of a greenish substance with the consistency of liver in the field around the bush. He knew that it was the fairies' blood and that a battle had taken place the previous night.

This information lay on a tape on one of my shelves for years until one day in 1999, on my way home from work in Limerick, I noticed excavation in progress in the field close to the bush. I stopped, inquired the reason, and was informed that the big new Ennis relief road, a $20 million project, was to pass here and an overpass was being built in this very field. I asked what was to happen to the *sceach*, only to be asked, "What are you talking about?" I pointed it out, but to the engineers it meant nothing. They had plans to complete and that was that, even though I warned them that if the bush were destroyed, the fairies would have their revenge: There would be many accidents, injuries, maybe deaths here as a result.

I wrote a letter of protest to a local newspaper and was interviewed on the local radio station. This was picked up by national radio, a report which in turn was noticed and carried by the *New York Times* and, from there, the affair mushroomed, with eventually over forty newspapers in the U.S., U.K., and Europe carrying the story, as well as at least a dozen TV stations in the U.S., Canada, and Europe.

As a result of all this publicity, and an accession of common sense, Clare County Council and the National Roads Authority agreed to vary the route of the road slightly, sparing the bush. It was a civilized decision, one that illustrates clearly that fairy belief, in spite of all vicissitudes, still has power to influence decisions even at a high official level and where much money is concerned.

I cannot imagine it happening in most other European countries. So why should it still be possible in Ireland? Because the fairies in Ireland are not a vague, impersonal force. They are people like ourselves. Of a different, a parallel, world, maybe, but similar to us in enough ways to be understood by us sufficiently to make us wary of Them, respectful of their habitations.

Unfortunately, as this manuscript was going to print, the Latoon fairy bush once again featured in practically all the Irish national daily newspapers, this time for wholly the wrong reason. Some person, on the weekend of August 9, 2002, took a chainsaw to it and very deliberately cut off every single branch, but left the trunk standing bare. What obscure point this person was trying to make with this cowardly act (done under cover of darkness, naturally) is hard to fathom. But an old man of that locality, one with a deep knowledge of such things, as soon as I phoned him with the bad news, replied, "Is he still alive?" I have no way of knowing that. What I do know—and what this book shows time after time—is that the Good People do not suffer destruction of their property without response.

The stories in this book will, hopefully, make clear the following about the Good People:

- There is considerable and respectable proof of their existence.
- They have been described in some detail.
- Their origins have been speculated on.
- Their amusements are similar to ours—dance, music, games, etc.
- They have specific dwellings.
- They protect their property.
- They travel from place to place.
- They have specific roads and pathways.
- They may be good or bad neighbors.
- They buy and sell.
- They are sometimes belligerent, but also placatable.
- They have their own (often mysterious) agenda.
- They have their fears and dislikes.
- They can be thwarted.
- They observe certain holidays.
- Time is different in their world.

In Ireland, do we portray Them thus because we project onto Them what we would wish Them to be, i.e., not so different from us, because if They were They would be *too* strange, unimaginable? At least while They are like us, we have some hope of understanding Them, therefore not offending Them too much. If that is so, it may display a basic fear, an uncomfortableness.

Why? Because we're not sure. We pretend to be so, nowadays, in a world where everything seems to be measurable, open to scrutiny. But that illusion-bubble is popped every time we are confronted by a particularly horrible fatal accident, such as the death of a young person. "Why? How?" will always be with us. Hopefully. Without them we would be reduced to mindlessness even as we elevated ourselves to certainty. While they are there to taunt us, there are certain aspects of existence we will not be able to take for granted, including the Other World of the Good People.

Perhaps the fairies are a cultural thing, of a particular time and place, like those who believe in them. A proof of this might be that they ride horses, never drive cars. They play hurling, Gaelic football, never soccer, bowls (iron!), chess, etc. They fight with sticks, hurleys, not with guns, knives (hardly, since they fear steel). Note: These things they are associated with are natural, of the landscape. Leading from this, a question might be asked, one which rarely is: Have they a religion and have they revealed it to anyone? Can it be inferred?

I think it can: respect for things old, for tradition, for the landscape, for nature.

The fact that they seem mostly to be experienced at night or in gloom could be interpreted in more than one way:

1. They belong to that indefinite, unclear time when we are, even nowadays, most susceptible to insecurity, uncertainty—because our sight (our most important

sense)—is reduced and because all our subconscious fears come to the surface then.

2. At that time we normally have more silence in which to think (or be frightened, if we're that kind of person). Consider here that the fairies are not usually experienced where many people congregate—in towns, well-lighted places, etc. This, for skeptics, is the sure proof that they are just a figment of the imagination. But is this a correct conclusion? Could it not be that lights and crowds and movement distract us so much that we no longer are in a frame of mind that allows us to experience Them, make contact with Them?

CHRISTIANITY IS clever here. It says that we are to see Christ in our fellow man, that this is how we may see God. But could anyone imagine seeing the fairies in his fellow man? The very notion would provoke laughter nowadays. Yet it need not, for the same notion is allowed for in the idea of a changeling, where indeed a person may be a fairy, or a fairy a person. And another similarity (once we have got over our initial skepticism) is that we see the otherworldly in our this-worldly "fallen" fellow man in order to improve him, just as we recognize the changeling as that same, in order to help him become what he really is, or get back to what he once was.

I have very few answers. I am still, after a search of over twenty-seven years, fumbling to ask the questions that will make some sense of all the responses I have got in innumerable talks with old Irish people whose belief in that other world of the fairies is unshakable.

Are they fools? Am I a fool? Those are matters you will have to settle for yourself as you turn the pages of this book.

Eddie Lenihan
Crusheen, County Clare, August 2002

PART ONE

"The Queerest
Thing I
Ever Saw"

WHO THEY ARE AND
WHAT THEY WANT

"The Other Crowd, they're the Devil's crowd. I wouldn't
be for saying that them'd see Heaven. No."
KILCOLUM, KILMALEY, AUGUST 11, 1999

The Vicious Fairies

EVERY COUNTY TRIES to make out that it has the best
o' this and the best o' that. I s'pose 'tis only natural. But wouldn't
you wonder, though, why anyplace might want to lay claim to
fairies that were vicious. And even be proud to have 'em! But
that's what they say about the Clare fairies more than any of the
others in all of Ireland—that they're the most vicious of all.
And how did that come about, you ask. Well, I'll tell you if you
want to know.

They say 'twas here in this parish o' Crusheen it happened.
There was a parish priest here one time, and he was well liked,
respected. And the reason wasn't because he said a short Mass
on Sunday and let the drinkers off to the pub early—the same
crowd, they'd go, anyway, 'cause their thirst kept 'em near the
church door! No, 'twas because he took his job serious, and not
the kind o' serious that persecuted people for nothing, either;
there was plenty o' them kind o' priests around. The reason that
man was liked was because anytime there was someone in
trouble in the parish—sick, especially—he was there to tend
'em, no matter whether 'twas in the middle o' day or night.

People appreciated that, too. Like I said, he was well respected. And rightly so.

Now, there was this certain man in the parish sick, an old man, and he wasn't expected to live long. He was nearly ninety! Four times the priest was called to him in less than six months, and each time he came, anointed him, and said all the prayers. And d'you know what! In each case the man recovered.

Naturally enough, the local people said, "Aha! There you are! The priests have the power, if they want to use it."

But time went on, anyway, and 'twas later on that same year, the month o' November. And the parish priest, this night, he was long gone to bed—and the curate, too. 'Twas well after midnight, in the dead hours, in fact, when all of a sudden there was this knock on the presbytery door.

The parish priest was a very light sleeper—used to being called in the night, I s'pose. He sat up in the bed and shook himself, wondering was he hearing things.

But he knew he wasn't when the knocking started again. He jumped out o' the bed, pulled his overcoat across his shoulders, and off out the hall with him. He opened the door, and standing there outside was a young man. The priest knew him immediately—he was from the house where the old man was sick.

He wasn't even asked in, only, "What's wrong?"

"He's sick again, Father. Bad. They want you to come, as soon as you can."

"Go on back, now, this minute. Tell 'em I'll be there after you."

He went in then, to dress himself, but as he passed the curate's room he knocked.

"Get up," he says, "and tackle the horse. We have a call to go on."

The curate woke and started muttering and cursing under his breath, "God blast 'em, but wouldn't you think they'd pick some better time than this to be dying? . . ."

"None o' that kind o' talk out o' you!" says the parish priest "Tackle up the horse. I'll be out in a few minutes."

That's the reason, you know, why curates were never given a parish in them days until they had about seven years served—so that all kinds of impatience and other dirty tricks could be knocked out of 'em first by an older priest. Just like training a dog or a horse, you know. But that isn't done anymore, o' course, and more's the pity.

But . . . back to the story.

The curate tackled up the horse and trap, anyway, and by the time the parish priest had his bag packed—holy oil, candles, his book, and all the rest—there was his transport ready and waiting at the door.

Now, you might ask why was it that the parish priest wanted the young man to go with him. Grandeur? It wasn't, but for company. And why? Every one o' the old people that time—and some of 'em even today—could tell you that a priest, or minister, going on a sick-call at night was in fierce danger.

From who? The Devil, o' course! That's the time, when a person is dying, that he'll try his best to sink his claws in him, to carry him to the Place Below. And the last thing he wants is a priest putting in on him. And you know, yourself, that the Devil can take any shape he likes. The Devil could be the person sitting next to you, your nearest friend. And often that's proved. He could be on the road—no, he *would* be on the road, on a night like that, to put the priest astray if he could. And there was only one way to get the better o' him: take company. And what better company than another priest!

That's the main reason he called the curate, whether the younger man realized it or not.

By the time he was dressed for the road, anyway, and had his bag packed, there was the curate outside the door with the horse and trap, all ready.

They started out, off down the Tulla road, and I s'pose with the jogging and swaying o' the trap, they were dozing off to sleep. But it didn't make any difference. The horse knew every foot o' the road. Why wouldn't he? The priest's horse, in them days, he'd know every road in the parish, day or night. Wasn't he traveling 'em full-time!

They went on, anyway, a couple o' miles south o' Crusheen, and I'd say the priests were maybe asleep by the time they came to Sunnagh Cross. But the horse knew the way as well as themselves. He turned left at the cross, up that Sunnagh road. He knew where to go, I s'pose, from all the times that year they visited the man that was dying.

Whatever 'twas, they were only gone a few hundred yards up that road—narrow country road, overgrown with big trees, like it is to this very day—when the moon came out from behind a cloud. And at that very minute, out from behind a big old bush—'tis still there, on the right-hand side as you're facing for Ballinruan—a man stepped out, into the middle o' the road.

The horse shied, o' course, reared up. But the parish priest, he was awake while you'd be counting one. Wide awake! And he was a good horseman, too. Calmed the animal in a few seconds.

But . . . there in front of 'em in the road was a man. No doubt about it! The first thing that came into their minds was, *a robber*. But no. There was no weapon, no orders. They could see him clear enough, though, all except his face. He was wearing some kind of a hood, and his face was in shadow.

Then, while they were half-wondering what they'd do, he reached in under his right oxter and pulled out a fiddle. He reached under his left oxter then and brought out a bow. And there, on that road, that very minute, he started to play—the most lonesome music that them priests ever in their lives heard. It brought water out o' their teeth, so it did. Never heard the like of it before!

And when that man—whoever he was—turned around and walked that narrow road in front of 'em playing that music, every bit of it, what could they do? Only follow him. They couldn't get around him. The road wasn't wide enough. And they were hardly going to drive out over him—priests in them days wouldn't do that, whatever about today!

Step for step they followed him, until they came to the gateway to the house where the old man was dying. He walked three steps beyond it, still playing, and just as the curate was turning the horse in between the piers, glad enough to get on with their business, the man stopped, turned, and held up his hand. He looked at the parish priest

"One minute, Father!" says he. "I want you to do something for me."

They looked at him. Then the parish priest says, "If—if 'tis nothing sinful or unholy, o' course we'll do it. What is it?"

"I want you to ask a question, Father, to that man that's dying above there in the bed."

"What . . . kind of a question?"

"I want you to ask him what's going to happen to the Good People on the Day of Judgment."

The priest looked at him.

"You what?!"

"Isn't it simple enough?! What's going to happen to the Good People on the Day of Judgment?"

The priest only nodded. He was half frightened.

"All right," says he, and the curate whipped on the horse. But the man had the last word.

"Remember this, Father. I'll be here, waiting for my answer."

On they went then, up the passageway to the house, and when they arrived into the yard, there was the woman o' the house, the wife o' the man that was dying within in the bed, standing there in the doorway. I s'pose she heard the wheels o' the trap coming.

"Thanks be to God ye're here, Father," says she. "Hurry on, please. He's very low."

The parish priest took his bag, left the curate to tie up the horse, and hurried in after her. And there inside, the kitchen was full o' people. All the neighbors were there; that was the custom o' the time, and still the same today when someone is laid out at home. They were there to help, to console the poor woman, like any good neighbors would. And when the priest arrived in, they all stood up, out o' respect.

"Welcome, Father. Good night. And thanks for coming."

He nodded. But first things first, talk later. He headed for the sickroom, closed the door behind him, and looked at the bed.

There was the dying man, not a move out o' him, eyes closed, hands folded. No sign o' life at all, and that gray-green color on him that you'll see on dying people. But the parish priest had it all seen before. That kind o' thing was his job, wasn't it? He opened his bag, took out all the bits and pieces he'd need—his prayer book, the holy candles, the oil, holy water.

He lit the candles on the little bedside table. He got down on his knees then and heard the man's confession—although I s'pose he didn't actually hear it, when the man was so far gone. But you know what I mean. In cases like that the priest could give absolution even if a person was unconscious. They had a name for it, too: conditional absolution.

Anyway, he said the prayers, and when he was finished, and the last blessing was given, he quenched the candles and put his stuff back into his bag.

He had full intention, now, of asking the question, just like he promised, but . . . in them few seconds, while he was putting his bits and pieces away, there was silence, o' course. And I s'pose the woman o' the house, she was listening at the door, worried, naturally. And when she heard nothing from the room, in she went to find out how things were—and in her hand a glass o' whiskey for the priest. She wasn't alone, either, 'cause in after her came most o' the crowd that was in the kitchen.

And that's when the damage was done, 'cause the parish priest wasn't a drinking man at all. He might have a few small ones when friends called to the presbytery, or maybe at Christmas, but that was all. Still, when the mourners were there now with him in that room, what could he do? Only be sociable and take what he was offered! He was a friendly kind o' man, like I said.

He sipped away, anyway, while the talk went on all around him. And 'twas mainly about the man dying there in the bed— the good neighbor he was, a decent man, kind and charitable, never turned anyone away from his door. All that kind o' talk. And you could understand that! What else would you say about a dying man, when he can't talk for himself? That's only ordinary decency. We'll all need that when the time comes.

He finished the first glass o' whiskey, anyway, but when he did, a second one was put into his hand. And the bother was, 'twas neat. You see, the woman o' the house wasn't a drinker either, knew nothing about it! So she filled the glass up to the top. Left no room at all for water! Thought she was doing the right thing. What chance had the poor parish priest with that kind o' drink?! I often said it, and I'll say it again now: Non-drinkers do more harm than drinkers ever do! They have no notion how to handle drink, at all. And she proved it that night. A full glass o' whiskey and no water!

The priest, in the middle of all the talk, sipped away. And when that glass was finished, the third one was put into his fist.

But, by the time he was gone down halfway in that one, he was beginning to go sideways. Why wouldn't he when he wasn't used to it!?

Lucky enough, the curate saw the way things were. He leaned over, took the glass, and said, "We'll go, Father. We have to be up early for Mass in the morning."

Now, the parish priest, he was never a troublesome man. Even with drink in him now, he made no objection, only stood up, and said to all the people there, "We . . . we'll see ye . . . in the morning. Good night! 'Night."

They stood, o' course, out o' respect. They knew the way he was, but not one of 'em there was going to say a word against him. Why would they, a man like him!?

The curate took him by the arm and led him out.

"Good night, Father," they said, "and thanks again for coming."

There was the horse outside. Same place, tied. They got into the trap, and off down the passageway to the road. But when they passed out the gate piers, turned right, for home, there in front of 'em on the road was the lad, with his hand up. The horse stopped.

"Well, Father," says he, "have you my answer?"

They looked at him.

"Answer?" says the parish priest. "What . . . answer?"

"You promised you'd ask a certain question for me, Father. Have you an answer?"

He was moving towards 'em all the time, and for the first time they saw his face. 'Twas yellow and wrinkled, a face that must be as old as . . . as the hills. 'Twasn't natural.

The parish priest—he was sobering up quick, now—he says, "Stay where you are! I forgot. But I'll go back this very minute, and find out for you."

He threw the reins to the curate.

"Here! Hold these till I come back."

"Me? I will in my backside! I'm not staying here alone."

He threw the reins over a bush, and back they went, the two of 'em, up the passageway to the house.

And when they knocked at the door, the woman came out. She was surprised to see 'em back, o' course.

"What is it, Father? Is there—?"

"Nothing. Nothing. I forgot something, that's all," says he.

He made for the bedroom, left the curate there to keep the crowd talking, and closed the door behind him. There was going to be no mistake this time.

The man was still the same way inside in the bed—stretched, no move.

The priest, he went to the bedside, down on his knees, and whispered into the dying man's ear, "What's going to happen to the Good People on the Day of Judgment?"

I don't know did he expect an answer or not, but, by God, he got it!

The man in the bed, his eyes opened up, as wide as saucers,

and he began to pull himself up on the pillow. The priest jumped back.

"Father," says he, "isn't it a strange thing, but I was just thinking about that same thing myself."

"I'm glad to hear it," says the priest. "But can you give me an answer?"

"I can."

"Do so, like a good man."

"I will."

"Ah, God—" He was going to swear, you know, but he didn't. Cool man! "In God's holy name, will you tell me whatever you know," says he.

Silence for a minute, then he stared at the priest and said, "All I'll tell you, Father, is this: If one drop of blood can be found in their veins on the Day of Judgment, the Good People will see the face of God."

"Wha—?"

"One drop of blood, Father. That's all."

And with that, he fell back on the pillow, dead.

The priest, he said a prayer, blessed him, and then out quick to the kitchen. He beckoned the curate and off they went, the two of 'em, out, and down the passageway. Left the people there wondering what in the name o' God was going on.

They came to the gate, turned right for Crusheen, and home. But when they did, there was the horse and trap in the middle o' the road. And there, in front o' the horse's nose, was the stranger. He held up his hand.

"Well, Father," says he, "did you get my answer this time?"

"I got an answer all right, but I don't know if 'tis the one you want. It didn't make much sense to me."

"Ahh!" says he. "So you have it!"

He started towards 'em, but the parish priest held up his hand.

"No, no!" he says. "No nearer. Stay where you are and I'll tell you what I know."

He stopped a couple o' yards from 'em, but they could see that wrinkled face of his clearly.

"Tell me!"

"He said . . . if one drop o' blood could be found in their veins on the Day o' Judgment they'd see the face o' God. Does that make any kind o' sense to you?"

"One drop o' blood," says the lad. "Only one drop?"

He stared at the priests again then, and it frightened 'em, the look in his eyes. They thought something bad was coming. But no. All he did was to put down the fiddle on the road, and then the bow across it, very neat.

And when he straightened up they were so busy watching his face that they never saw his hand going to his belt, slow, slow. 'Twas only when he pulled up a dagger and held it out before him that they jumped back, sure he was going to attack 'em.

But not a bit of it! All he did was hold it there at his full arm's length, nodding away at it all the time, like he'd be thinking to himself.

And then, while they were still wondering what to do, he stuck that knife straight into his chest, pulled it out, and stabbed himself again. And again. Twelve times in all he stabbed himself.

And not a drop o' blood! What came out o' him was thick green stuff like . . . like stewed apple, for all the world.

He looked at the knife, then at the two priests again, then flung it into the darkness. He turned around, and they could see a fierce change in his eyes now. Something . . . something they didn't want any part of.

"Father," says he, "for the last five thousand years and more, I and my people are traveling the roads of Ireland, and in all that time we never did harm to man, woman, child, or any living creature, only playing sweet music for all of 'em in the dark, hurting no one. But from this time on, Father, there'll be no more music."

He turned to the fiddle and bow then, where they were left on the road. Then he jumped on 'em, danced down on 'em until he had matches made of 'em.

"There'll be no more music, Father. But there'll be this!" He stepped into the dark, picked up the knife, and held it under their noses.

"Go home. Tell your people what you saw and heard here tonight. And tell 'em that anyone we catch on these roads after dark anymore . . . this is what they'll get. Now that I know we're never to see the face o' God, we have nothing to lose. So, make sure you have your message right, Father, 'cause there'll be no other warning."

He turned into the darkness then, and they saw no more of him.

They were frightened men, I can tell you, when they turned to the horse trap to go home.

But there was no "go home" there. The poor horse's legs were shaking under him and he was foaming at the mouth with fright. I always heard that—horses know when the Other World is near 'em. 'Twas they had to bring home the horse. Whether they brought the trap or not I can't tell you, but they got back to the presbytery very different men than when they were starting out. They went to their beds, no more said. They had plenty to be thinking about!

And there was no more said about it until the following Sunday, at eleven o'clock Mass in Crusheen church—the parish priest's own Mass.

The people were in, and waiting for the prayers to start, but while they were sitting there, or kneeling, they noticed that there was something out o' place. You know, now, yourself, the way 'tis in a church. Nothing ever moves much from one end o' the week to the next. But they couldn't make out what 'twas until the sacristy door opened and out came the priest. 'Twas then they saw it—a stool against the wall outside the door. But that wasn't all. Out after the parish priest came the curate, and then the altar boys. And that was unusual, 'cause the curate had his own Mass said earlier on.

They were all looking out of 'em now, to try to see what was going on. What was this concelebrated Mass for? But the parish priest started as usual—"In nomine Patris, et Filii, et Spiritus Sancti . . ." You remember, the grand old Latin prayers.

And still nothing strange, until it came to the sermon time.

Now, the other thing about the parish priest, as well as being a nondrinker, he was a hopeless man to preach a sermon.

Useless entirely. I heard he was so bad that every Sunday, when he'd start, the people used to go to sleep while he'd be at it, and the ones at the back and up in the galleries, they'd curl up on the seats to do it. And that's no easy job on church seats!

But on this Sunday no one went to sleep, or yawned, either. 'Cause all he did was to tell 'em about what he saw and heard on that road near Sunnagh bridge the few nights before. And there was the curate, sitting on the stool near the sacristy door, nodding at every word.

And you can say what you like—one priest might tell you a lie, but two priests together? No such thing! I wouldn't believe it, in spite of all the bad things we're hearing about the clergy for a few years back.

Anyway, he told 'em every bit o' what happened. And the man that told it to me, he said 'twas the damnedest thing he ever saw—people's hair beginning to stand above on their heads with the fright. And 'twas even funny in one way, to see old lads that were bald and whatever few ribs they had behind their ears sticking out!

But I can tell you, by the time Mass was finished, the last blessing given, and people stood up to go, there was a good third o' them people who couldn't rise out o' where they sat. Stuck to their seats! He frightened the . . . you know what . . . out of 'em.

That was fair work for a man that couldn't preach a sermon, hah!

From there the word went out, o' course, into all the parishes around—into County Galway and Tipperary and Limerick, and farther, too.

After that, night walking stopped entirely in all this part of Ireland. And they say it got so bad for a finish that country pubs started to go out o' business—no customers once dark'd fall. Publicans started to take the train and the boat to England, America, even to Van Diemen's Land—and by God, that's a place you'd persuade no Irishman to go unless 'twas a last resort! There was pubs selling here in Clare that time for forty pounds—and no takers!

'Twas only in the late '50s, when cars began to get a bit plentiful, that people started traveling out again at night. 'Cause you know as well as me that people are very brave when they have lights in front of 'em and maybe a radio to be listening to.

But I know this much, and you can believe it or not, whatever you like: That road isn't right. The whitethorn bush where the priests saw that lad, I often passed it in the dark, cycling home, and I'd always feel safer when I'd be past it.

I regard it as no shame to admit that I also have had that feeling on that same Sunnagh road at night. For I have done, on several occasions, what would surely have confirmed many people's opinion of me as a lunatic if they had seen me (and maybe some of them have, for in a small community one can never, even in the remotest place, darkest time, presume that one is unobserved) stop there, look around me as if I were expecting something unusual to happen. For, to country people, natives of these very same places, the last thing a person should do is stand, silent, waiting. They would laugh. "Waiting for what? For God's sake, have a bit o' sense. 'Tis only children believe in them old stories, that old kind o' nonsense."

And yet, later that same night, in the pub, when all the laughing and mocking is done, the serious talk will begin, hesitant at first, then more freely, until at last, many pints of Guinness later, even those who mocked earlier in the night will finally—and not for the first or last time—admit that, yes, "There's something there, all right. Petey (or Johnny, or Paddy or whoever) is no liar, whatever else he is."

And in such unpromising companies, by not retreating from impending scorn, ridicule, I have very often come away with a completely different knowledge of people I thought I knew before.

And such confrontations have, I think, brought to the surface for some of those mockers, too, something deep, something that may have been forgotten in our hurly-burly world of "acquire, have, experience, spend"—life as advertisers and their victims see it.

An oasis in the midst of crassness? Yes. But a great deal more, too, a lifting of a corner of that veil that separates us from a world that is right beside us, but for most of us as far away as Heaven . . . or Hell!

The Fallen Angels

NOVEMBER, as you know, is a very lonesome month. There
was a lot o' people long ago, they couldn't go outside the door in
the month o' November. They say if you're born at the dead
hour o' the night, between twelve and one, that you'll always see
ghosts and fairies and that kind o' thing. That was a well-known
fact long ago.

Everyone knows there were two or three different kinds o'
ghosts or fairies or spirits, or whatever you like to call 'em. But
the most plentiful kind of 'em was the evil spirit and the wandering souls. The wandering souls, all they wanted was your
prayers, and say Masses for 'em. But the evil spirits were different. They were out for destruction of every kind, devilment of
every kind. And I'd say a lot o' these plane crashes and car
crashes that happens to very careful people, they're behind 'em.
The only weapon against the evil spirit was the holy water. 'Twas
handed down here in west Clare that when people was tackling
horses they'd always shake the holy water on 'em, or going to a

fair with cattle you'd always shake the holy water on 'em. That was the only weapon, they said, against the evil spirit.

But, as well as them two, you have the fallen angels. The time Lucifer rebelled, millions upon millions o' the fallen angels went out in sympathy with him, and they fell all over the world. But however it was, for a country the size of Ireland and the small population, there did more of 'em fall here than in any other country. A missioner was in Miltown one time and he said, "Every step you're taking, you're walking down on 'em." He knew a lot about 'em, the same man. He said on account of Ireland being that kind of a country—long ago 'twas known as the Island of Saints and Scholars—that was why he thought that more of 'em stayed in Ireland than any other place.

But, that was all right, anyway. There was this man, and he came from the same quarter as myself—only about a half mile over there. He lived with his mother and his uncle and the servant boy. The four of 'em lived in the one house. And she was keeping him for the land. There were a good few in the family, but they were married here and there; the girls married local farmers and some o' the boys went to America and Australia. And one of 'em joined the RIC; he was a big strong man.

She was keeping this boy for the land, anyway. And he was a fairly strong farmer. He had a hundred acres o' land—mixed land, you know; it wasn't all good.

This uncle of his was over eighty years, but he used to do a lot o' handiwork around the farm—mind the cows, bring the cows to be milked, feed young calves, and boil spuds for pigs, and that kind o' thing.

'Twas the month o' November, anyway, and the uncle got a kind o' sick. There wasn't much wrong with him, but he wasn't feeling so good. The woman o' the house used to bring down the dinner every day to him, spuds and bacon and cabbage—they were after killing a good pig—and he'd eat as much, now, as any man. But still he wasn't getting up. He was keeping to the bed. And after three or four days o' this, she was inside one night. She had a good fire down and she was knitting a stocking. No one used to be idle that time! And she heard terrible talk coming up out o' the room. She went down, anyway, but 'twas how he was raving. He was talking very strange things. He was a great foot-baller when he was young, and he was talking about football. And he was a great man for breaking horses, and he was talking o' horses. And he was a great man in faction fights—they were very common at the time. He was a great man with a stick, and he was talking about 'em.

But the woman could make no sense of him; when she'd ask him a question he wouldn't know her or anything like that. She came up again in the kitchen, anyway, and she didn't know what to do. Her son came in about half past ten o' clock and she told him the story. And he went down in the room, and 'twas the same story: He was raving away. So the son said he'd go for the priest.

"No," says the woman, his mother. "You won't stir out o' this," says she. "I'm no good around people that'd be dying. You must wait now until the servant boy come in."

And they did wait until he came in, about eleven o' clock, and they told him their story. The servant boy was a great friend o' this old man, and he went down in the room.

Now, this servant boy, he was in service all over the country in different places, and he was often slowed up for a week minding old people. 'Twas a terrible crime that time to die in a hospital or the county home or them places. The servant boy went down, anyway, and looked at him.

"That man is raving," says he. "That man is dying. But we have plenty time. He'll go on till about the break o' day," says he. "Them people does. The month o' November it won't be day till about seven o' clock. We have plenty time," he says.

That was all right, anyway. The man o' the house said, "Will you go for the priest for him?"

"I will," says he, "and welcome."

The servant boy went out, anyway, and he used to keep a great bicycle, and he got it and cycled into Miltown. And he didn't go to the parish priest at all—the parish priest in Miltown that time was a bit old—he went to the curate. He knocked, anyway—the servant girl wasn't gone to bed—and he told her his story and she sent down this curate. This curate was only in Miltown about a year and a half. And that time, priests without power, there wasn't much thought of 'em, but this curate had a lot o' power; he had a good few people cured. At that time, a priest without power, you see, he'd be very old when he'd get a parish. Folklore is full o' the power o' the priest. Sure you know that.

Okay, anyway, the servant girl woke the curate, and the curate came down.

"I know these people well," says he, "but I don't know where they live. What way o' traveling have you?" he said to the servant boy.

"Oh," said the servant boy, "bicycle."

"Oh, grand," says the curate. "You'll show me the road," says he.

The two of 'em went out, anyway, and the curate went in the stable and took out a good horse, a good five-year-old Irish draught horse, a good clean-boned horse, and he put the saddle on him.

And himself and the servant boy rode down the street o' Miltown as far as Canada Cross, up Faiche na Muc, past the Ballard graveyard, up along, and up the Ballinoe Hill. And they landed near the place where this man lived.

The servant boy said to the curate, "There's a stable there. There's a man gone selling a horse," says he. "You can put in your horse there."

The curate did as he was told. They took off the saddle, and settled the horse, and went in to where the man was dying, in along the road. And the curate was talking away to him and the servant boy talking away to him. They arrived inside, anyway, at the house, and the curate went down and gave him the last rites. And he said the same as the servant boy. He said the man was dying but he might go till the break o' day.

And the woman o' the house was a very friendly woman. She wanted to rise the heat o' the fire and make tea for him, but he said he wouldn't, that he wasn't cold.

He went out, anyway, and the man o' the house said to the servant boy, "Go down with that man, now, till he take out the horse and see that he's all right."

And the servant boy said that he would.

There was about half a mile o' road into this house—there's parts o' the old house there yet; the rest of the place is planted with trees.

But they went down along the road, anyway, and they were gone about four or five hundred yards when the curate said to the servant boy, "I'm afraid you'll have to go back."

The servant boy said, "Didn't you hear what the boss said, that I have to go down and settle the horse with you, and get you going for Miltown?"

"I did," he said, "but you'll have to go back."

The curate and the servant boy walked nine or ten more steps, anyway. And the curate made a hoop of his hand, with his fingers on his hip, and he said to the servant boy, "Look out there and you won't be long going back."

The servant boy looked out through the hoop of the curate's hand and saw the five-acre field nearest 'em was full o' the finest people he ever seen in his life!

"Who're them?" says he to the curate.

"Them are the fallen angels," says the curate.

They had a human form, no wings. God took the wings off of 'em after Lucifer rebelled—that way they couldn't go back, d'you see. They had no wings. But there was so many of 'em that you couldn't drive a knife down between 'em. They were as thick as hair on a dog's back. They were the finest people he ever seen. And whatever way he looked at 'em, some o' the finest girls he ever seen was in it, he said. They *had* to be good-looking, you know! 'Twas the sin o' pride put Lucifer down, d'you see. The best-looking angel in Heaven, 'twas the sin o' pride put him down. I s'pose they were nearly all as good-looking.

But that was all right, anyway. The curate went on alone another bit until he came to a place where there was a little bridge crossing the road—*ciseachs* they're called here in west Clare, these small little gullets or bridges. But this man, a fine-looking man, stopped him there.

"I have a question for you, Father," says he. Oh, he styled him; he called him "Father." He had respect for the cloth.

"I have a question for you."

"What is it?" says the curate. "I'll answer it if I can."

"Will the fallen angels," he said, "*ever* be saved?"

Begod, the curate had his mouth half open to answer him, to tell him they wouldn't by all accounts—they won't you know—but he was lucky he didn't. Something tempted him to say, "I'll be here at this very place tomorrow night. I'm a man to my word," says he, "and I'll have a look at the good books tomorrow, and I'll have an answer for ye," he said.

Okay. They let him go, but they were very disappointed. He was going out along the road now, and they were very disappointed, but no one of 'em ever left a hand on him.

That was all right, anyway. He went home, went to bed. He couldn't sleep. Every time he'd think about sleeping, this five-acre field'd come before him, and it full o' fallen angels.

At that time there was none o' these tablets, now, these sleeping tablets or any o' these things; the only cure they had was to walk three times around the room backwards, and you might sleep. It used to work in some cases. The curate tried it before and it worked, but this night, mind you, 'twouldn't work. 'Twouldn't work at all. He was turning and twisting all night, but no sleep.

He got up early in the morning. 'Twas his morning to say Mass, and he went out and looked after the horse—brushed and settled him, gave him water, and brought in an armful of hay to him. After that he went out and dressed himself for Mass. He said Mass, anyway, and he came in again. And the servant girl had the breakfast ready for him. He told her not to prepare any dinner for him, that he wouldn't be around. He didn't tell her where he was going or anything.

He put the saddle on the horse again and rode down the street o' Miltown and out the Ennis road, on east Cloonanaha, into Inagh, down Kilnamona, and into Ennis. And he turned in the bishop's gate.

The bishop that was in Ennis that time had a couple o' hundred acres o' land, and he used to keep a lot o' cattle and milk cows and everything. He had three or four men working for him. One of 'em took the curate's horse, anyway, and put him up, and he went in to the bishop. The bishop had a terrible welcome for him, a great welcome. And they talked away for a start.

"You just came at the right time," says the bishop, and he told the servant girl to bring in two dinners. She did, and the curate, after riding a horse down from Miltown, had a fair stroke.

They went to eat, anyway, but faith, the bishop had a good stroke, too. And about halfway through the dinner the curate told him the story, what happened to him last night.

"What answer did you give him?" says the bishop.

"I gave 'em no answer at all till I'd see you."

"Well, you're a smart man," says he. "And a lucky man. If you told 'em the truth," he said—I s'pose the truth is they'll never be saved—"they'd rip you from ear to ear," he said. "D'you get the papers?" he said to the curate.

"Well, I don't get every day's paper," says the curate, "but if I was down the town I'd buy a paper."

"Well," says the bishop, "there was a man killed above in south Armagh, in Forkhill. He went out on a sick-call with a bicycle. He was found on the road dead and the bicycle thrown against the wall. He was destroyed," he said. "Another parish priest down in Cork," says he, "he went out the same night on a sick-call, and the same story, the same thing happened him. The pony was found grazing over the lockspit* o' the road, and the parish priest was found farther and he destroyed. You're a smart man. There's only one answer to that question," says the bishop, "and I'll tell you."

And he did tell him.

After a start, anyway, the bishop lit the pipe. And that time, when you'd fill the pipe you'd hand it around till it'd be empty. They used to generally rub it to the sleeve o' their coat. I often

*Grassy margin.

saw it. They'd hand it to the next person, hand it around till it'd be empty. 'Twas a common practice at the time. The bishop, I s'pose, was from the country himself and he knew it. He handed it to the curate, and the curate took a good smoke out of it, and he said he'd leave for Miltown.

And he had the answer. He went out, anyway, put the saddle on the horse again, and he hit out for Miltown. The same story—up into Inagh, hither along to the Five Crosses, and on to Miltown.

He landed in good time and the servant girl had the supper ready for him. He ate it. And he told her to call him at eleven o'clock, and he went to bed.

The same story again. No sleep. He couldn't sleep. Every time he'd think about sleeping, he'd see this five-acre field out in front of him, full o' these people, the fallen angels. He couldn't sleep.

About eleven o'clock, anyway—he had to be there about twelve—he tackled his horse, went in the saddle again, put his horse in the same stable, and walked in the road. The night before 'twas coming out he was, but 'twas going in he was this night. No man ever said a word to him. But, talk o' people! There was a three-acre field near him and 'twas full o' the same people. They were along the tops o' walls and everything. He had only just room to walk up the road.

No man ever said a word to him until he landed at the water again. And the same story again. But when the man asked him, "Will the fallen angels ever be saved?" he gave 'em the bishop's answer.

"That won't be known till the end o' time, till the Last Day."

Well, d'you see, 'twasn't a yes or no answer. He kept 'em in hope, anyway. They never rose a hand to him, or done a bit o' harm to him. But they were disappointed, and wicked-looking.

He walked out the road again, anyway, and he went home and slept that night. But that isn't the end o' the story. The bishop o' the diocese o' Killaloe—and that goes down to Tipperary, and some parts of it goes up to Longford, I'm told—he sent for one priest out of every parish in the diocese. And the idea of it was, d'you see, to tell 'em how to answer the fallen angels if they ever met 'em.

And there was never, as far as I heard, a priest killed in the diocese o' Killaloe ever since with the fallen angels.

That's the way the story goes.

This story, which was told to me in west Clare, within sight of the Atlantic Ocean, by one of the best and last of the great traditional storytellers of that area, is useful for the distinctions it makes between several categories of otherworldly creatures that are very often confused in Irish folklore.

But it is far more than that, of course, as is obvious from how it is told. It is, in fact, pure drama: gripping, compelling stuff, that takes us into the world of these strange beings and shows us life from their perspective, a lonely exile of frustrated waiting that makes them potentially deadly to meet for the unwary or slow-witted traveler by night, particularly during that most dangerous of months, November, traditionally regarded as the month of the dead in Ireland.

As in so much Irish lore the priest figures largely, but in this case his knowledge places him in a position where his spiritual power may avail him little against the forces of the dark. It is verbal ambiguity that protects him, rather than any holiness.

*"But the fairies, o' course, to do anything right, they had
to have one live person, d'you see. An' they'd sweep 'em. Any
wedding, or any wake, or any big football match, they used say
that they'd have to have one live person to carry it out right."*
MILTOWN MALBAY, JANUARY 17, 1999

A Fairy Funeral

WHEN I WAS about nineteen years old, now, I came home
one night about one o' clock, and my father sent me up to the
back o' the hill to have a look at a cow that was on the point
o' calving. I went up, anyway. 'Twas a grand night in the month
o' May. There was a kind o' frost in it, a dew. And that time
there was corncrakes, and you'd love to hear 'em on a soft night
like that.

I looked at this cow, anyway, and I felt her bones and I
looked at her udder, and I knew she wouldn't calve that night.
She was grazing out along with the cows.

And I was coming back—I often came out o' this field fifty
times a day. I knew where the stile was and everything. But I
s'pose I missed the step. I couldn't get it, anyway, and I knew for
a finish that I was going astray. I was going around in circles;
I knew well.

But 'twas the old plan, if you were going astray, to turn your coat inside out. I s'pose the idea o' that is the brain'd be gone inside out and by turning the coat you might bring yourself back. I done it, but it didn't bring me back.

I went on, anyway, and I was going around for, I s'pose, a couple of hours, and I saw a light. I thought 'twas someone at the back o' the hill that was up with a cow calving or a mare foaling—'twas that time o' the year, in the month o' May. I made for the light, anyway, and when I came into the yard 'twas a long thatched house. I knew by the look of it 'twasn't any house around. And I was passing the window, and whatever look I gave, I saw a big crowd inside. The door was open, anyway. I went in. And when I went in, the house was full. And there was a girl of about twenty years, a grand-looking girl, inside in this coffin in the middle o' the floor.

I knew it was a wake by the looks o' things and I went over and said a few prayers, but I didn't shake hands to anyone, for I knew no one.

I went back over by the wall, anyway, and 'twas like any wake, now, boys and girls. There was only four or five small little wizened, withered people that was right fairies, I thought, in it. The rest of 'em, I s'pose, was people that was swept* sometime or another, d'you see?

I went over by the wall, anyway, and I started talking to a couple o' lads that was near me, and spoke about the weather,

*Taken by the fairies.

and cuttin' turf. They knew it as well as me. We spoke about football matches and things like that, and they seemed to know what I was talking about.

The porter came around, anyway, and I took a drink o' porter. And the pipes came around, but I never smoked a pipe. I didn't take any pipe. The snuff came around. I took a sweep o' the snuff.

That was all right, anyway. They were calling us down to the supper, below in the room. And I was good and hungry now. And you could smell the baker's bread and the fresh tea and jam and everything.

But the girl near me told me, "Drink all the porter you get, or smoke all you get, and take the snuff, but don't take a bite with 'em. If you eat one bite with 'em, they have you. That's how they trapped me," she said.

I was on my guard then.

They went round the house and brought 'em down to the room, one after the other, and when they came to me, I found all kinds of excuses: that I wasn't hungry, and on like that. But they knew well, I'd say, that 'twas telling lies I was. They forced me and forced me, but I didn't go down.

After a couple of hours, anyway, when the supper was over, they started to put the lid on the coffin. There was no undertaker there; 'twas themself was doing it. They put the lid on the coffin—three boys that did it, about my own age. And they said to the old woman that was in charge (she was one o' the four or five fairy people I was telling you was in it), "Who's the fourth to take out this coffin?" one of 'em said.

"Who," says she, "but Francie Kennelly?" I nearly dropped dead when I heard my name called out like that.

The four of us took the coffin out the door. We didn't put it on our shoulders at all—like any funeral now. We put it on our shoulders outside, and one of 'em, a good-sized man, said, "Follow me, now."

We followed him, anyway, but grass was under our feet the whole time. And we crossed no wall, and sure, west Clare is full o' walls. I s'pose we traveled for about a mile, anyway, but the coffin was leaning on our shoulders now. And there was no change; we never changed.

But we landed at this fort, anyway, with a grand, dry grave opened. And when we were coming near the fort, this red-haired young man came out with a round collar on him. He was a priest. I s'pose he was one that was swept with the fairies. They have to have every kind of a person, you know.

He came out to meet the corpse, anyway, and walked in with us. And the coffin was left down. And he read the burial service, now, the same as you'd hear below in Ennis or Crusheen where you're living. 'Twas much the same as our own. He started off, "I am the resurrection and the life. He that believes in me will never die. Even though he die he shall live again." All that. And he said Christ was the first to rise from the dead, and by the three days He lay in the tomb He made holy the graves of those that believe in Him. Just the same as our own now. But in the diocese o' Killaloe here they says ten Hail Marys and an Our Father in honor o' the resurrection. Well, I noticed they didn't say it there at all. For sure, now, they had the same religion as ourself, but that was the only thing they left out.

He started to praise this girl, anyway, and he praised her up to the sky, but he never mentioned her name or anything about her—praised the great qualities she had, but nothing about her family.

The coffin was lowered in the grave, anyway, and there was two or three men there with shovels. I s'pose they were fairy men, too. They had the thing ready. There was no delay. They filled up the grave, and the very minute they filled up the grave, when they had it flattened out with the shovels, a cock crew.

And like that!—inside five seconds there was no one there but myself.

I looked around. And there was one big house, a slated house, and another small thatched house. They were both farmhouses. But 'twas in one o' them two houses the cock crew.

I looked around, and I seen the Ennistymon hospital—'twas a landmark—and I knew where I was then. I walked home, anyway, but 'twas nearly six o'clock in the morning when I landed at home.

As far as I know they done me no harm or I done them no harm. But they have to have a live person. And I s'pose in that case, I was the live person.

This tale, from the same source as the previous one, shows us many facets of fairy belief in Ireland—that a person may be taken from this world of ours to the World Beyond while going about very ordinary tasks (mainly in the twilight or in the hours of darkness). A universally tried remedy when put astray by the fairies was to turn one's coat inside out in hope of fooling them. In this case it does not work. Just as well for us, for as a result of this man's night adventure we see that the Good People are in many ways like ourselves: that they have the same rituals—wakes, funerals, burial services . . . almost. We are even told where the burial will take place: in a fort.

Here and there, however, we can glimpse, through significant details, danger signs: the warning not to eat, the strange journey with the coffin, the red-haired priest, the prayers not said.

Cock crow, that division between the realms of darkness and daylight, intervenes, luckily. He arrives home in the early hours, unhurt; convinced, though, that they need a live person to conduct their business properly. The very way he phrases it: "But they have to have a live person," is interesting. If he emphasizes the word "live" (which he does), what then are they to be regarded as? Dead? Or something in between? It is a question that finds no easy answer among philosophers and theologians, never mind folklorists.

"Footballers coming home after a game, or hurlers,
wouldn't like to be by theirself. They'd have someone with 'em.
They might be asked to play a game with the fairies, you see.
They used like to have someone with 'em. If there was a
second with 'em they mightn't be asked, they said."
MILTOWN MALBAY, JUNE 27, 1999

Refereeing a Fairy Hurling Match

THERE'S A FORT a couple o' miles from here, on the road to Askeaton, and this man I know, he told me he was coming home one night at about twelve o'clock. 'Twas a moonlit night in the autumn. And there was a hill where this fort was, so he had to get off his bicycle to walk up.

Next thing, this small little man, a fairy man, stood out in front of him and said, "Will you referee a match for us? We have two teams waiting, a very important match to be played, and there's no one to referee it. He never showed up, wherever he went."

Your man, anyway, was kind o' slow in venturing into this unknown territory. Would you blame him? He had heard enough stories about people who were asked to oblige the fairies and didn't, and what happened to 'em. So he laid up his bicycle and said he'd do whatever they wanted, as long as the people at home wouldn't be waiting too long for him.

"Don't have no fear about that," said the small man. "When the game is over you can go your way."

So he went in. 'Twas in a field just off the road, beside Haugh's Fort. I know the place well, a fine level field. The fort is there yet, as good as ever. No one ever put a hand to it.

They had all the field marked out when he went in, goal-posts up and all—'twas a hurling match—and they were all there waiting for him, fifteen a side. And they had different colors. They were all dressed in different colors so that he'd make no mistake.

They had great welcome for him. The two captains stood out, shook his hand. I don't know did he explain rules or anything like that to them. I s'pose he didn't.

But, anyway, he threw in the ball and the game started.

And 'twas a game! Up and down, and up and down, hell for leather. They were able to play hurling. There was no easy ball there. And every now and again he'd have to blow the whistle—they were fouling one another so much. He was amazed. The size of 'em and they were tougher than the biggest fellows he ever saw playing! Several times he had to warn 'em he'd send 'em off.

Anyway, he had a pocket watch, so he was keeping the time, and when it came to halftime he got a drink o' water and all.

But no one talked to him, and he was wondering what would he do.

The second half started, and he said to himself, "If I do the wrong thing here am I in trouble? Could they take me away with 'em?"

He blew the whistle, anyway, and the second half went on. And 'twas up and down, point for point. I think he played twenty minutes a side. He said a half an hour'd be too much for 'em, that they wouldn't be able to keep going—at least, by the size they were.

So, the last five minutes was an awful problem to him. He was saying to himself, "If I can at all now, I'll make this a draw. I'll be in no trouble then."

So, coming up to the last couple o' minutes, there was one side a point behind and they were pressing and pressing. But the other fullback cleared away out into the center o' the field. And then, however 'twas done from out there, didn't the crowd that were behind get a point to level the score.

He looked at his watch. And there was still a minute or two to go, but he blew the whistle . . . 'twas safer to do it now. He mightn't get the score level again.

Well, if he was wondering what they'd do, he needn't. They all gathered 'round him, and such thanks as they gave him! 'Twas the best match they ever had, they told him, a great night's entertainment entirely. And they asked him would he come again if they wanted him. He told 'em he would, and glad to. Maybe 'twas glad to escape he was. They went then and left him there.

But ever after he took a different road to Askeaton.

To be hijacked on your way home at night by the Good People! No small matter, especially when one of their hurling or football matches is in question. For they take their games deadly seriously. In this case the man in question should have been more careful, since his road home ran right beside a fort, moreover one where he was at a disadvantage, laboring up a hill.

Yet, the manner in which he answers their call when they summon him proves that obligingness, and after that a cool head, may save one from even dire possibilities.

And in this case the worst would have been the loss of a hurling match. Obviously the Good People are desperately competitive, and their sports are the traditional Irish ones of hurling, Gaelic football, perhaps wrestling, horse racing—not road bowling, though, since that involves iron or steel, which is anathema to them. And the notion of them playing soccer is . . . is . . . well, odd. So un-Irish as to be almost laughable. It would be the same as them driving cars: somehow ridiculous.

The man who so successfully referees their game that night on his way home towards Askeaton learns a salutary lesson, though: One meeting with them is enough. He knows well that the next time he may not be so fortunate, and modifies his behavior accordingly.

A Queer Walk

THIS MAN who used to live up here in Tullaroe, he had two sisters married over here. He was above in Kilkee this night, and he came along for Tullaroe. And when he came to one house they were in bed.

"Well," says he, "I won't disturb 'em." So he went to the other sister—she was only the pelt of a stone away, married there, too. And they were asleep. He made for home, anyway. And when he was about a mile down the road, he said he could see the crowd and they were kicking football.

He said he didn't get any way upset or afraid, but when he came back as far as Carrigaholt, he said he met a funeral. That'd be about one or two o'clock in the night. And the priests that were in the funeral were dressed in black and white, he said, and they were coming with the hearse. It stirred him up then. He got afraid because he had to go as far as Fódra.

When he met the funeral he said, "I won't go no farther. I'll go in to my friend's house."

So he went in. Wasn't it a queer walk!

He lived above there and he told me that one day when we were coming from Kilrush.

A story such as this one begs several obvious questions: Is the teller, perhaps, telescoping two separate tales, heard at different times in the past, into one? Was the man who told him the story, maybe, so frightened that he became confused? Or was he under the influence of drink on his night journey from Kilkee?

That a crowd would be playing football at night, or that there would be a mysterious funeral in the dead hours, both of these are well-attested happenings, but that they would occur to the one person on the same journey on a single night, without any negative consequences, seems somehow odd, something of a letdown—showing, maybe, how dependent we are on the teller of a tale for its coherence. But on the other hand, life being by no means as neatly packaged as we might wish, perhaps this is how that man's journey from Kilkee was that night— a walk with the otherworldly, that of the fairies and that of the dead in succession.

"They couldn't be seen, only in the nighttime."
KILCOLUM, KILMALEY, AUGUST 11, 1999

A Skeptic's Story

THE GOOD PEOPLE? Well, there was a lot o' them stories, now, and they were coincidence, I think.

There was a couple o' men from here one time . . . at that time you'd have to go into town for a coffin with a horse and car when somebody'd die. There was no hearse or anything else, only the horse and common car. But these two boys went to Gort for a coffin in a horse and car one evening. They took a few extra drinks and 'twas very late when they came back. And coming home, the band came off o' the wheel. And o' course, that was it. They couldn't go any farther. They hit it in a small bit, anyway, and they took off the coffin and they left it beyond there at Waters' crossing. Then one of 'em went away down for the loan o' the horse car from the man down the road, d'you see. And they left the coffin there. The other fellow stopped there with the coffin to wait until he came up with the other horse car. And he was sitting down on the coffin, sure, smoking his pipe, when a couple o' people came along. And, sure, Lord save us, they saw the coffin left down and a man sitting above on it. They definitely did conk out! One of 'em wasn't in the better o' that for a long time. He was full sure that 'twas the lad inside came out for a smoke.

Here we see a seemingly rational man coming to a rational conclusion about what in reality was a case of mistaken identity at night. And his testimony is useful in that it reminds us that, yes, many sightings of strange things at night by travelers in a pre-electric age must have been magnified by their imaginations into whatever they wished to see.

But his inability or unwillingness to distinguish between the fairy and the ghost world is typical of many Irish people, and even more interestingly, when I asked him a few minutes later whether he believed in retribution by the Good People on those who interfered with fairy places, his reply was, "I wouldn't believe in one bit of it."

Yet straightaway, he went on to add that he himself would not interfere with such places, bulldoze a fort, or move it: "I mean, you could trim it up a bit, but I wouldn't ever agree in taking it away. No. You could be wealthy enough without the little bit o' land that was taken up with a fort."

It is this strange mixture of sentiments and beliefs that I find so fascinating, and which has been far more effective in protecting these sites than the most stringent laws. (*To knowingly destroy a fort nowadays carries a penalty of up to €75,000.*)

*"I was telling you about the fairies I saw that had the sports
in the big field below; they'd remind you much of something you'd see
in a film. They flit from A to B. They're as if they'd be carried
in the breeze. That kind o' thing. But they were there. Sure I saw 'em
performing, an' the races they ran an' the games they played were all
going around in a circle. There was no go two hundred yards
on the straight in a race. They went round in circles."*
DRUMLINE, JULY 10, 2000

Man Carried to Play Football

IT HAPPENED about a half a mile up the road there, towards Camp. This man living below here, his daughter was married in Camp, and the mother had something to send down to her, so she asked him to take it down to her.

"I will, o' course," says he. She gave him a sixpence and he went off walking. He found the daughter, anyway. And her husband—they weren't long married—came up to Camp with him. I don't know is it Barry's or Ashe's pub they went into. 'Twas one o' the two, anyway, and they had two pints out o' the sixpence. And they had two pence left. And if they had another halfpenny they could get another pint and halve it.

But 'twas about ten o'clock when he left the pub and all the drink he had was two pints. He was coming along for Glenagalt and next thing he was taken into this field.

There was a crowd there, he said, but he didn't know any of 'em. They were normal size.

He could hear the ball kicking and any ball that came 'twas a goal. They put him in the goal. Two uprights and a bar across 'em.

And they were talking and everything, but he couldn't understand any word o' what they were saying. He understood, all right, that they wanted him to keep goal. But he didn't know was there a man in the goalposts on the opposite side o' the field or not.

'Twas nearly two o'clock when he got home. "The wife started at me," he says, "that we spent the night in Camp drinking."

But he went over the following morning then, he said. There was hay cut off o' that field and a nice bit o' young grass, but the only place that there was any bit o' trampling or anything was where he was standing—and he could see the holes for the goalposts.

So 'twas no dream. But they did him no harm.

Here we see, once again, that the Good People seem to need a human being if they are to do their business properly, even if the person in question seems to have only a poor grasp of the proceedings. The man in this story seems not to understand their language. Maybe not surprising, this, since the Good People speak Irish. His night visit with them is certainly a confused one. Can he, or can he not, see the football? Does he manage to prevent any scores?

Yet he can see and hear the players. And, significantly, they are normal human size. He comes to no harm, either, probably because he did not resist their summons.

And when he checks the place the following day, he finds that, sure enough, the marks of the goalposts are where he recalls them having been. But there are no other player's footprints there but his own.

The man who told me this story was ninety-eight at the time and died only in 2000, aged one hundred.

A Midnight Ride

I WENT OVER to my uncle in Feakle one time, and we went on *cuaird** one night. And we were coming home about twelve o'clock in the night and this terrible noise came along the road of horses galloping. And my uncle was coming behind me and he says, "Will you come for a drive tonight?"

"Where?" I said, "Or what?"

"Oh, you haven't much time now," he says. "First horse that'll pass you, shout, 'A cap and a horse for me!'"

Faith, no length till the horses came, and I heard my uncle shouting behind me, "A cap and a horse for me!"

And I shouted the same. The next thing, we were gone. No idea in God's glory where we went, but we were traveling for a long time. We could be gone back as far as Loughrea. We had terrible jumps here and there—you'd hear an old man shouting now and again to hold the reins tight. We could be back around Loughrea or Ballinasloe, but all of a sudden it stopped. And you

*Night visiting.

could look round. See nothing. You didn't know in the hell what was up, but there was terrible sound o' people now and again, great commotion o' talk.

But every now and again a light would flash over and hither, and it seems a football match was on. Whether 'twas Cork or Galway or who was at it between the fairies, this huge crowd was inside in a field by the side of a grove. Some of 'em was dressed in white and more in green. But the light'd flash now and again, just to let you see 'twas on. And the terrible shouting was going on inside, every now and again.

I have no idea how I was able to stick it out, but after about an hour and a half we started again with our horses. An old man came and shouted. They must have won the match. There was terrible shouting started.

But we came along—I s'pose we had to cross the Shannon. He let one unmerciful shout: "Boys," he said, "stick tight. This is a big jump!"

And we landed, I s'pose, in Tipperary or someplace—in across the Shannon. And off we went.

We was going all night long, until we landed back again to where we were, and felt these things coming down to the ground. And down we was, the very same as when we were picked up, at six o'clock in the morning.

Wasn't that something? Wasn't that an experience! And my uncle says to me, "If they ask you where you was," he said, "say we were playing cards. Don't let on we were out driving."

So I never told anyone for years where we was that night.

Not very often does one hear of a person brave (or mad!) enough to invite himself into the fairy host on its travels, but here we have such an account. The older man obviously has gone on such outings previously for he knows the magic formula that will allow them to obtain transport for the night's adventure. The younger man, however, finds the night frightening, confusing, yet exhilarating, a kaleidoscope of sounds, movements, colors, and impossible feats like jumping the Shannon, the largest river in Ireland.

No wonder his uncle tells him to mention nothing about where they've been all night when they get home!

Here again we see the competitiveness of the fairies in their games and the long distances they travel on important occasions to meet rival teams and support their own—just like the followers of hurling and Gaelic football to this very day, in fact!

*"They were famous for music. An' 'twas the pipes the most
of 'em played. An' different people heard it."*
MILTOWN MALBAY, JUNE 27, 1999

A Musician's Story

I KNOW A MAN, now, that went out in the night, and he heard the music, the violin music, playing. And he was a great musician. Faith, he associated it with the fairies. And I said to him, "Did you bring ever a note out of it?"

"Believe it or not," he said, "anytime ever I heard a new tune or music played anywhere, I always brought the air of it. But," he said, "not as much as a note did I bring out o' that fairy music."

I said, "Would you be able to get your bow and put it on the string on the same note?"

"Not a hope in hell," he said.

And that man was full o' music, could read music, was a great musician. No! The music, he said, was unnatural, 'twas windy, 'twas very twisty music. So I can understand that he didn't. Different people, now, that heard music in the night, I asked 'em the very same question: Did they bring a note out of it? And they said no.

Well, I have an instance o' something like that myself, now. Take the coral that grows in the coral reef in Australia. If you can break a piece off that coral there's no known adhesive that'll stick that. And 'tis like the fairy music. There's nothing to bond it. The ordinary musician that'll hear the fairies' music won't bring it.

And if the man I knew couldn't, no one would. I grant you that.

On the face of it, this story seems a little unusual, for there are many instances of wonderful music being brought back from the fairy world, such as "The Fairy Reel" or "Port na bPúcaí," etc. The vital differentiating factor would seem to be that if the music is given freely by the Good People to the human being (as a reward for a favor done, for instance) it will be brought across that divide between their world and ours. Otherwise, as in this case, its complexity defies even the best human musician's skill.

Not just to the luxuries of life, like music, does this apply, but to the very basics, like time itself. For a millennium and more Irish people have listened spellbound to stories of The Land of Youth—Tír na nÓg—with their message that to attempt to go beyond our natural sphere of space and time can end only in disappointment and ultimate disaster.

*"There didn't appear to be any dilapidated people in 'em.
They all appeared to be in good shape. They were a
lively crowd o' people, an' merriment was their
business, as far as I could see."*
DRUMLINE, JULY 10, 2000

A Fairy Request Thwarted

THIS MAN NOW—I only just remember him, but I remember my father talking about him many's the time—he was Dr. Walsh. At least he had the name of a doctor, 'cause he was a bit knowledgeable. He was in Listowel one day at the market and he came home, very early, of a summer's evening.

Now, he had a brother, and it was just the harvest time, and he said to the brother, "There's a rail o' turf yet in the bog. We'll go back for it before the harvest'll start. And d'you know what?" says he. "I'll take the shortcut, and let you go around the other road. I bet you I'll be back before you."

Why the two of 'em didn't go together, I can't tell you that, but this is the way my father told it to me.

The doctor went his road, and whether 'twas tired he was or not I don't know. He was, I s'pose, after his day in Listowel. But after he crossed this glen that was on his way, he sat up on the side of a bank and he fell asleep.

He slept for a while, and when he woke he was inside in the finest house, I'd say, that was ever built. There was nothing like it in Dublin, or in London, either. And still, he knew where he was in spite of all of it. And he knew the time he left home. Oh, he didn't lose the run o' his senses at all.

Next, a door opened and a man came in, a man of about seventy-five years of age.

He stood, oh, for a good five minutes with not a word out of him, only staring at the poor man. Then, when he had enough looked, he held out his hand.

"Welcome here, Mr. Walsh," says he.

"And tell me, how's Seán a' Carraig?"—that was Walsh's father's name—"and how's all the Walshs in Carraigín?" . . . and all that kind o' thing.

They started talking, and they had a great chat. But after a while the old lad says, "I know that my father'd like to see you."

"You don't mean to tell me, surely," says Walsh, "that your father is alive yet."

"My father? Indeed he is, and hardy," says he.

He got up, went to the door, and called for the father. He came in, a fine hardy man, right enough, and they talked on— "How're all the Walshs in Carraigín?" . . . and more to that.

But after a while the lad, he says, "I must call my grandfather. 'Tis a pity to leave him out of a grand friendly meeting like this."

Begod, 'tis then that Walsh was getting afraid. The grandfather came in, anyway, and begod, he was a fresh enough man, too, for his years, no crutches or nothing. But they weren't too long talking at all when the music started, and begod it must be good 'cause the whole lot of 'em got up and started in at it. 'Twas great sport and Walsh danced as good as any of 'em.

At last, the music stopped and a table was laid. And that was the time he says to himself, "Ah! If I take anything now, I'm held."

They wanted him in the worst way to have something. There was stuff on the table the like o' which he never saw before, but he'd eat nothing.

He must have great courage, the same man. What did he say to the man that came in the door first? He was sitting there next to him. "Well now," says he, "if 'twas the Man Above Himself sent ye here I don't know, but I'm passing here since I was a child and I never see this house here before."

"We're here," says he, "with . . . I don't know how many years. Hundreds o' years. And you'll put us back at the age o' thirty-three years now if you'll do this for us. We came from Mountcollins, and I'll give you a rod here now," says he, "and if you go to Mountcollins there's a field there. They call it Páirc na Búistéirí, The Butchers' Field. There's a well in that field and if you'll only touch the flagstone that's over that well with the rod, you'll be handed out a razor. Bring it back here to us, and when we'll shave ourselves with that we'll be back to thirty-three years again, myself and my father and grandfather. Will you do that much for us?"

"I will," says he.

He took the rod and he slept again—maybe tired after all the dancing. And when he woke there was no house. He was there on the side o' the bank. But the rod was beside him. He was looking at it! He was nearly afraid to pick it up, but what could he do, after promising 'em? So he went on home.

His wife asked him where was he and what kept him. She was a saintly kind of a woman. He didn't want to be worrying her, you know.

"Oh," says he, "I was with your cousin behind there. There was a cow sick to calve all night, and I didn't like to come home," . . . and all that kind o' talk.

But she mustn't have believed him, 'cause in the windup she got the real story out o' him. And she was at the well before him. Whatever chance he had, she took the rod, and she never again gave it back to him. Whether 'twould be effective or not, I don't know.

You'd think he'd be dreaming but for the rod being there when he woke up.

I heard that from the man himself. He used to be at our house, rambling, when we were young. But they say that kind o' thing was in his family. His mother's family was from Brosna, and his uncle had land going down to where Mountcollins creamery is now. And there was about a half acre o' land taken up by a fort in his place, near the creamery. And when they had the hay finished one year, himself and the mowers went over to Mountcollins to have a few pints. So, they were just crossing the bridge and one o' the mowers gave a look back at the fort.

"By God," says he, "'tis a pity to see that fine crop o' hay going for nothing. I'll cut it."

"Don't mind it," says the uncle. "Leave it there."

"No," says he. "I'll cut it."

He went back, whatever was picking him. He drew the first sweep. And he stuck the scythe in the ground—a thing that no right mower'd do.

"Come on. Come out of it!" says the other man.

"Well," says he—he was stubborn—"if it takes until cock crow o' me, I'll cut it."

That very minute a cock crew up in one o' the bushes!

"Will you come out of it! Leave it there!"

And they did.

'Tis there today, that fort. And if you look at it you'll see that no one goes next or near it 'cause 'tis all overgrown with bushes.

In tangible terms, all that remains today of the elements of this story is the fort near Mountcollins creamery. All the human actors and tellers are dead, and no one could point out to me the well or even Páirc na Búistéirí. That proves nothing, though, for names change, and land reclamation has gone on at an ever more rapid pace in every parish in Ireland in recent years.

This story appeals to me because of its undoubted antiquity—the notion of the chosen coming back to the same age as Jesus Christ, thirty-three years, especially for resurrection, was a common one in the Middle Ages throughout Europe. And a person's wandering into a fairy mansion, where the laws of human time no longer apply, is extremely old in Irish telling.

And yet, the miracle is that I was able to hear (in 1978) these echoes of ancient times from an ordinary, so-called uneducated man living in a roadside cottage! I was fortunate to do so when I did. Otherwise he would now be no more than just another member of that vast legion of great storytellers silent forever in the graveyards of Ireland.

Man Borrows a Fairy Horse

THERE'S SUCH A THING there as a *fíor-lár*. The *fíor-lár* is a fairy horse, a fairy foal. And how that foal comes to be a fairy horse is this: You see, ordinarily it takes approximately ten, eleven months, or a little over it, for a mare to breed a foal. But for a *fíor-lár*, from the day the mare has left the horse until the day she has the foal, she has to carry that foal for three hundred and sixty-six days. Not a leap year, now, but any year—a year and a day. 'Tis very rare. You might get one in five thousand. But it happens. And if you get that foal, you have a fairy foal. People don't particularly like 'em. They can be funny fish.

There was a fellow over the road and he had one, an Irish draught mare. She was a grand animal. And the stable was right up to the back of a fort. When she got to be a two-year-old, he trained her. Fine farming horse—or she'd hunt—excellent horse. As quiet and satisfactory an animal as you could possibly meet.

People around here used to be carrying hay, turnips, and everything to Limerick market that time. They used to start in the middle o' the night. Every fellow'd be looking to try and get a quiet horse that'd stand inside in town, stand inside in the market. If you had a quiet horse, they'd borrow him.

Nearly everyone used to borrow this one, the *fíor-lár* one. But the man that owned her, he'd always say to you, "You have no business coming for her until after two o'clock." They should be starting out at two o'clock in the morning to be in the market for five o'clock to sell a load o' hay or turnips.

But this one fellow, he lived about a mile away, d'you see, and he was a bit of an unbeliever in them things. "You know," he said, "I'll bring her home, and that way I won't have to be coming at two o'clock in the morning for her. I'll bring her home at seven or eight o'clock and tackle her."

"Okay," says your man.

So he collected the mare and took her home. And he started off for town at about twelve o'clock with his load o' hay.

Bejasus, when he was coming for Bunratty the load o' hay got two or three most terrible bumps. The car heeled up with him, man! He didn't know what in the hell was the score. But it settled down again. He went on to town. But when he got to the market and when it came daylight, it wasn't the mare that he borrowed that was under the car at all, but another one, a different horse!

So, begod, he carried on, but he couldn't understand it. He sold his load o' hay and came home. And he had to go on towards Newmarket with his horse and car.

Bejasus, when he came above to the fort at Smithstown— Walsh's Fort 'tis known as—the horse stopped. No power on earth'd move him. He stopped dead. Begod, he was a clever old boy. He decided that he'd untackle the horse and take him out from under the car and push the car a bit up the road and tackle him again to it. He knew 'twas the fort was stalling him. He got suspicious, you see. How could it be that a horse would change from under the car at Bunratty the night before? He knew he had something strange on his hands.

Well, anyway, he untackled this new horse, and the very minute he untackled the horse and pulled him down the road a bit, the horse shook himself. He shook off what tacklings was on him, jumped over the wall into the field where the fort was, and left him there—tacklings, car, and all. Ran for it.

He had the car there, anyway, and sure, he was nearly home. But by God, he was terrible confused.

So he went up and he collected his own horse and he got a fellow along with him. They tackled his own horse to the car and brought it home.

But he contacted the man that lent him the mare and the man said to him, "Christ, did you go to town with the load o' hay, at all?"

"I did," says your man.

"Begod," he said, "didn't I give you the mare to bring the load o' hay?"

"You did," he said, "but something happened in the meantime."

"Well, by God, I don't understand that, now," says your man. "That mare is below in the field. My own mare. She was in the stable this morning when I went out."

The man that owned her knew that the Good People had her picked up at Bunratty. They swapped him a fairy horse, another nag there, and let him off to Limerick.

The fairies wanted that horse for the hunt. That mare was gone with 'em that night. How well they left something instead of her, though. I s'pose they couldn't let him down there with no way o' going.

There are different definitions of what constitutes a fíor-lár, but what is not in doubt in Ireland is that some horses are special—are, in fact, fairy horses. This detailed story shows clearly that such a horse had an agenda of its own, well understood and accepted by its human owner if he was wise. She was needed at specific times by the Good People for their own pursuits, and when a human got in the way of those, he was unceremoniously pushed to one side— but not left helpless, as so often one human will leave another.

The Good People have a sense of fair play, we see. They will not let a person who is dependent for a livelihood on the services of the fíor-lár without a horse when they need her. Another horse is substituted.

A sad postscript to this story is that Walsh's Fort has been demolished of late to make way for a new highway. Not without promises of dire consequences-to-come from some very knowledgeable local elders. And, strangely enough, there have been several fatalities and injuries among those associated with its destruction. Coincidence? Maybe. Maybe not.

"Several cows around here was taken. They want the milk,
you see, in the forts, the fairies. They want the milk!"
LISCANNOR, JULY 17, 1999

A Fairy Cow

THERE WAS A STORY TOLD, 'twas common knowledge in this area when I was going to school, about this cow, a fairy cow. She used to billet above where the bush is in Latoon and she used to come down every morning via Clonmoney. And of course, the people o' the parish used to all milk her on the way down. She supplied milk to the poor people o' the parish. She was something on the same principle as the manna in the desert. She was a white cow. And you could milk her a million times and she'd still supply milk.

I inquired of a man that knew the story from his elders. I always heard it when I was going to school, but in order to back up my belief, I asked him. And he told me that some smart aleck on the way bet his neighbor he'd find a utensil that she wouldn't fill.

So he produced a sieve and milked her into that. She couldn't fill that, o' course. When the facility was abused, she came along until she came to Clonmoney, below the Hurler's Cross. There's a stream crossing the road there called the *Sruthán.** She took a drink out o' that stream and she showed up no more.

*Irish for "stream."

If the Good People take from us what they need when they need it, they can also be generous and helpful neighbors, as in this case, where one of their cattle is sent to help poor people.

Yet how depressingly predictable that human nature so often seems to find a way to abuse kindness—and for no other reason than the pleasure of doing so!—to the ultimate loss of everyone.

This story is told in various versions not just all over Ireland (in Irish the cow is known as the Glas Ghoibhneach*), but also in Scotland, Wales, and parts of England.*

"An old woman told me one time, if you ever heard it,
there's only a veil between this world an' the next."
BALLINRUAN, AUGUST 17, 1999

An Old Woman Changes Shape

THERE WAS AN OLD LADY, she used to turn into a hare and go off and clean what milk and butter'd be in the parish. I know, 'tis very hard to imagine for a person in their sober senses that a human being was capable o' doing it. Common sense would tell you otherwise. But still, it used to be done.

'Twas never heard of in a man—always a woman that did it. And if the wind changed while the person was in the shape o' the hare, she wouldn't be able to change back.

The Church used to denounce it, you know, strongly. So there must be something in it.

This old woman, anyway, that I heard about, she was definitely *piseógaí*.* You wouldn't be safe to have hand, act, nor part, or to meet her on the road, or anything.

Her neighbor had a pair o' greyhounds and he was out this day for a hunt. He was off a mile or two down the country when this hare rose. And the two old hounds—they'd be only old half-bred hounds—begod, they went at the hare. And she ran for it, straight for the house. There was a half-door in the house. And just as the hare was going over the half-door, begod didn't the hound grab her by the backside and brought a piece off o' her. The man that owned the two dogs, anyway, followed up, and he found the old lady inside in a pool o' blood on the floor. The hunt had the backside brought out o' her. So that's how he knew she was the hare.

The hare was an animal felt as being notably close to the Other World, to be regarded with suspicion if seen among cattle or too close to human habitation.

In this case the Good People are not involved, but might easily be, since this was one of the animals favored by them in their shape-shifting into our world.

*A charm setter.

The teller of this widespread story is adamant that only women were capable of this kind of shape-changing. But it had its dangers. Later, we will see that people who, similarly, "went" with the fairies could, in the long run, pay a terrible price for short-term gain. But if we can believe that women are more sensitive to, more capable of contact with, the World Beyond than men are, we need go no farther than County Clare for proof, for Feakle, in east Clare, was the home of Biddy Early (1798–1874), the greatest of all such. Regarded by the prejudiced and ignorant as a witch, she was in reality what the Irish called a "bean feasa"—a woman of knowledge. (There were no such things as witches in the Gaelic tradition. That was an imported aberration. Anywhere in Ireland that witches were burned—such as Kilkenny and Carrickfergus— was in the English sphere of political and church influence.) And to this day, Biddy is vividly remembered in Clare and the surrounding counties as one who cured not only physical ailments, but also advised people successfully on all and every kind of difficulties they might be having with their otherworldly neighbors. Her remedies are still remembered and some of them still acted on—well over a century after her death! No mean achievement for a mere "peasant" woman. *

*Cf. my *In Search of Biddy Early*, Mercier Press, Cork, 1987.

"They say she used to be with the fairies,
an' she got herbs an' cures an' every kind o' medicine."
MULLAGH, FEBRUARY 5, 1988

The Rats from the Ashes

THERE WAS A HOUSE down there one time—'tis gone now. There isn't even a trace of it there; all the stones were sold and took away. But 'twas a great house for *cuaird* one time. All the crowd around used to go in there at night.

'Twas the time o' Biddy Early, anyway, and the man o' the house, his cattle were dying, one after another. And his wife said, in the finish, "Wouldn't you go over to Biddy Early? She might do something for you."

"Ah," he says, "no. 'Tis some old plague on the cattle. And, sure, one that isn't able to do anything for her own daughter, she could hardly do anything for me."

She was a bit handicapped, Biddy's daughter, you see.

But, anyway, there was a few old lads in that night, and they all advised him to go over to her, that he couldn't be worse than he was. So, after a couple o' more dying, he decided he'd go over—off on his horse and saddle.

But when she saw him coming, she says, before ever he opened his mouth, "I know what you're coming for. And I know what you said about my daughter, too."

Nearly stuck him to the road, she did. Frightened the life out o' him!

"But notwithstanding what you said about us, I'll do what I can for you."

It transpired, anyway, that when he was going away she gave him a bottle. She told him to throw this bottle into Kilbarron Lake and all his troubles'd go.

And he did.

And she also asked him, "Have you an ash pit"—or an ash hole, as they call it—"in your house?"

He says, "I have."

"Open the back door and the front door," says she. "Stick down your spade into the ash pit and you'll see."

So, he went home and he did what she told him, stuck down the spade. And 'twas a lucky thing he had the doors opened, 'cause up came two big rats out o' the hole, and out the door with 'em. They were as big as a tomcat, each of 'em.

And them people never saw a poor day after.

But surely be to God, them were no ordinary kind o' rats— if they were rats at all. 'Twas something else that Biddy was putting out o' the place, you can be sure.

Human nature being what it is—proud, defensive, stubborn, and much more—we need not be surprised that the farmer in question here is reluctant to go to Biddy Early with his problem. It would be an admission of failure, perhaps incompetence, on his part. But when imminent ruin forces him at last to make a reluctant move, he finds that his problems are being caused by . . . by what?

The use of steel in Biddy's remedy suggests that the Good People are involved. But why? What did he do to deserve this treatment from them? As in so many tales, we will never know what that, perhaps smallest of mistakes, is that makes—even today—the critical difference between living a life of peace or turmoil.

During Biddy's final illness in 1874 the local parish priest, Father Andrew Connellan, before he would give her the Last Sacrament, is reputed to have demanded from her her famous blue bottle (a gift from the fairies) and thrown it into Kilbarron Lake, a short distance from her house. In the 1970s the lake was dredged in hopes of discovering this bottle but, alas, dozens of bottles were brought to the surface. So the mystery remains.

"There's bad fairies, an' there's good fairies.
Just like people. Take now, for instance, people seeing
a dog, now. He's the evil spirit, you know.
An' a pig is dynamite altogether. You might as well
pack it altogether if you meet a pig at night."
DRUMLINE, OCTOBER 17, 1992

A Strange Pig

THE MAN NEXT DOOR was coming one night, and he was frightened. There was a long house abroad there. As a matter o' fact 'twas a lot longer than my house, and there was a platform o' flagstones, a footpath, up to it at the front—the ground was low, you know. And he'd have an awful length to go around the house if he went around it.

A pig followed him over the road there, after he came round that crossroads over there. The pig was grunting and running.

Instead o' going around to the back door, with fright, he put all the force that was in his body against the front door. He pushed it in and shoved it out again. The pig didn't get to come in. He put the table against it.

The hens used to be in the houses at that time, inside in timber coops. They were made out o' laths and a space o' two or three inches between 'em. And the hens'd have their heads out.

They were double-decker coops. There was a low partition and a high partition. And there was a special peg in the wall for hanging up the horse's straddle.* And the cock used to never go in the coop. He'd be above on top o' that.

The cock crew three times, above on that perch that night, and fell down and died. What d'you think o' that?

That was no ordinary pig. Not at all! If the cock didn't die, your man would.

Here we can see the fear—no, mortal terror—even familiar animals could inspire in unfamiliar circumstances, and the close attention paid to details that a present-day, modern-minded observer would see as mere coincidence.

Why were certain animals associated with the otherworldly, e.g., the hare, the black dog, the pig, an broc sidhe (the fairy badger)? And which of these were evil spirits, which fairies in animal shape?

An extraordinarily difficult question to answer, this, especially since the Good People can take whatever shape they please, though they prefer some to others.

*Part of a workhorse's back harness.

*"There was a path, a fairy path there,
into Ralahine, an' there was always a dog on that."*
DRUMLINE, SEPTEMBER 19, 2001

Meeting the Black Dog

MYSELF AND MY BROTHER—we were barely going to
school at the time—we had an uncle up in Doora, up in Kil-
breckan. He had a little limestone farm and lived inside in a nice
thatched house in the middle of it. He never kept a horse—he
had only a small area o' ground—but he kept a small little dexter cow, with big wide horns. And she'd follow you to bed,
nearly, she was so tame. He was very thrifty. He'd have his own
little dexter calves, and they'd be sold to special people, people
like himself. He had a grand little shed made for the cow with
hazel wattles and covered with grass. Lovely! And the big old
grandfather clock with the weights, inside the kitchen. He had a
grand orchard at the back o' the house and he'd dig a grand
kitchen garden and he'd have spuds and cabbage and strawberries. Oh, we used to love him for the strawberries.

You'd love to meet him and talk to him. He was a great man
to explain to you, and trace, and go back on old times—a real
old-timer.

By God, didn't he give us this calf, a heifer calf, to keep for
ourselves in the house in the small little farm at home. So, we

minded this calf, o' course, like you'd mind a baby. And the calf grew up and became a cow. And when she'd be going to have a calf—you see, she was very small; she was a little dwarfy breed of an animal—we'd have to stay up for a couple o' days or a couple o' nights. She'd have to be attended to all the time. You know the old people, what they were like, now. There's no way they'd say, "Let her calve herself, and she'll be all right." That little cow was minded from once she showed signs o' going to have the calf until she *had* the calf.

So, myself and the brother was anxious to see this little calf. We hadn't a clue. But my father used to go up in the night. He had a setup under the hedge and he used to stay with the cow all night, for two or three nights, until she'd calve. And, sure, she might calve in the day, for that matter. But he'd be always there, anyway.

So, we'd be commissioned to make tea and provisions and bring it to the farm to him. And o' course, we were only delighted to be going up and down with the donkey. The donkey knew the road so well, man, that she'd trot flying up along and in. We'd deliver the tea and examine the cow and rub her and talk to her, and come home again.

But, when we were coming down, there was a big dog sitting up on his backside at this particular gate. He was two feet and a half high, sitting up—a big black dog. So, o' course, we were young lads and as far as we were concerned he was only a black dog. We were clever enough, though: Who owned him? Because we'd bring the eye out o' that dog with the throw of a rock, or a belt of a stick, if we didn't like him. But who owned him? That's what we were trying to figure out.

So, at ten or eleven o'clock the dog was there. We went again at midnight—and coming back, the dog was there. The dog was there till daylight in the morning for the two or three nights we were going up and down. And faith, I was smarter than the brother. You see, I was a year or two older. I was putting two and two together about the way he was sitting in the one spot all the time, and the size of him, that he was a bit unusual. But, right! We passed within feet of him, anyway. He didn't molest us and we didn't molest him.

The years rolled by and I discovered that the dog *was* there, and that he was no ordinary dog. There's a big fort forty yards from the gate, a mighty fort, and a farmhouse just under it. The farmer and his family were after eating the supper, and when they looked out at about six o'clock in the evening of a summer's evening, wasn't this big animal, like a bear, abroad, and he rooting around the yard. He frightened 'em, faith. One o' the workmen didn't come to work for a month after it. It frightened the life out of him, this big dog.

And that farmer and all his family, and his people before him, that came in and out o' that gate, they'd never admit to him being there. "No! He's not there. For sure!"

Well, they had seen that dog—and the whole country besides 'em—as often as there was fingers and toes on 'em, as the saying is.

O' course, they denied it for fear 'twould be a kind of stigma, that their place was haunted or something.

As an indicator of the otherworldly, the Black Dog is known in many lands, and in Ireland is regarded as a frequenter and protector of fairy sites such as their dwellings and pathways. Normally, the same dog is seen over several generations in the same location, huge, often immobile, watching menancingly, though rarely dangerous if left in peace. Few of those who encounter this creature choose, after their experience, to investigate more closely!

"Provided that you didn't interfere with 'em,
they wouldn't say or do anything to you."
DRUMLINE, OCTOBER 17, 1992

The Eel

YOU KNOW YOURSELF, that when the landlords were in charge here times were tough. Well, there was two days that people were afraid of more than all the others in the year. They were the gale days, the days when the rent had to be paid to the landlord's agent. It varied from place to place—April and October, maybe, or June and December. But if you hadn't that money in your fist for the vulture when the time arrived, you could be thrown out on the side o' the road. And he had the police and the courts behind him, so there was very little you could do, only pay.

Now, in them times there was a man and his wife living down the road there, not too far away from the next lake below. Decent people they were, too. Hard-working. And they had a bit more comfort than their neighbors. The reason was simple enough—because he was a thatcher. Remember now, thatching at that time was a trade as big as the blacksmith's. Every parish had one at least, because nearly all o' the houses were thatched, as well as all the stables and outhouses.

But, this man, he was good at his trade, and well liked 'cause he'd always give you a choice o' the kind o' reeds when he came to you to thatch: freshwater or saltwater. The difference between 'em? 'Tis a big one, I can tell you. Saltwater reeds, they'll only last above on a roof for about eight years, but freshwater reeds will last the most of fifteen years. That's the reason why nearly everyone wanted the freshwater ones. And 'twas the reason why he was so popular, 'cause he never charged anything extra for that type.

But they had to be cut, o' course. And even today, if you're cutting reeds there's only two ways to do it—either with a reaping-hook or a scythe. It'd take forever to cut 'em with a hook, so naturally he used the scythe. But the bother with a scythe is that you need the ground clear in front o' you. If you strike a rock you'll make bits o' your blade—and that was a dear enough item in them days.

But, sure, he knew all the lake shores like the back o' his hand, and year after year he used to go back to this grand, level sandy beach, a couple o' hundred yards long, no rocks there and plenty reeds.

So, this particular year 'twas in the month of October, fine frosty weather, ideal for cutting—he was there, working away at the side o' the lake. And 'twas shoving on to evening. He had enough done, he said to himself. Tomorrow was another day. So he began to bind up the reeds into sheaves, then into bundles, and carry 'em home. Now, he was only about a quarter of a mile from his house, so between home and back, home and back, it wasn't long before he was down to the last bundle. He was pleased with himself, too. A good day's work done and nearly finished. So he took his scythe, threw the bundle o' reeds over his shoulder, and headed for the gap out onto the road.

But he was only halfway across the field when he noticed something up in the field to his left. He stopped to look at it. And there, down out o' the corner o' that field, came a wheel! 'Twas the size of—d'you know the big wheel of a penny-farthing bicycle?—the size o' that, rolling down the field towards him. He didn't know what to make of it. What would you do yourself if you saw the like? But it rolled out along, about twenty feet from him, and as it passed him he saw that it was no wheel, but an eel or a snake with its tail inside in its mouth.

It couldn't be a snake—in Ireland?—so it had to be an eel. But it did him no harm, didn't interfere with him in any way, only went off about its own business into the gloom.

He stood there a while, wondering if he was dreaming. But 'twas getting dark, so he went away home. He was wondering, though, as he came near the house, should he tell his wife about what he saw, or not.

He knew her well enough—why wouldn't he, when they were married for over twenty-five years?—and he was full sure that if he mentioned it to her the first thing she'd do was attack him, accuse him o' being up in the pub drinking porter when he should be working. So he decided, no. Maybe he was only imagining it; he'd say nothing.

She was waiting for him at the yard gate.

"Anything strange?" says she.

"Nothing at all," and he put away the scythe and his bundle.

He went in then, had the supper, smoked his pipe by the fire awhile, and then went to bed.

But he couldn't go to sleep thinking about the strange-looking creature, wondering did he see it or didn't he. He was turning and tossing, this way and that, until his wife sat up in the bed.

"What in God's name is wrong with you?" says she. "Is it fleas you have, or what?"

That quietened him. He turned in to the wall, but he couldn't put it out o' his mind. And the last thing he said to himself before he closed his eyes was, "I'll be there again tomorrow. We'll see what we'll see then."

And he was. In the same place, cutting, cutting away with the scythe. He had great work done by the time 'twas beginning to get dark.

"Enough," says he, and he began to gather the reeds up into sheaves, into bundles, then carry 'em home. And by the time he was down to the last one, the light was nearly gone. But he waited. Five minutes. Nothing. Ten minutes. Nothing moving. He gathered himself to go.

"Wasn't it just as well I didn't tell her, and make a fool o' myself. She'd be throwing it at me for the next month!"

But just at that very minute he saw something moving, in the very same place as the day before, the same corner o' the field. He stopped, watched it as it came closer and closer, in the very same path as the evening before. And as it passed by him—only about maybe ten feet from him—he saw that 'twas the same creature, a huge eel, or at least like one, with its tail inside in its mouth, rolling along. But this time he noticed something else: It had a big, long mane o' hair down along its back, just like a horse.

"Well, by God," says he, "that's the queerest thing I ever saw," as it went off into the gloom. Never did him one bit o' harm, only off about its own business, whatever that was.

He went home, anyway, and this time there was no doubt in his mind. He could tell his wife about it. He was sure o' what he saw.

She was there waiting for him, as usual.

"Anything strange?" says she.

He only smiled while he was putting away the scythe and his bundle.

She knew there was something different this evening.

"What happened?" says she. "Was there something—?"

"Time enough for that later on. Where's the supper?"

That only made her more curious than ever. She kept on at him until he told her what he saw. But did she believe him?

All she said was, "You're drunk! Above in the pub drinking, when you were supposed to be working!"

And, sure, if she had any eyes in her head she should know by all the bundles he brought home before that that couldn't be true. But she had her mind made up!

"Well, I knew it," says he, "that I should have mentioned nothing!"

And he breathed out, then—"Ha-aaagh! There now. Is there a smell o' drink off me? Is there?"

She had to admit there wasn't. But she still wouldn't believe him. And maybe 'tis hard to blame her. 'Tisn't every day you're asked to believe a story like that.

Well, he went off to bed by himself, straight after eating. No smoke, no more talk. He was in a temper with himself for mentioning anything to her about it. But he swore to himself that if the eel was there the following day he'd do something about it. He wasn't going to be treated like a fool in his own house!

He made full sure to be back at the same place the next evening. He was working away like before with the scythe, cutting away before him, and by the time the light was fading he had enough done, so he started making up his sheaves, then bundles, and bringing 'em home.

And when there was only one last load to bring, he stopped. And waited. He looked around him. Nothing stirring. He waited there ten minutes. Still nothing. The moon was starting to rise now, the makings of a fine, cool night. But no sign o' life. He took up the scythe then, and his bundle on his shoulder, and walked for the gap. But every so often he'd look back, hoping, I s'pose, that the thing'd come back. But nothing.

When he came to the road he stopped, looked all around him again. Still no move. He waited a few more minutes. But there was nothing there. What could he do except go home! And that's what he did. But every few yards he'd peep in over the ditch, between the bushes, back towards that far corner o' the field. But maybe 'twas his misfortune he couldn't leave well alone. Because he was only gone maybe twenty yards along the road when, what should he see, in the very same place, only something moving! He knew straight away what 'twas; dropped the bundle o' reeds and ran back to the gap with the scythe in his hand. 'Twas halfway down the field now, coming towards him in the very same track as the other two days. And this time, by God, he was going to do something about it!

He stood there in its way, the scythe ready in his hands, and as it passed him he stabbed out, up with the blade, and cut it about a foot from where its tail was inside in its mouth.

It flopped down, into the grass, and 'twas only then he saw the right length of it—ten feet at the very least. But he didn't care, only stuck the point o' the blade down into it, threw the scythe over his shoulder, kept the thing well out from himself, and headed for home. O' course, the creature was wriggling, going mad with pain, I s'pose. He didn't care. Now he'd show his wife whether he was drinking or not!

He arrived home in ten minutes or so and there she was in the yard, waiting for him.

The Eel

"Well," says she, "did you—?"

But she got no chance to finish. He threw down the eel in front of her.

"Now," says he. "Now was I drinking? Was I imagining it?"

The poor woman jumped back, of course, when she saw this thing, especially when it started wriggling down along the yard—trying to escape, I s'pose. But he wasn't going to leave things so. Oh, no! He ran for the door, into the kitchen, to the dresser, and snapped the knife out of the drawer, the sharp knife they had for cutting the bacon. He was out again before the eel was gone two yards, and he clapped his boot down on it, just behind its head.

D'you know what he did then?! He slit it with that knife from his boot down to its tail—what was left of it. I don't know what was he expecting to find. Gold? Some other kind o' treasure? I don't know. But all he got was blood, that small bit o' blood you get when you cut up an eel. And he was so annoyed that he kicked it from him. He was disgusted. Worse than disgusted!

He went in home, left the eel to the cats—and there was plenty o' them there, like you'd find in every farmyard.

His wife saw the temper he was in. She said nothing to him during the supper. Or after it, either. He went to bed. There was no more said that night.

But the following morning, early, about six o' clock, he was up—his usual time, like all the other farmers o' the place. He got out o' the bed, nothing on him but his shirt, and started for the back door, for the water, to wash himself and wake up right and shave.

Remember, now, that in them days in Ireland there was no hot and cold water in houses at the turn of a tap—not like today! The last thing that had to be done at night—and 'twas usually the women that did it!—was go to the well and bring in the water, two buckets of it. One of 'em was for drinking. That one was left inside the door, in case animals might be paddling around in it in the dark. The other one was for washing and shaving, that kind o' thing. That one was left outside. It didn't matter so much.

Well, here was your man now, just out o' the bed, half asleep, scratching and stretching himself. He opened up the door like he did every other morning, stepped out onto the flagstone in front o' the same door. But when he did, there was something waiting for him.

What? Something that was going to change every day o' the rest of his life. That's what!

D'you remember the old razors that were there before these modern safety-razor things? Cutthroats they were called. They looked like a big sharp knife. Well, when he stepped out onto the flagstone to get the bucket, there, just outside the door, was one o' them cutthroats, the sharp edge up.

He stood straight down on it, o' course—he was half asleep. When he did, 'twas his wife inside in the bed heard the screech he let out o' him. She leaped out of it, ran for the door, and found him there, thrown down on the flagstone, holding on to his foot.

There was blood pumping out of it.

"Quick!" says he. "In the name o' God, get something, quick, or I'm dead!"

'Twas lucky for him that she was a cool-headed woman. She ran and got a cloth, tied it tight around his foot—he was split from his toes back to his heel, and bleeding like a stuck pig—then she ran for the neighbors, and they brought the doctor.

He was carried into Ennis hospital and when they saw the damage they had to operate there and then. They sewed up the wound—it took over thirty stitches—from his toes back to his heel. Then they put a plaster cast on his foot and most o' the way up to his knee.

He was kept in there, o' course, in the hospital, for nearly two weeks. And when he was let out, 'twas with two crutches. They told him to go home, put up his leg, rest himself, and do no standing for the next three weeks. He was glad to hear that, I s'pose. Nothing like sitting down and letting the woman do all the work!

But, when the time came, after the three weeks, he went back to Ennis hospital to get the plaster taken off. He was brought in and he was lying back in the bed, with a nurse and a doctor tending to him.

He had no pain in the leg at all, so he was expecting nothing unusual. 'Twas only when he looked up at the nurse, while the doctor was cutting away the plaster, that he knew there was something wrong. She was watching his leg as the plaster came off, and then he saw the strange look on her face. The same look was on the doctor's face. The two of 'em were staring down at his leg, not a move out of either of 'em.

He pulled himself up in the bed to see what they were looking at. And there was his foot, shrunk to the size of a five-year-old's!

What could he do, only stare at it, too?!

There was nothing that could be done for him. Even though they examined him upside down and back again. When he was let out o' there that day, 'twas with a step and a half he went.

And until the day he died he never thatched another roof. How could he! For thatching you need two sound legs under you. Standing up there on a ladder, working above your head? Ha! You'd want no weakness in your legs for that job, I can tell you.

But d'you think he got any sympathy from his neighbors? He didn't, not one bit!

And why? Because any one of 'em—especially the old people—could have told him that was no eel he met. That was one o' the people that live in those lakes, carrying a message to some other lake. 'Twas going about its own business, doing no harm to him or anyone else. And he should have done the same, mind his own business. But he didn't, and he paid the price of it—like you always will when you interfere with the Other Crowd.

A surprising fact about Crusheen parish is that there are, within its bounds, thirty-seven lakes. But an even more surprising thing is that the number of fishermen who take advantage of this wonderful amenity could be counted on the fingers of one hand. This leaves the field open for foreign visitors and, over the years, several of these, Germans in particular, have come to be almost Irish, enjoying the relaxation, the Guinness, the friendliness and conversation of the local pubs. And the silence of the lakes, of course.

But, I have often wondered, as I hear them enthuse about that wondrous solitude that attracts them to those same lakes year after year, whether they might change their minds, moderate their enthusiasm a little, if they knew what lurked in some of those murky waters. For, as we can see from this tale told to me by a man who lived all his long life close to one of those lakes, more than fish inhabit them. And the other livers there do not appreciate being disturbed, particularly when going peacefully about their own private affairs.

"Well, I wouldn't like to meet 'em, anyway.
They could bring you or maybe injure you in such a way
that they'd have you, d'you see. They could."
LISCANNOR, SEPTEMBER 2, 1999

The Fairy Frog

I'LL TELL YOU ONE THING, now. If a poor man had a good-looking daughter in the times when the landlords were in it, 'twas bad news for him. He'd like to keep it quiet and get her married as soon as he could. Why? Because if the landlord found out about her, or the agent, even, they could send for her and do what they'd like with her. And 'twouldn't be good, you may be sure o' that. And what would a poor man be able to do? If he didn't let her go, they'd all be thrown out on the road, more than likely. Evicted! And no coming back either.

There was this man and his wife living near Mount Callan, and all they had in the family was one daughter—oh, as fine a girl as ever you laid eyes on. She was about fifteen or sixteen years old, and they used to send her out to the upper field minding the cow when the day'd be fine. Sure, 'twas grand. She'd be there looking around her, the finest view in the whole world.

She was in it one day, anyway, and what came in a gap—only this frog, jumping, jumping, until 'twas up beside her. Sat down there looking at her with the big black eyes. And 'twas then she noticed the belly sticking out, down to the ground, nearly.

She didn't move. Maybe she was afraid. But after a few minutes looking at her, the frog turned around and went off back the same way, out the same gap.

"Begod," says the girl, "I'd love to be there when that thing that's holding you back sees the light."

But there was no more about it. She brought home her cow that evening and never said a word.

And she forgot all about it.

But . . . about a week after, she was gone to bed this night and the father and mother were still sitting up by the fire when they heard a saddle horse coming along the road.

"Begod, he's in a hurry, whoever he is," says the father.

Anyway, the horse stopped just outside the house and they heard the sound o' the man getting down. Then the footsteps came up to the door, and next thing there was a knock.

They were in no hurry to open it at that hour, I can tell you. The knock came again.

"Who's there?" says the father.

"Open up! I have an urgent message."

Maybe 'twas the way he said it . . . I don't know. They were only poor people. They opened the door, anyway, and there was a gentleman standing there, riding boots on him, grand clothes, and a cloak over his shoulders. A fine cut of a man. Like one o' the gentry.

They asked him in, o' course. What else would they do? And the talk started. They asked him would he have the tea. He thanked 'em. No. He had business to do.

"Ye have a daughter, I'm told."

"We have, sir," says the father. "Why?"

"Well, 'tis like this," says he, and he looked right close at 'em. "I want her to come with me until this time tomorrow night. Will ye let her come? And I give ye my word of honor that no harm will come to her. I'll bring her back here safe and sound tomorrow night."

They weren't so happy with that, you may say! But what could poor people do in them days?

The mother went up to the room and called the girl.

"Come down," says she. "You're wanted. This gentleman here wants you to go with him."

Oh, she was in an awful state, and would you blame her? To go out into the dark o' the night with a stranger? But he spoke nice to her, promised her again that she'd be back safe and sound the following night.

In the finish up, anyway, she went, but she was crying when the stranger put her up on the horse behind him, and I don't know but maybe the father and mother were crying, too. I s'pose they thought they'd never see her again.

They went off, anyway, in the dark, a long distance, until they came to this hill. And above, on the top of it, was a fort. They kept going till they were in front of it.

"Now," says he, "we're here."

He took her off o' the horse and brought her into the fort. And such a place! She never saw the like of it in her life. There was lights, and crowds o' people walking around. And they were bowing to the man that was with her, like they knew him all their lives. And, sure, I s'pose they did! But he was someone important, anyway; you'd know that.

They walked down this big long hall and upstairs, up and up and into this room above.

The first thing the girl saw was the big four-poster bed and a woman inside in it, nearly ready to give birth. The midwife was there, and servant girls, all waiting and ready.

"Go on," says the gentleman. "Go over and hold her hand."

She was frightened but she did, and the woman in the bed was watching her with big black eyes. And 'twasn't long before the child was born.

But . . . wasn't he dead! And what did they do! The midwife, she passed him over to one o' the servant girls, and she dropped him into the fire. Into the fire, mind, and covered him up with the sods o' turf. Burned him up!

Sure, the poor girl was looking at that and she didn't know what to do. But at that very minute this woman came in with a child in her arms—oh, a real child that was carried, you can be sure!—and she handed it to the woman in the bed.

All right. That was fine. The woman in the bed started breast-feeding the new child, but her own child was burned away in the fire until there was nothing there, only ashes.

The girl was watching all o' this and she was amazed, o' course. And frightened.

"Don't be one bit afraid," says the man that was with her, "only come on now. The supper is ready."

He brought her out into a big hall where all the people were sitting down at tables, eating—oh, the finest o' food and drink, better than you'd get in any hotel.

And a servant came to her and asked her what would she like. But no. She always heard that you shouldn't touch any food in a fort or you'd never leave it, so she wouldn't eat. But she thanked him. A couple o' times he came back, but she took nothing. And the gentleman was watching her all the time.

When the feast was over the music started, and the dancing, and they were at that for the rest o' the night, until 'twas nearly daylight. No one asked her to dance, though, and she was looking around her. And she saw these servants going into the room where the woman was in the bed. They went to the fire, raked out the ashes where the child was burned, and one of 'em brought out a shovel o' them ashes. And just inside the hall door there was a big . . . 'twas like a holy water font you'd see outside a church, and full o' water. The ashes were thrown into it and mixed up.

And when all the dancing was finished and the crowd started to leave, every one of 'em, they'd put their fingers into the water and rub it to their eyes. And when they were all gone she was wondering what would she do. And the gentleman says to her, "Sit down awhile. Take your ease." So she did.

She must've fell asleep, 'cause when she woke 'twas getting dark.

"Come on," says he. "We must be going. But first, herself wants to see you above in the room."

The poor girl, she didn't know what to say. She was took up, anyway, into the same room again, and there was the woman in the bed with the child.

"Come here," says she.

She shoved over near the bed. Frightened.

"I'm thankful you came when I needed you," says she. "I'll have to reward you for that."

"Oh," says the girl, "I don't want no reward. I'm glad if I was any use."

"Even so, you'll have to get something," and she reached in under her pillow and brought out a bag o' gold and a necklace.

"Here," says she. "Take these with you, now."

And the girl did. Delighted, o' course. 'Twas little o' the like she ever saw at home.

The Fairy Frog

The man came back.

"Are you ready to go home?" says he.

She bowed to the woman in the bed.

"Thanks very much," says she, "for these. They'll be a great help to my father and mother."

They went out then. But when they were going he dipped his fingers into the water inside the hall door and rubbed it to his eyes, just like the crowd that went out earlier on. She saw him, so she says to herself that she better do the same, whatever 'twas for. But she had only rubbed it to her left eye when he turned around and caught her by the arm.

"Hurry on," says he. "We must leave this very minute."

He took her out, anyway, up on the horse behind him again, and off they went as fast as the horse'd go, and never stopped till they came to this grove o' trees.

He pulled up the horse and he says, "Did herself give you anything that time she called you back?"

"She did," says the girl.

"What was it?"

She was half afraid o' him, that maybe he was going to rob her.

"Tell me," says he, "what was it."

So she told him about the bag o' gold and the necklace.

"You aren't the first one to get the like," says he. "And if you'll take my advice, and if you want to see your father and mother safe and sound again, take that necklace now and tie it around the branch o' that near tree there."

Oh, she didn't want to do it, o' course—to give away a grand thing like that! But he let her down, anyway, and he told her again, "Put it out o' your hands, like I told you. Hurry!"

So she did what she was told, and they went on. But they were only gone a small bit when there was this fierce blast o' thunder behind 'em, and a flash o' lightning. And when she looked back the tree was broke in two halves. Burned up!

"Now," says he, "weren't you lucky you took my advice."

They went on again, and when they came near her own house he stopped.

"Show me what else herself gave you," says he.

She took out the bag o' gold and showed it to him.

"Listen to me, now," says he, "and do what I'll tell you. If that gold isn't used up in three days," says he, "you'll have nothing in that bag, only leaves. If you'll take my advice you'll get rid of it as fast ever as you can."

They came to the house, anyway, and when the father and mother saw her back home safe, they couldn't hardly believe it. They thought they'd never see her again. Oh, they thanked him, and asked him in for the tea, but no.

The only thing he said was, "Remember what I told you." And off with him. Gone!

"What was it?" they said. "What did he tell you?"

So, she told 'em the whole story, from start to finish. And they were amazed, o' course. They didn't know was she making it all up.

But when they saw the bag o' gold, and took it up in their hands, 'twas then they knew there was no lie in it.

"We better get rid of it, like he told you," says the father.

And the following day they started buying, cattle and a horse, things for the house and clothes for themselves, a lot of it in the town of Ennistymon. And by the third day all was spent except one or two o' the gold coins—sovereigns, you'd call 'em, I s'pose.

But the following morning, when the old father put his hand in his pocket where they were, to get 'em, there was nothing there, dry leaves.

And 'twas the very same with all the people that got that money for the cattle and all the rest of it. When they went looking for it there was nothing there, only leaves.

Wasn't she the lucky girl to do what the lad told her!

They lived away, then, and 'twas richer they were getting by the day. They used to be at this fair and that fair buying and selling cattle, and the girl'd always go with the father. She got nearly as good as himself at it in the finish-up.

But this fair day they were in Kilrush. A big fair. And while he was settling up with a couple o' buyers she walked down the street, just looking at the shops—maybe she had something she wanted to buy for her mother or herself. Whatever 'twas, she was only gone a small bit when she saw one o' the crowd from the fort that night.

She stopped, o' course, thinking she must be mistaken. But after a small while she saw two more of 'em. And then she saw the gentleman who carried her to the fort and he walking up the footpath towards her. She saluted him, o' course, delighted to see him. But he was looking strange at her.

"D'you see me?" says he.

"Hah? O' course I see you. How could I talk to you if I didn't see you?"

"But . . . tell me, now," says he, "d'you see me with . . . your right eye?"

"How d'you mean?" says she.

"Just tell me," says he. "Do you?"

She closed her left eye.

"That's strange," says she, "I can't see you now."

"And you won't, either," says he.

He stuck his finger into her left eye. Blinded her. She never again saw anything with it, for all her money.

And 'twas that way always with the Good People. You might get something from 'em, but maybe you'd be better off without it.

How careful we should be in making wishes, lest we get what we wish for! In this tale we see how the natural world may be a mere cloak over a world we have little understanding of and whose denizens may summon us at short notice for their own mysterious ends.

The unfortunate girl who is the human essential to the fairies' business in this case knows enough not to eat their food in the great mansion to avoid being held there. Unfortunately for her, there is a dark and vicious side to their nature that her innocence does not allow for. The loss of her eye in the end is a high price to pay for the gold she receives, but as the teller of the tale says, and as was widely accepted in Ireland, a person might be better off to have nothing at all to do with the Good People. Too often the liaison ended in tragedy for the human.

PART TWO

"There Since the Start o' the World"

FAIRY PLACES AND SIGNS OF THEIR PRESENCE

"I know that the whitethorn is always associated with the sióga. *
That's why 'tis called the fairy tree. But 'tis the lone whitethorn
in the middle of a field that's the dangerous one.
There was a reason why that was left there, you see.
No one but a fool would interfere with that."

CROOM, OCTOBER 12, 2001

The Bush That Bled

YOU DON'T REMEMBER the bad times, I'd say. You're too young. But I do. I do, and well. After the war, and the '50s, there was nothing in this country except hunger. If you had a job that time you were a lucky man, for sure.

I was working for the county council them years, and my brother was, too, God rest him. And glad to have it. But I remember to this very day a thing that happened one time during them years, above Tubber, not so far from Lough Bunny.

The council was making a new piece o' road, to shorten the way across from this road here to another road going down there, nearly half a mile over. 'Twould save people going three miles all around when 'twas finished.

The engineer came; 'twas surveyed and all marked out. We started work on a Monday morning, a big gang of us. Pick and

---

*The fairies.

---

shovel and sledgehammer, that's what we had—none o' the big machinery they have today. Sure, the lads doing that kind of a job now don't be working at all, only stand and look at the machines doing it for 'em. But more luck to 'em. We had to slave for the few bob we got. I wouldn't wish that on any man.

We were working on, anyway, and 'twas slow going, too, 'cause there was a lot o' rock there.

But this morning—I'll remember it all my life—myself and my brother arrived, and we were a small bit late. We had nearly ten miles to cycle and the weather was bad. But there was no one working when we got there—everyone standing around idle.

"Lord God," says I to my brother, "surely 'tisn't break time. We couldn't be that late, could we?"

"No," says he, "'tisn't that."

There wasn't a stir from any o' the crowd there, only standing up, leaning on their shovels and the foreman talking to 'em. We found out quick enough what 'twas all about. He was laughing at 'em. But, faith, you could see he wasn't too pleased about something.

I fell in behind a man and asked him—quiet, you know—what was happening.

"The job is stopped," says he. "He wants us to cut the *sceach*. 'Tis in the way o' the road."

"What?" says I. I didn't know what he was talking about.

"That *sceach* there," says he, and he showed it to me. Oh, 'twas there, all right. Plain to be seen. So I said nothing, or my brother, either, when we weren't in it. Let 'em sort it out between themselves.

Oh, they argued for a good long while, but no! There'd no one cut it. He was a decent enough man, the same foreman, only doing his job, sure. He tried to persuade 'em first.

"Look," he says. "That's no *sceach*. Surely to God if that was a *sceach* the engineer'd know it. He wouldn't have the road brought in on it, would he?"

"What do lads inside an office in town know about things the like o' this?" says one of 'em.

He didn't like that. He got ratty.

"Don't mind that old talk. Or tell it to the man himself if you want to. He'll be here tomorrow to see how things are going."

But still, they wouldn't cut the bush. And 'twas there, right in their way! Standing by itself. The man that marked out that ground, he mustn't have much sense, whatever else. But you'd often see that, fierce smart men, and still they can do awful stupid things.

The foreman, he says, "Look, men, no more talk about it. It has to be cut, that's all," and he picked out two of 'em.

"Get the crosscut," says he, "and do it."

Faith, they wouldn't stir.

"We all know one another, lads," says he. "Don't make me use no threats."

He was a decent man. I'll say that much for him. I knew him well. And what else could he do? He'd be in trouble himself if the job wasn't done.

But no move.

He had to say it, I s'pose, in the end: "All right, so. If you won't cut it, you'll be without jobs this evening."

I'm not blaming the man. Maybe if he didn't do that, maybe *he'd* be without a job if the engineer came and the work not done. But, anyway, when 'twas put like that—and I s'pose with jobs so scarce, and they were married men, the two of 'em— what could they do?

They took up the crosscut and started at that whitethorn.

But . . . Lord God . . . I saw it with my own two eyes, and every man there saw it! . . . they had only two draws o' that saw pulled across that *seach* when it started to bleed! I tell you, I never saw men jump back as fast as them two. And threw the saw away from 'em. 'Twas a wonder they didn't cut someone with it. 'Twas blood that came out of it—nothing else, only blood!

And who'd cut it, after that? All that was worrying them men that marked it was, would they live or wouldn't they?

'Twas left there and 'tis still there. And I hope it'll be there when I'm dead and gone.

Would *you* take it out o' there, after what happened that day? You'd be the brave man to do it.

This story might be dismissed as the ramblings of an old man whose memory had begun to fail him in his ninetieth year, were it not for the fact that in 1999 a far more important highway, costing millions of pounds, met a similar obstacle at Latoon, at the opposite end of County Clare (see Introduction). In this latest case, something at least seems to have been learned: the seach *in question was not harmed. Instead, the road was varied slightly around it, a civilized solution to what might otherwise have been an ultimately very costly ignoring of powers that cannot be ignored—unless very unwished-for consequences are to be invoked.*

"Now, there was one man round our part o' the country that did cut a lone bush. An' he was cutting a tree, maybe within two years after, an' the tree spun on the butt an' killed 'im."

MEATH, MAY 6, 2000

A Fairy Bush Moved

A BUSH LIKE THAT surfaced in the entrance to Ferenka in Limerick, and several machines and machine men approached it. Couldn't care less! They'd shift it.* And each machine, as they went in to shift it, stalled, for no known reason. So it remained there for some time, and there was a new machine man who came to the job. He wouldn't be aware o' the happenings at all, you see, the new man. The rest o' the lads were. So they asked the new machine man if he'd move the bush.

---

*I.e., they were determined to move it.

He examined it, anyway, and he sized it up, that it wasn't his kettle o' fish.

He said, "Yeah, I'll move the bush. But on one condition."

They said, "What's that?"

"That you'll gimme an alternative place to plant it."

So they said, "Yeah. We'll search 'round, and we'll find a place for you."

So he went down and he dug out the alternative place, and he drove up and got his big scoop of a machine in under the bush, brought it down and replanted it. No problem after that. He replanted the bush. He didn't destroy it.

But o' course, Ferenka didn't prosper much ever after. There was always controversy about the place.

As the speaker says, "there was always controversy." The fact was that Ferenka, one of those flagship companies that employed a huge number of workers in Limerick in the 1970s, was a symbol of the "new Ireland." This story of the problem about its building persists even to this day. But was it the disturbing of the sceach that brought about the demise of the plant in 1979, or was it the woeful industrial relations that prevailed there?

The interesting fact in the Ferenka saga is that city as well as country people believed in the sceach version of events—some even going so far as to claim that the industrial mayhem at the plant was a direct result of disturbing the Good People.

> *"I heard about this man who cut a fairy tree, a whitethorn tree,*
> *an' when he went to bed in the night, the bed was full o' the*
> *needles o' the whitethorn. He couldn't sleep. An' often in the*
> *nights when he'd turn in the bed, that part o' the bed'd be*
> *all thorns for years after. He cut a fairy tree, a lone tree.*
> *He'd always have to sleep in one side of the bed ever after."*
>
> MILTOWN, JUNE 27, 1999

Man Cuts Briars in a Fairy Fort

OH, 'TISN'T RIGHT TO DO IT, to interfere with a fort. Oh, I wouldn't do it. A lot o' people'd laugh at you today to say that, but 'tis no cause of a laugh.

We have a fort above there now, behind the house, and I'd never take the timber in that fort. Any of it that fell, I'd throw it in the fort and let it rot away there.

But I remember cutting the briars in it. D'you know why? Because I used to have sheep at that time, and they'd get tangled in the briars. So I'd cut 'em. But I'd leave 'em there, shove 'em to one side. I'd never take 'em out of it.

My wife—God rest her—she wouldn't even like to see me doing that much. She'd rather I'd leave it alone entirely, put no hand to it. And I didn't interfere with the bushes, either. Only cut the briars.

But, anyway, I got a lump there on the back o' my hand. Jeez, it rose up a good bit, and I couldn't know in the name o' God what was it.

And she said to me, "Did you interfere with the fort?"

"I cut the briars."

"Oh," she said, "you had no right to do it."

Well, 'twas there on the back o' my hand for a couple o' years, not giving me any pain or anything. And you know the two men I used to be gambling with—Lord have mercy on the two of 'em now—one of 'em used to always be joking, "Leave out your hand here and I'll flatten out that thing for you."

'Twas half the size of an egg, you know.

But this night, anyway, wasn't I collecting up the cards to deal 'em, and he was as good as his word. What did he do, only hit my hand a welt—hurt it. I made nothing of it then. How could I, in the middle of a game? But the following day 'twas sore, and in a couple o' days after didn't it fester.

'Twas paining me, so I had to go to the doctor with it. There was only one thing to do, he said, and that was to let out the badness. And that's what he did. Lanced it. But d'you know what came out of it? A thorn about an inch long!

I don't know was it in the fort I got it or not, but when I told my wife about it there was no doubt at all in her mind.

"Now, will you leave it alone?" she said.

I won't say that I did or I didn't, but 'tis still above there, anyway.

The man in question here I know very well. At over eighty he still plays the cards he describes here and today shows no trace of the lump that disfigured his hand. I recall seeing it, though only two years ago did he tell me this story.

Note how reticent he is in putting any blame on the fort or on the Good People. But his wife is far more certain of where the truth lies. To the very end he will give no definite answers, but the facts speak for themselves: steel used in a fort; a mysterious ailment; an impossibly painless thorn; the fort left since unmolested. The message is clear enough.

*"Personally, I never cut even as much as a thorn in that fort.
'Tis belongs to . . . the unknown. I'll put it that way. The Good People.
'Tis there for generations, for longer than we're aware of, or know of.
We don't know what the origin of it is, nor we don't know
what them people are about. Just leave 'em alone."*

DRUMLINE, SEPTEMBER 19, 2001

Respecting the Ancient Forts

LONG AGO, the Tuatha dé Danann* and the Fir Bolg† and all
those tribes used to have fights, and after one o' those battles the
crowd that lost—I don't know was it the Fir Bolg or the Tuatha
dé Danann—retreated into the spirit world, and they are the
fairies today. As we know, the spirit world lives forever. That is
why they were before Christ and they wouldn't have entered the
eternal mansions when the spirits moved over. 'Tis because their
spirits stayed around their own property. They still hadn't been
converted to Christianity. And that is why the fairy raths, or
forts, or whatever people want to call 'em, people feel that
they're protected. Their property is still protected.

I'll tell you this story, now. One night we were visiting this
local man—he had got a bad bout of sickness. There was three

---

*The principal otherworld race in Irish mythology (literally, "the people of
the goddess Danu").

†A people who reputedly inhabited Ireland in ancient times.

of us. And the three of us had fairy forts on our land. O' course, naturally, the discussion turned to forts.

"Well," I said, "I never interfered with it at all, never touched it. It was there thousands o' years before I came, and hopefully 'twill be there thousands o' years when I'm gone. I wouldn't interfere with their property at all, at all."

And the other man that was there, he said, "Well, I cut the bushes out of it all right, but I left the rings there."

And the third man came in and said, "I brought in the bull-dozer and made the fairies homeless." He was laughing at the idea. Thought 'twas a big joke.

I said, "Watch it there, now, Pat. *They'll* make *you* homeless."

In one week a shed fell on him and killed him. In one week! That was a Sunday night we spoke. The following Sunday the shed fell on him.

And the other lad was dead one morning when his wife woke. He was dead alongside her.

I'm the only survivor of the group.

Whether the speaker here realizes it or not, the battle he refers to is the great mythological "First Battle of Moytura," in which the Tuatha dé Danann defeated the Fir Bolg aeons ago. His logic as to why the losers did not enter into "the eternal mansions" and why they became the sióga may be a little shaky, but there is no doubting the sincerity of his belief that their spirits still protect their property, i.e., the fairy raths and forts.

The story he then tells is meant to leave us in no doubt whatsoever that interference with such places will lead to certain and appropriate punishment, and that the best policy is to respect them, leave them be.

"They was in dread o' forts a lot in my time.
They wouldn't even cut a bush."

CORLEA, DECEMBER 21, 1989

A Sportsman Who Won't Interfere

THERE WAS twenty-five or thirty people demolishing Bally-caseybeg fort. If 'tis wrong, what was the county council going to do for you? They dropped you in and paid you to demolish it, but they didn't do it themselves. I think it was pure, sheer pigheadedness. Obstinacy. What does a government official know about a fairy fort?

Well, the man that owned it, his father before him, and his father before *him* again, they lived up against it. The house is still there.* Any o' them people—and they weren't superstitious, 'cause they weren't that kind o' people at all—'tis the last thing they'd dream of, to interfere with it.

Now, one of 'em was a hurling fanatic. You couldn't hear Mass with him of a Sunday. All through Mass he'd be talking

*It has since been demolished.

hurling. As a matter o' fact, I changed my chapel so I could hear the sermon and hear Mass.

There was a nice ash tree with a curve on the bottom of it growing out o' the side o' the fort. The hurling lads went up to him, and they had a great hurling debate. He went back fifty, sixty, seventy years o' hurling matches—he lived to be a man o' ninety, actually.

But they said to him, "What about the hurley that's growing up the side o' the fort above. Did you see it?"

"Oh," he said. "I did. I saw it."

They said, "What d'you think of it?"

"Ah," he said, "sure, 'tis a right one." 'Twas a grand clean stick. It grew out clean, turned and all. Nothing to do, only cut it. And he knew a good stick when he saw it.

They said, "Will you cut it?" He had a chainsaw.

"Will I what?!" he said.

"Will you cut it for us?" they said.

"No," he said. "I will not do any such thing. Look, if you want it, do what you like about it. I won't give it to you, nor I won't refuse you. I won't have hand, act, nor part in the removal o' that hurley. I won't refuse it, nor I won't give it to you. Look, the option is yours."

I own to God, d'you know what? They didn't take it. Wasn't I looking at it above when the county council sawed it up.

"Me, nor anyone belong to me, we never brought as much as one stick out of it," he said. "I went over to Derramore to Kilkishen, fifteen, sixteen miles, and I drew a half hundred o' turf out of it, bought it, every year, a thing I could ill afford to do. And there was plenty wood there, up to my ear, to go up with a hatchet and cut it. The wind even blew it down. But I didn't. And I'm here today, and I have no worries."

That was his version of it. Now, I'll give honor where honor is due. He was anything but superstitious, any o' his family. I never heard 'em passing any remarks on the fort. But I'll tell you, what I know to be a fact: They had very good reason to be respectful to it.

There was a black dog parked at the gate there. He was known as the Knockane dog and he used to come down from Knockane. He used to go in over the stile beyond at Macs at the Grove, just come nightfall. And they used to come out in the summer evenings to view him—big black dog—for a lifetime. If he was a local dog the most he'd live'd be ten or twelve years, not fifty, sixty, seventy years of a man's lifetime. You don't get dogs living seventy years.

There was a noble spring well there, and they'd no more go out to that well at nightfall for a bucket o' water. They'd just do without it, if they hadn't it. They wouldn't clash with that dog. It didn't ever harm anyone, but different people had queer stories about him.

The man telling this story had every reason to feel indignant. A fairy fort he knew as a fixture all his life, and the many tales attached to it, was demolished in 2001 during the building of the same new highway that almost caused the destruction of the Latoon sceach. Not only that, the very hill on which the fort was situated, as well as the farmhouse, all have been swept away.

Yet, according to this man, the powers of the modern, new Ireland of sur-face glitter may have disturbed something here for which it has no answer. Already at this place there have been some tragic occurrences, including deaths, that might perhaps even give cynics some pause. And when the new road is built over the site of the fort? Some local people look with trepidation to the future at this place.

"I s'pose, if a fairy is molested, if you go tampering or meddling with 'em, well, they'll retaliate. 'Tis only kind o' natural, retaliation when you're interfered with. Nearly everyone in Ireland is aware that it isn't the done thing. Was never the done thing. The most ignorant people in Ireland, people that were illiterate, wouldn't bring a thorn out o' them forts."

DRUMLINE, SEPTEMBER 19, 2001

Let Very Well Alone!

WE HAD a very healthy respect for them forts, I can tell you. And I know that our generation would not interfere with 'em on any account. In day or night you'd hardly visit 'em, day or night.

Now, as you see abroad there, I have any amount of fancy stones. I have stones from every part of Ireland. As a matter o' fact, I have stones from every part o' the world. I have stones from Beijing Square. I have a stone off the Wall o' China. I have basalt rock and the stone for the stone axes. I have all them things, but no way have I stone out of a fort.

If I did, how do I know but my lace might trip me and put me standing on top o' my head? By God, if people want to laugh, I can make jokes. I can be jocose. But I don't want to make 'em cry, either. If I only tore the backside o' my trousers wouldn't half the country laugh at me. I'm not worried about the laughing. But definitely, for my own peace o' mind . . . live and let live. Let very well alone!

I have three forts in my land. I never took a hatchet or a saw to them forts to cut 'em down. No way! Even now that there'd be government restrictions and orders to leave forts alone, not to demolish 'em or do anything with 'em, as far as I'm concerned the orders don't have to be there at all. I just won't interfere with 'em.

Didn't I tell you about the man that demolished the fort, and his two daughters? One of 'em she died laughing and the other one died crying. Got a fit o' crying.

I was talking to a man last Sunday and he was telling me about three of his neighbors that bought a bulldozer between 'em when there wasn't hardly another bulldozer in Clare. But they had a lot o' land and they decided that they'd spend a couple o' thousand between 'em for the bulldozer. They had young fellows growing up, and the young fellows would demolish all the banks and mounds and moots, and level 'em all out— which they did!

From that day to this, no one could ever go in with a machine to the forts they demolished, and cut the hay out of 'em. The machine'd break. This man that was telling me about it, he went in with his machinery to cut the hay there, and for the third time in succession it failed him.

The next year they didn't go near it at all. He had a difference with the man that owned the hay. He wouldn't cut it. He says, "There's no point in me taking down my machine and breaking it, and it costing me a heap o' money to repair it, for a bit o' hay. I couldn't cut that hay," he said.

"Ah," the man said, "I'll get it done." But, faith, he didn't get it done.

A neighbor arrived on the scene and he said to the man that had the machine, "Did you cut the hay?"

He said, "I didn't."

"No," said the neighbor, "nor you never will."

He knew the score. He never did. There's several instances o' that.

In the face of all the evidence—rumor, coincidence, skeptics would say—that interference with forts brings no rewards, and most likely misfortune, it may seem remarkable that there are still people who will do so. But we must remember that human nature may be homogeneous, but human society is rarely so. There will always be those who will "try their luck," for whatever reason.

In days gone by we might have seen fairy stories as a way of "keeping people in their place," but in a modern age of machinery this view becomes more difficult to sustain. And yet, it persists that no matter how modern-minded or well-equipped with up-to-date technology you are, some things should not be done; some places are out of bounds . . . if you have sense.

That the Good People should have anything to do with machinery may seem on the surface odd, given their aversion to iron, but look more closely at the story and you will note that whether it is a case of the madness of two daughters of a man who interfered with a fort or the self-defeating stubbornness of a man in a more technological age, one thing they know well: how to take advantage of our nature. They punish where it hurts most appropriately. They direct their vengeance at our weakest point, whether it be our affections or our greed.

In fact, one of the most depressing aspects of human/fairy contact seems to be that they need never be too troubled about those things that frighten them so much—such as iron. They will always get some human to do for them any dirty work that might need to be done, should it be necessary . . . despite the consequences.

"Do you know, there's a subterranean linkup between 'em all,
between all the fairy forts? They couldn't come out, you see,
that time, because o' wild animals, but they could
travel to each other underneath."

CROOM, OCTOBER 12, 2001

Mysterious Sounds from Two Forts

BOTH FORTS over here are in Derryulk, and there's a different story about each of 'em. There was music attached to one of 'em and churning to the other.

The near one here, there used be music played in it, and three lights would leave it and continue on down for a mile and cross the road. I often saw the three lights myself, and lots o' people besides me, in my time. The lights'd come across the road, and if they were coming, you'd make sure you'd let 'em cross before you'd come in contact with 'em. They went on for about a mile, and them three lights finished up in an old big gentry's house. They'd go into that house—'twas all knocked down, only the shell of it there. But them three lights'd disappear inside that house. Time and again they came there. And they'd be about two feet from the ground, coming along as if they'd be three people coming with three lanterns.

But the music . . . McNamara that lived over here—the fort is at the back o' the house—he often sat on the stile before he went inside, listening to the music playing the finest. He was a poet himself, and a singer, but he never heard finer music than he used to hear before them three lights'd start out.

Then, the other fort is over here to the left. My father—the Lord have mercy on him—he had a brother seven or eight years of age, and he was sent for the cows one evening. And a woman caught him, a small woman, and struck his knee against a stone. He told 'em when he came home. The stone is there yet to be seen. He had a pain in his leg, and he was crying. They couldn't do anything for him, so they sent for the doctor. The doctor came and he couldn't do anything for him. In four days he was dead.

They used to always say that the fairies took him.

In that fort, there used to be churning heard at certain times. Even my own brothers and sisters heard it when they'd be over there working in the garden late of an evening. They'd hear the churning inside the fort. There was a wall, and the big fort was inside under the ring o' bushes. And they used go to the wall to hear the churn. They'd think 'twas someone making the butter inside the fort, same as they would here at home. You'd hear the dash o' the churn up and down. You know, the dash churn they had long ago—the very same as the one they'd use at home. They'd come home then and they'd be around the house talking about "the churning in the fort this evening." Just like that!

This man came out to that fort one evening, cutting a big whitethorn with his saw, and a voice spoke out from the bush to get away out o' there, not to be "cutting the jamb off o' their door." So, he went away and left it there.

If proof were needed of the otherworldliness, yet uncanny ordinariness, of forts, surely this story provides it. Strange in the comings and goings and the lights, where no one was seen. Equally strange, when one of the inhabitants was seen—but with tragic consequences.

Then, also odd in its everydayness, one of the basics of life—churning of butter—seems to be going on in the fort. But then . . . when humans seem to be taking the place so much for granted that they take advantage, a sharp shock is administered: Beware of what you do in a fort. It is often repeated in Irish stories that the branches of whitethorn bushes in forts are the jambs of the doors to the world of the Good People.

*"There was a man in Kilfenora, an' he rooted a fort. An' his mouth
was turned back here the following day. His mouth was turned back.
But, he went to the friars in Ennis . . . an' the friars told him to go back
an' settle the fort, put back all the clay that he took out of it an' make it
the way it was again. An' he did it. His mouth came all right."*

LISCANNOR, SEPTEMBER 2, 1999

A Pregnant Woman Goes into a Fort

WOULDN'T YOU THINK, when people are living near a
place like that all their lives, they'd know something! Now, I
wouldn't want misfortune on anyone, but, d'you know this?
I think a lot o' people bring their own misfortune on themselves. A woman expecting a child, now, shouldn't she know
better than to go into a fort in the first place, in the name o'
God! What was she thinking of?

But, what happened was, she was well gone, six months
and more.

The house was only a small distance from the fort. One
morning, after all the rest of the family were gone doing whatever they were doing, she went lighting the fire. But she had no
kindling, so the nearest place to get some was the fort. She went
up and started collecting. But she was there only a few minutes,
working away, when she got some kind of a weakness and had to
sit down for a minute. 'Twas nothing serious, only a kind of a

blackout. She came to herself, gathered her sticks again, and went off down home.

There was no more about it. She told no one. Why would she? Not then, anyway.

But, a couple o' months later the child was born. And he was a hunchback. Oh, he lived, but he was a hunchback.

The misfortunate woman had plenty of time to be telling about it after, but what good was that?

Them places . . . if you have no respect for them, you have no respect for yourself. 'Tis as simple as that. And 'twill come back on you, sooner or later.

The tone of this story is what is important, more than what actually happens. If there is sympathy for the woman in her misfortune, or for the child, who was, after all, innocent of any wrongdoing, it is not shown. What comes across, rather, is a tone of "How could she have been so stupid? What other outcome could she have expected?"

And so it is the mother, not the Good People, who is blamed for the tragedy. It is almost always so in cases like this.

Fear of antagonizing the fairies? Or an unshakable belief that some things just are not done, and no more about it?

"Know your place" would seem to be the golden rule—the only rule!—when dealing with the Other People, since there is no leeway for error.

"But you can't tar 'em all with the one brush.
There's some o' them forts an' you could take your bed
into 'em an' sleep in 'em with no ill effect. But there's
some of 'em an' they're dynamite. They're highly dangerous,
for whatever reason. An' you won't know until you're burned.
An' what can you do if you have the damage done?"

The Man in the Coffin

YOU OFTEN HEARD IT SAID, did you, that there's no luck in interfering with forts? I heard that myself, and I'd believe it, too.

There was these two men living near Quin one time, poor men; they had only the grass of a cow each. They were next-door neighbors—we'll call 'em Seán and Pat—and there was nothing they liked better than to go out hunting in the fall o' the year, when all the leaves were gone and they could see what they were doing, you know. But they had only the one gun between 'em—'twas Seán had it—and Pat'd go with him just for the company, any time the day was fine in the month o' September or October. You'd often get a nice hardy spell o' weather at that time o' the year.

So this Sunday they were out, 'twas in the start of October, and they were after walking miles, and shot nothing. Didn't even see a rabbit, or a pheasant. Nothing. They didn't mind, though.

'Twas a grand fine day for being out, and they met several people to talk to on the way.

In the evening, anyway, they were coming back, chatting away, Seán with the gun over his shoulder. And they were passing Corbally fort—'twas there on the hill overhead 'em, a big double-ring fort, about a mile and a half from the village. And when Seán looked up, didn't he see a white thing above on one o' the bushes in the fort.

"Lord God, look," says he, "look at the goose!" and he loaded up the gun quick, and fired. Sure enough, he hit it, 'cause he saw the feathers scattering and the bird falling down through the branches.

But Pat was looking at him.

"What're you talking about?" says he. "I don't see nothing."

Seán wasn't listening to him at all, only in over the ditch with him, and off up the hill to get the goose.

But when he came above to the fort and reached in under the bush where the bird was—the feathers were scattered, now, and plenty blood around—there was nothing there when he touched it, only . . . stuff like frog's spawn. 'Twas like jelly. Well, he pulled back his hand from it like he was burned, but the stuff stuck to him, and even already 'twas turning black. He tried to wipe it off, but no. He couldn't.

"Come out of it," says Pat to him. "Why did you fire into the fort?"

They went back to Quin, to their own places, and they didn't see each other any more that evening. But the following morning Pat was up early. 'Twas a grand fine morning. And what he'd usually do on a morning like that, he'd stand at the door and smoke his pipe and be looking around him. And usually Seán'd be doing the same next door. But this morning there was no sign o' Seán. The door was closed.

"Begod, that's queer," says Pat. "He'd be there if 'twas raining."

After he had a drop o' tea and there was still no sign o' Seán, he said to himself he might as well wander over and knock. Just in case.

You wouldn't do that at a neighbor's house today, or you'd be nearly took up for trespassing! But there was nature in them days, when people had nothing. And now, when they have everything, they wouldn't give you the steam o' their piss. Oh, it's a different world entirely, boy.

He went over, anyway, and knocked. No answer. He knocked again. Still no answer. So he tried the latch. Door locked.

"Begod, that's strange," says he. Because in them days no one used to lock doors, no poor people, anyway. 'Cause what had they to steal?

So, he went around the end o' the house and looked in the bedroom window. There was no curtain. Seán wasn't a married man, no more than himself, and you know the way 'tis with old bachelors, now: The last thing that'd be worrying 'em is something like curtains.

So, he peeped in the room window—and, Lord save us, what did he see inside in the bed? Only Seán, and every bone in his body twisted. That's what it looked like. Hands. Legs. Neck. And even his mouth and eyes.

Pat, he tried everything he could to open up the window, but it failed him. He had to get a stone and break the glass to go in.

And when he faced the man inside in the bed, sure, Seán wasn't even able to talk, only croaking.

"Don't stir. Don't make one move," says Pat. "I'll get the doctor."

That's what he did. Into Tulla as fast as he could, and they came back together.

Well, the doctor only took one look at him in the bed and he said, "'Tis the hospital for you, poor man."

They lifted him into the doctor's sidecar and off to Tulla; the hospital was at Garruragh, outside the village. 'Twas a workhouse, but, sure, they're the kind o' places that poor people had to go to that time. The people hated 'em, especially after the Famine, but what could they do?

So, Seán was landed into Garruragh, anyway, and when they arrived he was put into this big room by himself. And I s'pose the only reason he was alone was that 'twasn't right winter yet. If 'twas the month o' December, now, that place'd be full.

Anyway, he was left there, and Pat says to him before he went home, "Don't worry about the cow or anything. I'll mind her. You'll be out in a couple o' days."

So, the night came on. But he couldn't sleep. Would you be surprised at that? And the moon came up. And 'twas shining in the small windows—they were up at the top o' the wall, near the roof. Oh, the lads that built them places, they didn't build 'em for your comfort or so that you'd be looking at the flowers! And Seán, he was watching it—'twas about all he could watch—when, all of a sudden, some time in the small hours, he heard this scratching noise down along from him, below in a corner. And the first thought that came to him was that 'twas rats. And, Lord God, if they attacked you they'd eat you alive, man!

He couldn't move, only his head and eyes, but, by God, when he did, he saw enough—and 'twasn't rats he saw, either. Only worse! 'Cause there, coming through the wall at the far end o' the room, was a leg—and another one next to it, and another, and another. Four of 'em. In through the wall, side by side. But that was only the start of it. Slowly and slowly they came in, the legs, an' then the rest o' the bodies . . . until he saw the elbows and the hands. And 'twas then he saw the end o' the coffin! Coming in through the wall, too! And that wall was built o' stone, at least two foot thick! All he could do was try to cover himself up with his blanket . . . but he couldn't. His hands wouldn't work.

They came in, and a third man holding the coffin behind. They started walking up the floor towards him, and he could hear every creak of every floorboard under 'em. Sure, he was near wetting the bed with fright.

When they came to where he was, they put the coffin down next to the bed. And one of 'em, he started to unscrew the screws at the four corners of it. He pulled off the cover then, and he says, "Look what you did when you fired into Corbally fort!"

Seán, all he could do was look down out o' the corner of his eye. But he could see enough. 'Cause inside the coffin was a man, all covered with blood from his feet up to his head, like he was shot.

"That's what you did to our brother when you fired into our house. And listen, now, and listen, carefully. If you don't get out o' that bed this minute, and pick every single shot out of our brother before the sun comes up, you'll be in that coffin with him, and we'll let the two o' you sort out your differences . . . *after* we screw on the cover again."

By the way the three of 'em were looking at him, he knew full well they were in earnest. But he was still crippled, so all he could do was roll out o' the bed, out on the floor, and start rooting around in the dead man, trying to find all them pellets. And, sure, 'twas like handling dead meat. But he had to do it. They were standing there around him, watching him. Hour after hour he stuck at it, and the nearer 'twas getting to daylight the more they were getting impatient, "Hurry on! Hurry up!" and on like that.

'Twas just close before dawn, and didn't he find the last o' the shot—someplace in the man's neck it was. But if he thought his troubles were over, they were only starting, 'cause at that very minute the lad inside the coffin, his two eyes opened and he started to rise up.

Indeed, when Seán saw that, I tell you he wasn't long getting back his movement. He made a dive under the bed and tried his level best to get out through the wall. But no hope.

The man stood up, and came out on the floor. Sure, his three brothers had a great welcome for him, naturally.

"Where's the wretch that shot me?!" says he. "Show me him."

They all pointed in under the bed where Seán was.

"What'll we do with him?" says the lad.

"We'll carry him with us," says one of 'em. "Wouldn't he be handy for carrying the coffin?"

"Him? A man that'd fire into a fort? Sure, a man like him has no religion at all!"

"He'd be handy, all the same."

"He wouldn't."

"He would."

"He would not!"

And the argument started. For a finish they were nearly coming to blows about it, until one of 'em looked up and noticed that 'twas very nearly daylight.

"Ahhh! Look! Quick."

And like that (!) they clapped the cover on the coffin, up on their shoulders with it, and out through the wall—the very same way as they came in.

But d'you think Seán came out from under the bed? Indeed, he didn't. And he was still there at half past eight when the matron came in with the surgeon.

O' course, as soon as they opened the door, the surgeon says to her, "I thought you told me you had a patient for me."

"Well, he was here last night, Doctor, whatever happened to him."

But, o' course, Seán, under the bed, as soon as he saw the legs at the door, he thought 'twas the lads back again for him. All he did was to make one buck-leap out between the doctor's legs, out the door, and legged it. He never stopped until he got to Ennis, and he didn't even stop there, only kept going till he came to the pier at Clarecastle.

There was a boat there, just about to sail for Limerick, and he jumped into it, caught a hold o' the mast, and no amount of 'em could make him let go. Pure terror!

For a finish the captain said to leave him there, or they'd miss the tide. That's how he got to Limerick. And he got going from there to America. Worked his passage, I s'pose, like a lot more. And I heard he did well in America, too. Got married there. Had a family. But never came back. And you know why? 'Cause if he did, if he ever set foot in Ireland again, you know who'd be waiting for him, don't you?

That's right. The three of 'em. And their box. And the second time they'd make no mistake.

It is a much-overlooked fact that not all of the thousands who fled Ireland in former times did so to escape hunger, deprivation, and persecution. There were also those who went to escape the wrath of the Good People. Many stories illustrate this, the one here being typical.

If proof were needed that the fairies can take whatever shape they wish, this tale provides it, and the relentlessness of their pursuit of the man who has violated their dwelling, and their ability to inflict ugly physical consequences, shows clearly why there was such reluctance among Irish people to have much contact with them.

To cross flowing water (in this case, the tide) was one of the few known and proven means of escaping them. But for the unfortunate one who had offended them, it was a one-way ticket.

"Can you tell me anything about fairy paths?"
"They go from A to B, usually straight, from one fort to another.
Maybe the fort, even, could be miles away. It mightn't be the
one in the immediate vicinity."
DRUMLINE, OCTOBER 19, 2000

A House Built Between Forts

THIS MAN AND HIS BROTHER—they were two elderly men when I knew 'em, two very nice men, two very nice, honest men. They had a house at the side o' the road, and they lived very comfortable. And they had an outhouse for the horses and cattle, and the outhouse was facing the road. And the dwelling house where they lived, the gable of it, was out to the road.

Apparently the outhouse was built between two forts. There was a fort at one side of it, up on a hill, about five hundred yards away. 'Twas known as Lios Árd, the high fort. And there was a fort at the opposite end, 'twas known as Crossa fort. That was a mighty structure altogether. There was a big mound and a big high hedge. 'Tis still there. The man that lives in that place today would no more touch that than he'd cut his right hand off.

There was, I s'pose if you like, a passageway from one fort to the other. And the house was in between. 'Twas a fine long house and there was a door in it, and that door could never be closed. Opposite the door there was a window, and the window could never be closed. So what happened was, he put in a half-door and he left the top vacant. And at the window at the back, he done the same thing. He always left way, for whatever came, to go through without the door hindering.

That's the way 'twas, and that's the way I always knew it. And that's the way it was until the day the house was knocked.

They had a little dog. Certain times o' the day, if they came out on the road with the little dog, 'twould be like a fellow shadow-punching. The murder'd start with the little dog. And nothing there to back it up. No reason whatsoever! He'd have holy open murder with something, but no one knew what, and they'd have to get him away. He'd fight to death with whatever he was clashing with on the road.

In later years they tied a dog near the door and he got involved, it seems, during the night. He got involved with whatever was passing through. He came out at the worst end o' things, though. He got killed. He was stone dead in the morning.

They maintained that in the month o' May they used to hear the music and the people up in the air crossing from one fort to the other. Such sweet music and noise was never heard of!

And they weren't the kind of people that'd be telling a tall tale. Oh, God, no. They were two fine, decent, honest men, very sincere. And proof o' their sincerity: We'd be there in the night, now. There'd be a crowd of us there, all the lads'd collect in, you see—they weren't married—and we'd say for a joke, "D'you want to build up the window, Pat?"

Oh, he'd go wild! He'd clear you, man. No way! On no account, don't interfere with it. And he'd watch you in case you did. Oh, Lord, no. That was sacred to 'em. And the fort that was above at the back o' that house, they'd have your life if you went near it, man. Oh, you need never go there again. They were out with you.

That was the story o' the house before ever they were born. The house was there maybe two hundred years. But 'twas built in the wrong place. 'Twas built on the track.

The fellow that came after 'em, then, he built a new house, but by God, when he did, he didn't build it across that path.

Formerly, great care was taken in Ireland in the choosing of a site for a house, and not merely for its physical attributes. If there was any hint that it might be on a fairy path, or track, it was sensible to avoid that place and let them have free access to their accustomed route.

The elders had their own ways of testing a dubious site. One such was to hammer down four hazel branches solidly at the four proposed corners of the house-to-be. If they were disturbed in the morning, it was unsafe to build there.

Sometimes the presence of a fairy path might be deduced, as in this story, where there are two very visible forts—though its route would only have been known by consequences. At other times, however, nothing but the knowledge of a person wise in the ways of such things could alert one to the danger of building in the fatal spot—as the next story, "The Fairy House," shows only too clearly.

This very year, an old man who was most adamant on the point, told me that the reason Ireland was having such a plague of marriage breakdown, child delinquency, drug abuse, suicide, etc., at the moment was because so many big housing estates were now being built without any regard to "the paths." What possible chance had families in houses on those paths, he asked, of a normal, peaceful life?

"If you built a house in the wrong place, on a fairy path, you had company!"
DRUMLINE, SEPTEMBER 19, 2001

The Fairy House

D'YOU KNOW, BOY, that this house is infested? With the fairies! D'you see that place there, just inside that door? Behind the plaster there they used to do their cooking. Frightened the living life out o' my grandfather and grandmother when it started first. They got used to it in time, though. They *had* to. 'Twas either that or move out o' the house entirely.

Did your father ever tell you, boy, that this is a fairy house? Well, 'tis. And I'll tell you how it happened, too, if you want to hear it.

'Twas after the Famine—sometime in the 1860s, I'd say— and my grandfather and grandmother were living in an old shack of a house, a mud-walled cabin you wouldn't put animals into today. The thatch was rotten and letting in the rain. The damp was down along the walls in streaks o' green moss. Now, my grandmother, she put up with that for a long time. But 'twas getting worse.

At last she said to the husband one day, "Look, I'm sick o' this cursed place. 'Tis damp and dark. D'you want us to get our death here? Surely to God, 'tis time to build a new house."

But no, he wouldn't hear of it.

"Have a bit o' sense, will you, woman. Can't you see the bad times that are in the country? Whatever bit o' money we have, we need, so don't talk to me about a new house."

But she had no intention of leaving the matter there. Day after day she annoyed him, more and more so as time passed. But he was a stubborn man, as well as all else, and as often as she asked, he refused. Until at last, she threatened him.

"For the last time, I'll ask you. Build a new house. Or if you don't, I'm going."

"Going? Where?"

"Back home, to my own people. That's where. Before I'm crippled by the rheumatism in this piggery."

With that threat he knew she was in earnest. He knew, too, that his back was against the wall now. And why? Because in them days the only reason a wife'd leave her husband was if he was beating her. If she went, what would the local people think—the men especially? There'd be ugly talk . . . "brave man, beating up a woman," and gossip like that. A man's reputation wouldn't be in the better o' that kind o' thing.

So he had to give in, even though he did it with very bad grace.

"All right! All right! But it'll have to wait until the new year." She was so surprised that she agreed to that. She kept a close watch on him, though, so that there'd be no backsliding. And there wasn't. In the month of April, the following year, he started. She told him what she wanted, too—how many rooms, the size of 'em, and all that.

O' course he objected. That's the kind o' man he was.

"Merciful God, woman, what do we want all them rooms for? You'd swear we had ten children."

"You'd never know," says she. "Maybe we might. Anyway, 'tis me that'll be cleaning and minding 'em, so don't worry yourself about it. Just build it."

That's what he did. And nearly all on his own, too. He wasn't going to spend money hiring workmen if he could do it himself.

So he picked out this site here. He could have picked a lot of other places, too, 'cause they had plenty land—even though most of it was only bog and rushes. But he picked this, I s'pose, 'cause 'twas near the road. And this morning he started to mark out the plan o' the house with a piece o' rope on the ground. That was easy enough to do when he knew what she wanted.

He was there on his knees, measuring away, when he heard a voice behind him.

"God bless the work."

He looked back. There, leaning on the fence, watching him, was an old traveling man, a beggar man, you know. There used to be dozens of 'em on every road in them days, so he wasn't a bit surprised to see him there.

"You're thinking o' building, I see."

"I'm not thinking about it, at all," says he. "I'm *doing* it."

The old beggar man looked at him. "I wouldn't, if I was you. That's the wrong place. If you build there you won't be short o' company, whatever else."

"Well, you're not me. This is my land and I'll build wherever I like."

He was ever a man like that, my grandfather. Hasty, you know. And stubborn.

"Oh, do. Build where you like," says the old man. "'Tis nothing to me, but you won't have much comfort in it. I can promise you that much."

He went off about his business and my grandfather forgot about him. The building o' the house went on and he did most of it himself. Some o' the neighbors helped him to roof it, and I heard that the timber for that roof came from Aghadoe. That's somewhere around Killarney, isn't it?

'Twas whitewashed then, and they moved in their bits o' furniture from the old house. They hadn't much—the bed, table, a couple o' chairs, pots and pans, and o' course the dresser. A fine big dresser made out o' bog deal.

And when everything was ready the priest came and said Mass in the house. That was the custom in them days, to bring a blessing on a new house. 'Tis still done by a lot o' people today.

When the praying was done, anyway, there was a bit of a party; nothing big, you know, just a half-tierce o' Guinness, a few bottles o' whiskey and *poitín*—and plenty tea, o' course.

The priest didn't stay too long and when he was gone the party started in earnest. They drank what was there, but they didn't get drunk. They did not, 'cause all of 'em had to be up early in the morning—farming people, you know. But they enjoyed themselves while they were in it, and they wished my grandparents well in the new house: *"Go bhfanfaidh sibh sámh agus socair ann."* (May ye live secure and peaceful in it.)

Then, coming on midnight, they started to leave, until there was no one left—only the two themselves. After all the excitement o' the day, all they wanted was to get a bit o' sleep. So they left everything there after the party. They could clear it up in the morning.

They took to the room, anyway, went to bed, thinking they'd sleep sound. But they didn't. Their heads were hardly on the pillow and their eyes closed, when there was this almighty crash below in the kitchen! Down came the big heavy dresser, down on the floor. They jumped up in the bed and heard the cutlery scattering, the crockery breaking. Their first thought—and would you blame 'em?—was, *Merciful God, there's someone in the house! Robbers!* Next thing, they heard the table and chairs dancing around the kitchen floor.

They leaped out o' the bed, ran to the room door, looked down—and there was everything where it should be. Table. Chairs. And the dresser standing by the wall. Nothing at all disturbed.

They stood there a couple o' minutes, staring, wondering if they were dreaming. But my grandfather, he was no coward, whatever else he was.

"I'll go out," he says. "There's someone blackguarding, trying to frighten us."

And he did go out, in his nightshirt, out the door and all around the house, to make sure there was no one there. But there was no one, not a sound. And their dog, he was sleeping on the flagstone outside the door. Surely to God, if there was someone there, the dog would have barked!

He was scratching his head when he came back to his wife, and said, "No one there. Maybe 'twas a dream we had."

They went back to bed, anyway. But, their eyes were hardly closed when the very same thing happened again—crash! Down came the dresser . . . cutlery scattering . . . crockery breaking . . . table and chairs dancing around the kitchen! They jumped out o' the bed again, ran to the door, looked down—nothing. Everything below was just the way it should be.

They went to bed again, but they got no more sleep that night. Or the following night. Or the one after that. By the time they had four nights put by 'em without sleep, they were walking around like two zombies. And remember, now, they still had to do all the work on the farm.

Things couldn't go on like that. It looked like they'd have to move out, back to the old house again, miserable and all as 'twas. At least they'd be able to get their night's sleep in it.

On the fifth day, his wife said to him, "Look, go to the priest. Explain to him what's happening and maybe he might be able to do something for us."

And he did, that very same day.

But as he made his way up Brosna village—the presbytery is above at the top o' the village, you know—he was getting more and more nervous with every step. And when he came to the gate, he stopped. How could he face the priest with a stupid story like that? Sure the holy man'd laugh at him, tell him to go away and have sense for himself.

But then he thought of his wife waiting at home and what he knew was sure to happen that night again if he didn't do something. So he knocked at the door. And as soon as the priest came out and saw his face, he knew there was something wrong. Why wouldn't he, and my grandfather falling with the tiredness? He invited him in, sat him down, and asked him what could he do for him.

The story came out, anyway, and d'you think the priest laughed? He did not.

"Yes, indeed," says he. "Things like that have been known to happen. Look, I'll go back with you and I'll do what I can."

That's exactly what he did. He took his prayer book and whatever else he needed, and they tackled up his horse and trap, and they went back to the house.

The prayers were said—for some kind of an exorcism, I s'pose—"And now," he says, "you should be able to get your night's sleep."

Well, that night they went to bed early. They had plenty sleep to catch up on, I can tell you! But 'twas little sleeping they did! Their eyes were hardly closed when the very same thing happened all over again. Down came the dresser with a crash, down on the floor, smashing crockery, scattering cutlery. Then the table and chairs started their dancing again, around the floor.

"God Almighty help us!" they said. "Not again, surely!"

But it *was* again. Not a wink o' sleep that night either.

The morning came, and she says, "I'm staying in this house no more."

But isn't it strange, too, how things turn out sometimes? What saved 'em was a complete accident. Or maybe 'twasn't. Maybe there's things that we don't know nothing about.

The rent day was coming up—the gale day, as they called it in them times. That was the day, twice a year, that Irish people had to pay the rent to the landlord's agent. And if you hadn't it, cash in hand, you'd be evicted, yourself and your family. And it didn't matter if you had ten children or two, out you'd go if you hadn't the money. And if the agent didn't like you, he'd send in the "crowbar brigade" to level the house so you couldn't come back.

Anyway . . . the gale day was nearly on 'em. And they had no money, but they had two cows they could sell.

The poor man could hardly stand, but he says to his wife, "Look, I'll take the cows to Castleisland fair in the morning. Maybe I'll get enough for 'em to pay the rent."

Castleisland is the nearest town to here, you know. Nine miles away. The following morning, he hit the road early. She wished him well, but he hardly heard her, he was so tired. Out by Cordal he went and, sure, the poor man hardly saw the road. 'Twas the cows were leading him, instead of him driving them.

But, at last, he got to Castleisland. And if you were ever there, you'd notice something unusual about it. 'Tis only a small town, but it has a fierce wide main street—the third widest in Ireland, they say—and ideal for cattle fairs, plenty space in it.

When he arrived there that morning 'twas full, that street, crowded with cattle and people, all kinds o' trading and buying and selling going on.

He wasn't there half an hour when he sold the two cows. He was well known, you see, and honest, so he had no trouble getting rid of 'em. But the last thing he wanted to do was go home. He was so tired he couldn't face it. He had to sit down someplace, rest for a while, have a drink, and think. So he went down to a pub there on the street—the one he always went into when he'd be in town. But as soon as he opened the door, a blast o' smoke and noise came out against him! The place was full up with people doing business, finishing up bargains, and all the rest of it.

And even though usually there was nothing he liked better than a bit o' gossip and conversation, he couldn't face it now. He was too tired. So he peeped into the snug—you know, the little private room where you can have a quiet pint, and order your drink through a little hatch into the bar—and 'twas empty. Talk about relief! He went in there, called the barman and ordered a pint o' porter. He got it. But all he could do was sit there, stupid with the tiredness, half asleep, hardly able to move or keep his eyes open. Could you blame him? What way would you feel yourself if you were nearly five nights without a wink o' sleep?

So he sat there dozing away, waking up, and then dozing off again. But one o' them times he woke, when he looked out the window, who d'you think he saw passing outside? Only the old traveling man who gave him the warning that day he was starting building the house!

Well, he was up out o' that seat like lightning and out the door. By then the old traveling man was gone maybe fifteen or twenty yards up along the footpath. But he called him, and in spite o' the crowd o' people between 'em, the old man heard him and stopped. He came back, and my grandfather invited him into the snug, ordered a pint for him, and sat down. But the old man, he didn't sit down, only looked at my grandfather across the little table.

He stared at his face and said, very quiet, "You look to me like a man that isn't getting his sleep. You have company, I'd say."

And my grandfather knew straight away what he was talking about!

"Look," says he, "what in the name o' God is wrong with my house? We can get no comfort in it, no sleep or nothing. Even after the priest's prayers in it. If he can't help us, what'll we do?"

"Didn't I warn you?" says the traveling man. "There's no use talking here about it. Finish up your pint and come on back with me. I'll show you what you did wrong."

They finished their drinks, walked out o' that pub, and out o' the town o' Castleisland, back over the hill, nine miles back to the yard o' his new house—the house we're sitting in now! There was his wife waiting for him, wondering o' course, were the cattle sold and had he the money for the rent. When she saw him coming into the yard with the traveling man she was a bit surprised, naturally.

But the old man, he didn't even salute her. He just walked to the front door there, where she was standing, pushed her aside—not rough or anything—and called my grandfather.

"Come here!" he says. And when my grandfather was standing beside him—there in his own doorway—he says to him, "Now, look out there and tell me what do you see."

My grandfather looked. "The yard?"

"No," he says. "Look again."

"The road?"

"No. Look careful."

"Oh, that old whitethorn bush? Sure, that's there forever. That could be there since the start o' the world."

"D'you tell me that, now?"

The old man walked out to the gable o' the house, called my grandfather, then says, "Come over here."

He did.

"Look out there, now, and tell me what do you see?"

My grandfather was beginning to catch on at this stage. He looked out from that gable end, and there, no farther away than the end o' the garden, was another whitethorn bush, standing alone.

"Now," says the old man, "I told you. I warned you. The fairies' path is between them bushes and beyond. And you're after building your house on it." He walked back to the door.

"Watch this, now," he says then. "Come in here with me."

They went into the house.

"Stand here in the middle o' the kitchen floor." Which they did.

Then he says, "Now, look out the front door there. And remember what you saw out the back. D'you realize now what you did? You have 'em stopped from passing through on their path. Every time they pass here at night they strike against the wall. And if you'll take my advice this time, you'll knock out a door there in the back wall. Let 'em pass in a straight line between their two bushes, 'cause that's the way they're passing since the world began. If you don't, I'll tell you this much: You'll never get a night's or a day's peace in this house. Take my advice if you like. If you don't want to, don't. I can do no more. Good luck and God guide you."

Off he went about his own business again.

I can tell you this much: They hadn't to discuss the matter at all! That very day, he did the job himself, broke out a new door in the back wall—the one you're looking at below there now. And 'tis that way ever since.

That, sure enough, is what I did find myself looking at that day in August 1975 as I talked to the man who told this story. And he made it quite clear that there was never after any disturbance in the house. Once that doorway was opened, once their path was straightened and cleared again, there was no more trouble. Except for one thing: Every three years, the people of the house would wake in the night to the smell of cooking and sizzling down in the kitchen. Each time it would be coming from the same place, under the plasterwork by the back door. And without fail one of their cattle would die three days later. The fairies, the Good People, had their own way of collecting the toll on their road.

And Tadhg told me something else: that from then on, in his grandfather's time, in his father's time, even in his own time, neither of those two doors was ever locked at night.

"Because," he said, "you can lock 'em. You can chain 'em. You can bar 'em. But in the morning the two of 'em will be open a couple of inches. They can't be kept closed."

I had no reason to disbelieve him. After all, he had to live there, alone, a man in his late seventies, in an isolated place. Why would he be trying to frighten himself?

"If you put a wall or barbed wire or a thing
on their path they mightn't like it. A man near here,
he planted whitethorns an' things started going wrong for him.
So he went to Biddy Early, an' she told him to take 'em out of it,
that they were in the path o' the fairies. . . . Seemingly
they have feeling, an' they'd tear themselves on the thorns
when they'd be passing. There must be a certain amount
o' natural life in 'em, then, you'd think."

CULLANE, TULLA, FEBRUARY 15, 1982

Planting on a Fairy Path

THERE'S A PLACE on that old road outside there, the old
Dingle road, and you'd be better off to have no dealings with it.

Over there, going into the land, there was a bit o' ground
between the old road and where the boundary fence was. We
were planting potatoes in the field—there's a couple of acres in
it altogether.

And my father said, "We'll fit in two ridges between the old
road and the fence."

'Twas a hard, cold day from the southeast.

"I'll have shelter there," he says. "After we have the dinner I'll
start, and we'll plant 'em."

We came, anyway, and there was six sheep in the field while
we were turning the two ridges. We had the dinner. We came
out. And my six sheep, they were in one bunch, dead there. I

called my father, Lord have mercy on him. He went over, any-way, and turned back the sods, left it there.

If they died from grazing, or anything they ate, they wouldn't be in one little bunch.

Could anyone tell you the cause o' that? I s'pose there was a certain amount o' Those People traveling there. I s'pose they're traveling there all the time.

For poor people, with little margin between them and hunger, the use of every inch of ground for grazing or tillage was necessary. But such intense land usage had its risks, as we see in this man's story. I know personally that they could very ill afford to lose the six sheep in question. But note that there is no out-burst, no recriminations against the Good People. The old man knows better; he accepts that he has made a mistake in invading fairy property, undoes the dam-age as far as he is able, and bears his loss. Such stoicism was, no doubt, bred of long experience of the futility of humans measuring themselves against the Good People and their power.

*"Building houses, now, when the foundation of a house
was laid out, if the masons came the following morning
an' if there was things knocked, they might remove it.
It might be in the path. An' if a house was built in
a path, strange things might happen."*

MILTOWN, JUNE 27, 1999

Electricity Poles Moved
from Fairy Path

AT THE TIME they were putting up the poles for the light over
in County Cork, they put down a pole, anyway, in a line with the
rest of 'em. And, sure, you know most of 'em was down six and
seven feet. I see the holes they made here in our place; they were
about six feet deep. The pole that was put down there, it was
taken up that night and laid down flat in the field. The one pole.
There was no digging around it, only pulled up out o' the hole,
and laid down in the field.

When the ESB (Electricity Supply Board) men came back
they put it in again, in the same hole. For, d'you see, they had the
poles in a line and they had to put it there.

By Jeez, didn't they put it down again.

And that night it was taken up *again!* I don't know, now,
about the third time, but they didn't put it down in that hole
then anymore. They changed the ground and put it in another

place. And 'twas left there then. I s'pose that was a path, a fairy path.

Without doubt, the coming of rural electrification in the 1950s had a profound effect on Ireland. Places were now made bright at night that had never been so before, and according to popular account, fairy lore and all things traditional began to wither from this time on. Perhaps. But what is certain is that in the laying down of the vast network of poles to carry the electric wires, ground was dug up that had lain undisturbed from time immemorial. And in the process it was only natural that things should come to the surface that consorted ill with the bright new way of things. A clash of cultures? Most likely. And have the Good People lost the fight (if ever there was one), since we rarely hear of such incidents as the one recounted here nowadays? Hardly. Most elders would say that they have merely adapted themselves—or not even that; that it's we who have changed as a result of all the modern "discoveries," not they; that the consequence has merely been that we are less able than ever to see, hear, meet, or experience them.

Fairies Violently Object to Their Path Being Blocked

UP HERE, at the back of us a small bit, we witnessed the fairies ourselves, sure, when we were playing cards. A step'd come to the door every night when we'd be playing the cards. We'd take no notice. 'Twould go away.

This night we were playing and the man o' the house was out milking the cows, and he came in. We had the table pulled out and I took the lamp and I was going hanging it on the pier.

So we played away—we'd be in no hurry home, up to twelve o'clock in the night. The old game we'd be playing, or forty-five, and a kitty the odd time—oh, a penny a game.

But, anyway, we was playing away, and 'twas around twelve o'clock when this explosion happened: The glass o' the lamp broke out over our heads on the table. So we all got a bit excited, I s'pose. But we didn't take much notice. We knew there was fairies around the place. We were told it.

He lit two candles and we finished our game and went away home.

We were there the following night and when he came in from milking the cows he brought in this flashlamp. 'Twas a bicycle lamp, but the glass in 'em them times was an inch thick. They were the first o' the battery lamps that came out for the bicycles. He brought it in and left it on the window, and around the same time as the globe busted, the explosion took place again, in the window. It shook the house from end to end and we discovered the glass o' the flashlamp had broke; it split in two.

Sure, we enjoyed that laugh going home, talking that the fairies was coming.

Next night, anyhow, 'twas the grandest night that ever came out o' the heavens. But when we went up the following night the bull shed was gone, clapped up against the end o' the house and a car house where we used to be going in—and not one nail was ever drawn out of it. 'Twas taken off of its walls and brought by the wind, the *sí-gaoith*,* out between a big, high cabin and an ash tree. So nine of us, and the two men o' the house, we caught that shed and brought it back down. It took two hours of us to bring it back in between the shed where it came out and the ash tree. And we put it up on the walls and nailed it down. All in one piece! A nail never drew out of it. Corrugated iron, ten-foot sheets, and three spars o' timber in it—and never drew a nail or broke a lath!

*The fairy wind.

'Twas the fairies swept it up. The fairies brought it and clapped it up where we were going in to stop us from going into the house, to block the thoroughfare. Brought it out across the yard and clapped it up. There was nothing else you could make out of it, only that 'twas stopping us from going into the house.

So, we played cards away and laughed coming home and said the fairies was in it for sure this time.

I met an old man, a neighbor of ours, the next day, and I told him my story.

"There wasn't a breeze o' wind heard in any part o' the parish the same night," he said. 'Twas the finest night that ever came, and the moon shining. "Let you leave there," he said. "We played cards there before you and we had to leave it. The fairies are there. Get out o' there."

So we went back there no more. That was the finish o' that.

Night gatherings such as card plays or dances often provided scope for pranksters to play tricks on the more gullible of those present, so stories from such settings need to be examined closely and with a little skepticism. The teller of this tale even seems to feel this way during the first two incidents, the breaking of the lamps. The fairies are mentioned, but only as something to be laughed about. But on the third occasion, when the fairy wind lands the shed in the way of the card players, on a dead-calm night (significantly, without disturbing a single nail in the process), the laughter is far less certain, and disappears entirely when an old neighbor confirms that the house in question has a long-standing otherworldly reputation—specifically that a fairy path runs beside it. Knowing that fact makes all manner of strange happenings explainable, for when the Good People are going about their business—usually in the form of the sí-gaoith—the powers of everyday nature are suspended for the duration and anything may happen.

"I used see the fairies. As a matter o' fact, I used see the fairies coming over the road. . . . An' d'you know how I used to see 'em, do you? I'll tell you. When you'd see all this sinneán gaothach, all this dust, rising, rising, rising an' blowing hither the road, an' blowing in—in the daytime."
LISCANNOR, JANUARY 12, 2001

Man Gets Warning
from the Fairy Wind

I WAS TALKING to this man the other day and he said to me, "You're the very man I wanted to see."

I said to him, "What's your problem?"

I had heard, though. A fellow had told me.

He said, "What's your version o' the fairy wind?"

The same man wouldn't believe anything like that. And you wouldn't frighten him with a shotgun. He had an iron nerve. He'd demolished a couple o' forts, and when I gave out to him,* he said, "Ah, bull! Yourself and your forts. What the hell about 'em. What are they? Mounds of earth."

That's what he came up with always.

But he had a fright got. That's why he was coming to me. He was out walking a greyhound about five o'clock in the evening. Broad daylight! He was getting the greyhound ready for Clounanna (a large greyhound meet in County Limerick). And the breeze o' wind came, the whirlwind. Out o' nowhere. And just as he came to the ash tree on the side o' the road, it stripped it. Cleaned it. All he had standing there in two seconds was the tree and the branches. It didn't leave a leaf on it.

I had heard and I had gone to see the tree. The man that told me said that the dog, if he was there since, wouldn't pass it. He yowled and he yelled and he wouldn't pass it.

So, I said to him, "Are you going to Clounanna with that dog?"

"I am," he said.

I said to him, "Will you do me a favor? And yourself a favor?"

"What is it?" he said.

I said, "Stay at home."

"What d'you mean?" he said.

---

*Berated him.

"That's what I mean. Do what you're told. Stay at home. Jeez," I said, "if the whirlwind caught you in the car, where was you? Stay at home. Yourself and your Clounanna!"

And he did. He got the message, because his nephew was cutting hedges and developing sites and doing a few jobs around the farm, and the one warning he gave him—this man who wasn't afraid o' the Devil out o' hell if he met him—"Whatever you do," he said, "leave the forts alone."

There's two or three of 'em left yet in the farm. But he was just lucky. If he interfered with the wrong forts, he wouldn't be around to be giving advice to anyone.

It can sometimes amaze one to see how patient the Good People can be in the face of human stupidity and destructiveness. Even when they are provoked beyond what we humans would call all reasonable bounds, they often surprise by choosing to warn the offender when swift vengeance might more reasonably be expected. That is part of their inscrutability. And here we see that the sí-gaoith is different than in the previous story—there is no hint of a path, merely a warning, and the dog recognizes what the man does not: the presence of the otherworldly.

The man in question in this story learns a salutary lesson, and perhaps the reason his fate is not violent is that he is of more use to the Good People alive, as a convert to spread a more civilized message. Or is it merely, as the teller says, that he was lucky in the forts he chose to destroy?

Three Brief Stories of the Fairy Wind

THERE'S A FARM NEAR HERE, and out at the back o' the
house there was a noble barn. I used to be always looking at this
barn because 'twas built with stone—but there was no roof on
it. Everything else was perfect, oh, a fine barn. And I said to the
owner one day, "How is it you never put a roof on that barn?"

He told me that when 'twas built and roofed the first time it
took fire. 'Twas left for some time and 'twas roofed again. They
finished it of an evening, and this whirlwind rose about an hour
after it being finished, what's called a fairy wind, the *sí-gaoith*, and
swept across and lifted the roof clean off.

They left it then, and they inquired, and they found out that
'twas supposed to have been built right in the middle of a path.

I KNEW THIS HOUSE where there was a good tablecloth, that
used generally be on the parlor table. 'Twas a very fine day and
they took out the tablecloth and spread it out, just to get the

sun, I s'pose. And the *sí-gaoith* came, and took the tablecloth and 'twas never seen again.

The contention was that because they were having a certain amount of pride in this tablecloth, that's why it was taken away altogether, that you should be very humble where Those People were concerned.

I REMEMBER, myself and my mother was above in a field we have up there—ah, that'd be fifty or sixty years ago, I suppose. My father wasn't at home at all at the time. We had loose hay in a field, you see. 'Twas after being shaken out and we had no way to gather it in, only forks and rakes. And we was gathering it in, and gathering it in, when didn't this big, big, big gust o' wind come out o' nowhere. And didn't it bring it above and in the gate for us. Blew it in! It did. My mother said 'twas the fairies. I s'pose they see we had no help.

The unpredictability of Those People, the fact that they might take exception to—and carry off—a luxury domestic item just because it was being displayed publicly makes us wonder were they class conscious, wishing to keep people "in their place." It is not certain why the displaying of the cloth should be offensive to them in this case, but it obviously is.

Far more understandable is the case of the fine stone barn that met with repeated misfortune, all for the lack of inquiring whether it might have been built on a fairy path—which, of course, it was.

But we see the other, the more kindly, neighborly, side of the Good People here also, a side that should never be forgotten. The speaker here showed me the field in question, and there is no possibility that any ordinary gust of wind could have moved the amount of hay it contained to the place he indicated. Either it was, as his mother said, the fairies, or else . . . what? There is one other possibility—that he is mistaken. But I know him too well. Even though eighty-nine, he is as clear-minded as someone half that age.

"Some people were very afraid of it. You'd hear it coming. It'd be twisting bits o' hay an' paper, twisting around. You'd get out o' the way when you'd see it. That was them passing."
MILTOWN, JUNE 27, 1999

A Woman Gets Knocked with the Sí-Gaoith

THERE'S A STORY about this man, he was out saving hay, himself and his wife and family. And 'twas broken kind o' weather. They shook the hay this day but 'twasn't fit to tram.*

---

*Make up into large heaps to await bringing home to the hay shed.

The following day was a fine day, and they got a fine night, and 'twas grand for tramming. The same day, the fairy wind came at different times. The old people at that time, if they heard the fairy wind coming, they'd throw theirself down. For if it knocked you, they said you might never again rise.

But this woman, she had a rake, an ordinary rake—'twas all handwork at the time—and she was clearing the ground, raking it clean with the timber rake. She was just out at the end o' the line o' hay and she was turning, when the fairy wind caught her and knocked her, herself and the rake. She wasn't down two minutes when she was up again.

But from that day out she didn't feel right. They lived on, anyway. And at that time women milking cows used to sing for the cows. She was a great singer, but the husband noticed that she stopped that, stopped the singing. She wasn't right ever after. She worked away, but twelve months was nearly up and she was getting weaker and weaker, and she wasn't fit to do much work—'twas neighboring women that was coming in, washing the clothes and making bread, getting the scholars ready for school. He had tried everything—she went to blessed wells, she went to doctors and everywhere, and they could find nothing wrong with her. But still she was ailing away, ailing away.

Twelve months was nearly up, anyway, and this day she was very bad, and whatever drove it into his head—he was outside working—he said he'd go to Biddy Early.

He struck off in the morning for Biddy Early's, and on into Inagh, and down Kilnamona and into Ennis, and out the Tulla road to Biddy. But he didn't know the house. He knew the direction. He went on, anyway, and he met a man bringing in cows for milking in the morning.

He asked the man, "Could you direct me to Biddy Early?"

But the man gave no answer, only pointed the way. He spoke no word. You wouldn't get absolution at that time if you showed Biddy Early's house to anyone.

He went on, anyway, farther, and who did he meet but the scholars going to school. 'Twas all walking, o' course, at that time. There was seven or eight of 'em together, and he was giving 'em grand soft talk about who was teaching 'em, what class was they in, and all that. And all of a sudden he asked 'em, "Could any o' you show me Biddy Early's house?"

And a young lad o' six or seven years, he said, "'Tis over there about a half mile, a thatched house."

He had no sooner his mouth open than a girl, she was nine or ten years, she gave him a dart o' the elbow, but he had the damage done; he had the man told.

He carried on, anyway, on the young lad's instructions, and he landed at this house. 'Twas in a bit from the road and this red-haired woman was rinsing the teapot to get the breakfast ready in the morning.

"Is this Biddy Early's?" he said.

"Well, 'tis," says she. "But you're Biddy Late. Where are you the last twelve months? And you living with an old fairy woman since the day your wife got knocked with the *sí-gaoith*?"

By God, she frightened the life out o' him, anyway.

"Come in," she said.

She brought him in and she gave him a cup o' good strong tea. Biddy's house was never without whiskey and baker's bread, for by all accounts she usedn't get much money. 'Tis things like that she used to get.

She gave him a glass o' whiskey, anyway, and he drank the tea and he drank the whiskey, and she went in the room and consulted her bottle.

"I have bad news for you," she said. "When you'll go home your wife is dead. There'll be a corpse house there."

She frightened the life out o' him. "Will you be able to do anything for me?"

"By God, I'll do my best," says she, "but I'll guarantee nothing."

'Twas a thatched house, and she went out the door. At that time they used to pick ash plants for walking sticks in the November darkness. That was the time to pick sticks, ash plants, handles for whips, or anything. They'd be right limber. 'Twas customary; they used to pick 'em in the November darkness, the dark o' the moon.

She took down the first ash plant, anyway, out o' the thatch, and she bent it, but it didn't pass the inspection. She took down the second. 'Twas a little better. She stuck it back up again. She took down the third and 'twas right limber.

"When you go home, now," she said, "there'll be a wake in progress, or a kind of a corpse house, for 'twill be daylight, you see. And when you go home, open the two doors"—there used to be two doors in the old farmhouses, a back door and a front door—"and put a stone to each of 'em," she said. "Go in the room where that corpse is laid out and belt enough at her with that ash plant, and you'll see what'll happen. But don't touch the ground with that stick or yourself till you land in your own yard."

He struck out, but the horse was getting tired and he drove him fairly hard. He was all the time afraid that if he got a false step, and if he fell, the game'd be up.

He landed in his own yard, anyway, and there was a couple o' horse carts there and they had the wake brought. He had a brother married nearby, he had a couple of uncles, and they had the wake brought—porter and baker's bread and jam and everything like that—and the woman was laid out.

He landed in the yard, and o' course they were shaking hands to him—"I'm sorry for your trouble"—but he was throwing 'em out of his way.

Into the house he went, and there was a good few women inside. 'Twas the same story—he was throwing 'em out of his way. He done what Biddy Early told him—put a stone to the front door and a stone to the back. He went in the room and beat the life out o' the corpse. And the fairy woman went out the back door and his own wife came in the front door. All was lost but for Biddy Early.

But it didn't stop there. One o' the uncles or one o' the neighbors said, "We'll bring back that porter and the publican'll take it back."

"You won't stir a bit of it," he said.

It so happened that Garret Barry, the blind piper of Inagh, he was staying in a girl's house not far away. They were home from America, a couple of the girls, and he used to be playing for 'em in the night when they were dancing. They sent for Garret—and the like o' the dance that was there that night! All was welcome. He threw the doors open. The like of it was never before in the parish o' Miltown. His own wife came back and she was a young woman all the time. She had two more children. She's buried over in Ballard. She died at her natural span, eighty-three years.

That's the story o' the *sí-gaoith.*

We can date this story probably to the third quarter of the nineteenth century, for the man whose wife has been carried by the fairies decides to go to Biddy Early with his troubles. Biddy's uncanny knowledge of his predicament frightens him, but after her consultation with her magic bottle, things become clearer, though no less intimidating. But, by obeying her instructions to the letter, he saves his wife.

This is a story full of dark hints, which shows a world in which people are at the mercy of mysterious powers, where the simplest of mistakes can lead to tragedy, but where help is at hand if only it is asked for.

Not too different, this, from our modern world, really, if we consider it, though all the surface points of reference may seem to be quite dissimilar.

*"They'd be another form o' life. A spirit.
They're not physical. D'you remember I was telling you
about the big field below where I was veered in the night?
I wasn't in any physical contact that I could see,
but the pressure I could feel. But the pressure o' what?"*
DRUMLINE, OCTOBER 22, 1999

Strange Gravity

ONE NIGHT this man was going to the fair o' Tulla. He used to have cattle to sell sometimes, but he had no cattle this night; he was going buying cattle. He got up and looked out, and 'twas so bright he thought 'twas all hours in the day. He didn't even wait to put down the breakfast, only started out on his bicycle, out and down the road. Once he got out on the public road, he pulled the bicycle to the side to go up on it—and no chance in God's earth could he go one yard! The bicycle wouldn't stir. If he was walking 'twas all right, he could push it on, but any time he'd go to go up on it, 'twas held. No move! Oh, a big, courageous man—he often told it—the sweat was teeming down off o' him.

He had to go about a mile. He was going down with the fall, and no hope in God's earth could he go up on that bicycle till he came down to where there was a little stream crossing the road. And the very minute he crossed the stream, he went up a little bit of a hill from it, got up on his bicycle, and into Tulla, no bother.

When he arrived into Tulla 'twas only half past two in the night. He thought they'd all be gone home, and he discovered that 'twas only half past two. There was some friends he had in Tulla. He knocked at the door and they let him in. And he was sweating! His shirt was stuck to his back with what happened to him for a mile o' the road, trying to push his bicycle—down the hill!

But they always said if you meet the Good People, once you cross a stream you leave 'em after you. They can't cross flowing water.

What happens to this man would be explained today in terms of "time warp" or some such phenomenon, perhaps, but to the person telling the story it is all very clear: Here was a man out at the wrong time and place—very likely when the Good People were on the move and wanted no witnesses.

By unbelievers, the disruption of time might be explained thus: People can sometimes wake suddenly and find themselves utterly confused (though rarely does the confusion last for as long as in this narrative). But how to explain the inability to cycle downhill as here described? A bicycle in a state of neglect? Hardly, since a while later the same bicycle is easily cycled uphill!—yet, significantly, only after a stream has been crossed.

The teller of the tale is in no doubt why things have gone astray, and he says so clearly: The Good People have been at work.

---

*"A man was telling me that he was passing this place in the road
one night where there was a fort, an' the horse stood up. An' whatever
he'd do, he couldn't get the horse to pass it. An' the horse was black
with sweat. He had to turn around an' go back. He couldn't get
him to pass it, whatever he seen. An' he could see nothing."*

TUBBER, NOVEMBER 30, 1984

Man Prevented from Passing

MY GRANDFATHER, my father's father, he hurt his finger.
'Twas building a wall he was, and a stone fell back when he was
putting it up, and it made faggot o' the finger. He went over to
old Hehir's father, a mile and a half, to settle his finger. He had
to put the finger together. And he put splints on it, you know;
old Hehir was a great bonesetter.

My grandfather took his stick, anyway, to go on home.

But, "I don't know would you go now, Paddy," says old
Hehir to him. "What time is it, Janie?" to his wife.

"Just half twelve."

"You won't go now."

"What're you saying?!" he said, catching his stick. He was a
hardy man, seventy-seven years of age.

"I don't know are you going now. But I'll go as far as the
door with you."

He'd come up the hill that time and he'd come out straight
by the quarry, out to Kilcolum, a mile and a half.

Faith, the cock crew.

"Look, go on in, now, and sit down." And he said to Janie, "Will you make a little drop o' punch there? Make a drop o' punch."

"I will, o' course," she said. "Come in."

"Don't mind your punch!" says the grandfather, and off he goes, out by the end o' the house, and back the end o' the cowshed—an old puddly place—and up the hill. He was only gone up the hill a piece when he could go no farther. By God, he stopped, and he sat down on this rock.

"What's here?" he said, whispering. . . . "What's here?"

He was hard to frighten, but he could go no farther. He was held.

He sat down, anyway, three times on the stone.

"Is it myself that's wrong, or what's wrong? Sure, that man inside was only trying to frighten me," he said.

He got up the fourth time, to go. He only could get up about a foot. He couldn't straighten himself.

He turned and walked back. Tapped at the door.

"Hah! We were expecting you. She has a drop o' punch made. Sit down," said old Hehir. "What did you see?"

"Nothing in the world," he said, "but I thought there was men hurling above on the hill. Or they're hurling very near there."

"They are," he said. "They're over on the hill opposite. They're hurling there."

'Twas one o'clock! One o'clock. He was a half an hour in the stones.

He sat down in a corner, and she made a drop o' punch, and the shivering went out of him. He was shivering like the devil!

Well, they started talking.

"Oh, them things are nothing," old Hehir said to him. "That's nothing. 'Tisn't long since I got blocked there myself."

God, he gave him great courage.

It struck two o'clock.

"Go now," he said. "Go away now. You can go home now."

And he did. Walked out. He went in the same place, and he stood in the same place. And he saw nothing.

By God, there was fun over on the other hill, beyond on Keane's Hill, at the match.

But there was no traveling that way while they were playing. That's a fact.

Here we see clearly that, at certain precise times, definite places belong to the Good People and they will brook no trespass by humans—as, indeed, why should they? Would we allow someone to stroll through one of our games in progress without an attempt to restrain him, even if only for his own safety?

The old man described here is inviting trouble by his stubbornness in ignoring a friendly warning by one who knows. That he is allowed to go in peace . . . could it be due to the fact that they were so engrossed in their game? Who knows. He did escape, though, obviously a wiser man, for the story has been passed down to his grandson (now in his late seventies), who showed me the very place where he was stopped in his tracks at half past twelve on that fateful night.

*"When a horse'll sneeze three times they used say he
sees something, something from the Other Side."*
MILTOWN, JUNE 27, 1999

Latoon Dead Hunt

D'YOU EVER HEAR tell o' the hunt in the middle o' the night?
Delmege's Mountain was the famous place for that, sure.

There was a man, Mac, he was coming from Ennis after
paying the rent. He had a few pints, and he went to sleep at the
side o' the road, above at Latoon bridge—there beside Lane-
Joynt's place.

In the middle o' the night—he didn't know what time—the
hunt came. He was a great horseman himself, Mac was. And
there was all the gentry and they woke him up and invited him
to join 'em. He woke, said he had no way o' joining 'em. So they
got him on some kind of an animal—he made out 'twas a bullock—and he hunted all night with 'em, until daylight in the
morning.

When he got dropped in the morning, he was below on
Delmege's Mountain, thirty miles away. And he didn't cross the
river, couldn't cross the Fergus.

He went to the priest after coming home, and he told the priest his story.

"Ah, my good man," the priest said to him, "you're in the deliriums. You have drink taken. You're imagining things."

"Oh, God, no, Father," he said. "There's no way I could walk it. And there was no means o' transport, one way or another," he said. "But I got up on that animal, and I steered that animal after the hunt all night."

And he named all the gentry. They were dead, all of 'em. He was positive that he followed that hunt.

The priest said to him, "I might be wrong, and you might be right, but don't ever be there, in that area, after dark again. After nightfall, make sure and certain that you don't be there. On no account."

"Right," says the man.

The following year, at paying the rent time, he went to Ennis again, had his few pints, and he was making good sure that he was coming home this time, that he wasn't going sleeping. He was killed, at the same spot.

He didn't take the priest's advice. And that's the rock he perished on.

Them hunts were seen in several places. There was one of 'em come from Quin, down across the country. They used have a stag hunt there at one time. It used to assemble around Fitzy Blood's in Ballykilty and hit off for Ballygireen—dogs, horses, the lot—full cry down across the country after the stag. Passed people out. No stag! Nothing there. Frighten the life out o' you.

And the funny thing about that is, I might see it and hear it, and you could be with me, and you'd be wondering was I gone queer.

There's something like this to it: Whatever star you're born under, or whatever hour o' the night you're born, that's what causes it.

Here we have a story that demonstrates how closely the fairy and ghost worlds are associated in the Irish mind. Take the fairy elements in it first: Very often the fairies are known as "the Gentry"; they are excellent horsemen, often given to night riding (cf. A Midnight Ride); they do not cross running water; they often provide a human companion with a mount that later disappears; this episode occurs very close to where the Latoon sceach *stands.*

The ghostly elements are less obvious, but present nonetheless. The man is able to name each of the companions he rode with that night, and he is sure they were all dead.

The teller then digresses to describe other such ghost/fairy hunts seen, and why, and his explanation is perhaps as plausible as any for those who need to know why these phenomena torment some while leaving others quite unimpressed.

*"There was a man out late one night, an' a woman. They had no clocks
in them days. They'd only get up an' go away to the town, the way they'd
be there early. An' this lake, anyway, when they came as far as where
'twas, d'you know what was in it? A big city, or a big town—
all houses, where the lake was. They went about their business.
An' when they were coming home, 'twas all right.
The lake was there. No houses."*

BALLINRUAN, AUGUST 17, 1999

A Fairy Mansion

N o w , Seán Maguire had a man working for him called Mick
Gallagher—he's only dead a few years. And, his match was
made, Seán Maguire's, and he was to be married in Tulla on a
Saturday morning. But the papers had to come from the canon
o' this area in Killaloe. Now, Jack McCarthy was a relation of
Seán Maguire's. By God, Friday morning came, and no certificate came in the post. Maguire was getting married on Saturday,
and I don't know if there was post on a Saturday, but 'twas leaving it a bit late, anyway.

He said, "I'll be in a show if I have to go up to Tulla in the
morning with all the people, and I have no certificate to get married. They'll say there's something queer, that maybe I was
married before. I'll be disgraced,"—which you would be at
that time.

Jack decided he'd cycle down to Killaloe and collect the

certificate from the canon and bring it back. Struck away on a bike. Begod, evening came, and dark came, and no account o' Jack coming back. He was very fond o' the drop, you know.

Seán Maguire knew enough. He says to Mick, "Begod, Mick," he says, "Jack is gone on the booze."

"There's only one thing for it," says Mick. "I'll hit away down, and if I search all the pubs I'll surely find him in one of 'em. He'll have the certificate in his pocket."

He struck away on his bike. I s'pose it was nine o'clock in the night when he went into Killaloe. Every pub he went into Jack had been there, but he was gone. Had drank enough in each one of 'em.

So, the last pub he went into, the man o' the pub said, "He's gone about an hour." You see, Jack's mother was from Ogonnelloe. "He's gone down to Ogonnelloe to the mother's place to stay the night," says he, "because he's too drunk to go home."

Now, you know where Ogonnelloe is, halfway between Killaloe and Scarriff, along the shore o' Lough Derg. Begod, Mick Gallagher didn't know where the house was, but he knew the general direction, and he said he'd hit away out—'twas getting late at this time, up to twelve o'clock.

He struck away on the bike. Driving out along the road, past Ballyvally, where Sarsfield* crossed the Shannon that time, Lough Derg at his right, the mountain at his left. He arrived,

---

*An Irish general who, during the siege of Limerick in 1691, led a column of men by night out to intercept and blow up King William's artillery at Ballyneety, thus saving the city for the moment.

---

anyway, at Ogonnelloe. So he said to himself, "I'll call, now, at some house and I'll inquire where his house is."

He didn't like to knock at a house that there was no light in and get the people up out o' bed, you know. So, he said, "The first house, now, that I'll see a light still on, I'll knock there and inquire my way."

He was only gone a small bit farther when he spotted this light halfway between the road and the shore of Lough Derg, away down in the fields. Left his bike up against the fence. He couldn't find a gate or an avenue into it, but it seemed to be a big place.

"Begod," he said, "I'll take the shortest route."

Hopped in over the fence and on towards the light that he could see, through the fields.

He wasn't traveling very long when he came out in front o' the house.

Oh, 'twas a big mansion, blazing with light, all the windows in it. Went up and knocked at the front door. There was no answer. Knocked again. No answer. He gave the door a push. It went in in front o' him, went into this magnificent hallway— chandeliers and everything hanging off o' the ceiling.

He said, "God save all here," and there was no answer.

There was doors to the right and to the left. He opened a door and went in. And he was in this most beautiful room with a big long table in it, and the table set for dinner. There was every type o' food that a person could imagine on the table, and wine. He was hungry and he was thirsty, and he got this terrible temptation to take a sup o' the wine. And the same man was fond of a drop, himself. But he resisted it, somehow—all the stories he heard I s'pose about not taking any food or drink in a place like that. Because if you did, you were finished. If you ate a bite or drank a drop, there was no coming back. All the old lads had that. And they believed it.

But all of a shot, he started to get afraid. He knew things weren't right. And he turned, and out. And he made his way across the fields again and he never looked back till he found where he left his bike—up on it, and off.

The first house he came to on the side o' the road, he knocked, and he said, "Am I far from—?" and he named Jack's mother's place.

They looked at him. The man o' the house said, "A couple o' hundred yards up the road, the first house you'll come to."

He went up. Jack was in bed, sleeping off the effects o' the booze. The family got up, though, and had great welcome for him, made tea for him. 'Twas in the summertime, and I s'pose the daylight would be three or four o'clock. The old man there was over eighty years of age. He got up, and he was drinking his tea, and Gallagher told him about the house that he saw down near the banks o' the lake, which was only maybe a quarter of a mile down the road, how he got into it, the things he saw there, and everything.

"Begod," the old man said, "I'm eighty years of age and my father before me was eighty when he died, and I never heard him talking about any kind of a house in that place. Or I never saw one."

They waited for the daylight, and himself and Jack struck

for Broadford with the documents. He found where he left his bike, and he got off and he stood up on the pier of a gate. He could see the whole country down to the shores of Lough Derg, and back across Keeper Hill, Silvermines, County Tipperary, up along nearly to the borders o' Galway. There was no type of a house. Nothing there, only the green fields.

Gallagher told that for a fact. And he's only dead a few years.

Stories of visits to fairy mansions are by no means uncommon in Irish lore. Cynics will say, of course, that they stem from dreams, drunkenness, or ragged peasants peeping longingly through the windows of landlords' great houses at the sumptuousness within and imagining impossibilities thereafter. Such peeping was probably done, but stories of fairy mansions did not originate there. Over a thousand years before the landlords were even heard of, "Bruíon Chaorthainn" ("The Fairy Palace of the Quicken Trees") provides us with something similar— a house that looks welcoming, but—! And that is the basic formula right up to our own time, no matter how the building itself may have changed—wood, stone, iron, or whatever. The main problem is: Once in, how does one get out? That part of the plot has changed remarkably little. Why? Probably because people themselves haven't, whatever their surroundings.

*"An ol' man used to tell me when I was young—there's a fort
not far from here, an' he said if you were passing it in the night
a man's voice would say, 'fan liom' ('stay with me'). Whether he
believed it or not, one thing I can tell you about him, after dark he
wouldn't go near that fort. He said he heard it himself, an' he named
several people for me that heard it, the voice saying* 'fan liom.'"
BAREFIELD, APRIL 18, 1982

*M*eeting *the* Cóiste Bodhar, *the* *F*airies' *H*earse

I MET the *cóiste bodhar* myself. I was coming back home from a
dance at two o'clock or half past two, maybe three. They used
always say the *cóiste bodhar* was the fairies' carriage, their hearse,
that they were going burying their dead someplace.

That *cóiste bodhar* was about a mile high; the rattle of it was
about a mile high. And it took nearly a quarter of an hour for it
to pass me.

I wasn't one bit afraid. I was cycling, and I thought 'twas a
lorry coming around the turn o' the road. I was expecting there
was a fellow in the lorry that'd know me, and I didn't want him to
know I was on that road at all. So, I pulled the bicycle into the side
of the road and I sat on it with my back turned from the lorry, as
I thought. But, you see, I suppose 'twas all for luck. I didn't realize 'twas the *cóiste bodhar*. Still, I felt the thing passing me, all but

touching me. That was why I couldn't look back to see who was in it.

Oh, 'twas my luck. If I realized that that was the *cóiste bodhar*, I might never have come home. The danger'd be that, sure, you might give way. An old man that used play cards with us, sixty years before that he met it in the same spot, the *cóiste bodhar*. In the very same spot.

The cóiste bodhar, *or the headless coach, is an unearthly vehicle much feared by night travelers—pedestrian and otherwise. Accounts of where it comes from and what its function is vary—devil's coach, transport for the banshee, omen of death, etc.—but the teller of this story is quite sure. It is the fairies' hearse. And, as always, when they are on the move, normality takes second place. Note the perception of its size, for example—as if a train were passing, but an impossibly high one.*

His turning away from it may have been a more instinctive than rational decision than even he realized, in fact. For most Irish people of his generation (over age sixty-five) knew that to see the cóiste bodhar *would be a calamity amounting to a death sentence. And he knows that despite any terror he might feel (though he says he doesn't), he must hold his nerve and his ground. Only thus can he remain safe.*

Here, we see again (as we did in the account of the Latoon sceach), *the Irish fairies as being subject to death.*

"They'll tell you that the banshee isn't there. Bull! She's there!
(A local man) saw her. A big tall veil . . . a white veil,
in the shape of a woman. An' a big long head o' gray hair.
An' every time she roared, she threw back the head.
That was his description of her."
DRUMLINE, OCTOBER 19, 2000

A Personal Experience of the Banshee

THERE WAS A MAN lived near me, he was a gentleman farmer. He wasn't one o' the landlords, as such. At the time he arrived on the scene, the old landlords had died out, but his place at one time was landlord property.

This old lad wouldn't like to see too many people shooting in his place. He was great to preserve wildlife, but when nobody would bother him to go into the place, the place filled up with rabbits. You see, rabbits are terrible to populate. Where you'll have two rabbits at the start of a year, you'll have five hundred rabbits at the end o' the year. They're a terror to populate.

So he discovered he had too many rabbits. And I met him on the road one day. He had a grand sidecar trap, big high wheels and a racy horse inside under it, and a big whip. And he'd be sitting back and the horse'd be flying into Limerick—a blood horse, man. He pulled up, anyway.

"Just the man I wanted to see," he said.

I said, "Yeah?"

"I'm going to town," he said. "If you agree to do something for me, I'll do something else for you."

I said, "Right. I will, o' course, if 'tis possible."

"I'll tell you my problem," he said. "My estate is infested with rabbits. I'll go into Newsom's now when I go into Limerick and if you agree to trap the rabbits for me, I'll bring you the ways and means."

I said, "Yeah. I'll do that." Little he knew that I was doing it on the quiet, anyway! But I had a quieter way o' working than a rabbit trap. I'd snare 'em. Wire.

I said, "Okay, I'll do the trick for you."

So off he went. He was delighted. He arrived back in the evening and he brought three or four dozen traps. So, I got some tape and I taped the traps, the jaws o' the traps, so the rabbits wouldn't be screeching. And the following day I collected the traps, got my brother, and we went to the far end o' the farm—there was over five hundred acres in it, a mighty estate!

I told him, "I'll be around the house probably in the night. So, if you hear any sounds you can know that I'm going in and out,"—because, you know, you could get yourself shot. He wouldn't bat an eyelid to blow the brains out o' you. He was a target for robbery, so you couldn't blame him for defending himself. And he wouldn't miss you, either!

We went off to the far end, so he wouldn't hear the rabbits getting caught, you see. If he thought there was any cruelty or anything like that, he could get sorry and tell us, "Out!"

So, we did our business out from the house first. We'd go in the night at about nine or ten o'clock, and we'd pick all the rabbits out o' the traps and snares, and we'd collect again at about two o'clock, and again in the morning.

Rabbits were a half-crown a pair, a brace, and that was a lot o' money, you know, where there was a thousand rabbits and money so scarce.

We had two good bikes, man, and we'd hit for Limerick. As a matter o' fact, a man with a car out o' Limerick came to us for the rabbits. Oh, 'twas well worth his while. They used to export 'em.

After about a week, anyway, we showed up near the house. And there was an orchard, and a big wall, and we took shelter at the back o' the wall. The first night we were there 'twas very lonesome! But I had told him in the day that we'd be in the vicinity and he said, "Okay. That's okay. I'll know you're there."

I assured him that I wouldn't wake him up or cause him any undue bother. "That's okay," he said, delighted. Asked me how I was getting on.

"Getting on good," I said.

He was thanking me, man. Normally 'twas the other thing you'd get, a shower o' lead!

We were around there for most of a week, and this night, 'twould be about two o'clock in the morning, we were contemplating going home. There'd be nothing happening after that. We were tired out, sure. By God, I thought I heard crying away down in the estate. And before we moved to come home, maybe ten minutes, the crying came nearer, louder. That's how we knew 'twas nearer. It got louder. More distinct. And we decided that we wouldn't move until . . . well, things settled down. So we stayed put. And faith, the crying passed within—ah, I'd say thirty or forty yards of us.

'Twas very loud and clear at that stage. There was two of us in it, and we were two young men, good hardy lads; it didn't frighten us that much. We waited until it had moved on and came away. We came home. And 'twas when we came home and put on the light—o' course 'twas only the light of a lamp; there was no electricity at that time—that's the time we got frightened.

We went away to bed, anyway, and forgot it. But we never forgot it, really. We thought we did, but 'twas pure fatigue. We slept, and delivered our catch for the night to the car man the following day. He arranged that he'd come again for more, and we said, "Yeah. There'll be more."

In order to meet our commitments, we had to go down again the following night, earlier in the night, around midnight.

I learned since that the banshee scarcely operates after midnight. 'Tis up to twelve o'clock, or one o'clock. And she can't cross a stream.

You know the big stream that runs down through most estates, a big watercourse, with pebbles inside in it, a drainage system? It ran down at the back o' this house, and, faith, she didn't cross it. She came directly down in line with the stream, parallel. By God, she came closer. 'Twas a female voice. But it had a funny intonation. It wasn't continuous at all. It went in spasms, very sweet, as if the head was being thrown back. It came out in volumes like that.

So we steadied ourselves. We weren't as frightened the second night as we were the first night. And she came via the front door, the hall door. Without a doubt in the world, it came past that hall door.

By God, we didn't go home that night; 'twas too early. We held on. And the banshee continued on her journey, out the main gate of the estate.

We weren't that brave, either, now, I might just as well tell you. 'Twasn't through bravado at all we stayed, but there was a few pound at stake! We had a discussion, anyway, myself and my brother, about this banshee thing, and the conclusion we came to was that . . . the man was going to die.

I had a chat with him during the following day, and he didn't show any signs o' going to pass away. Nor he didn't. But about four or five days elapsed, and he arrived out to us all spruced up, and he said he was going to his brother's funeral, that he had died.

I said nothing about what we heard at that time, but I was intending to ask him, to know had they anything like that in the family, when one of 'em'd be going to die, or when one of 'em'd get sick.

I got my chance a few weeks after. He thought to himself for a long time.

"Why did you pose me the question?" he said.

"Well, I'll tell you the truth, now," I said, "why I'm posing you the question. When I was trapping the rabbits, I heard something, what I reckoned was the banshee."

"Yes," he said. "Yeah. That was before my brother died. The banshee follows our family," he said.

Though regarded by most academic experts as not one of the fairies, despite her name, which suggests that she is, I have decided to include the banshee in this collection for the following reasons: She very clearly belongs to the otherworldly—though solitary and with a very specific function, i.e., to warn of impending death; she displays some of the traits of the Good People, such as an inability, or at least reluctance, to cross running water; and, most importantly, some of my informants were very definite in regarding her as one of them. Though nearly all, it has to be said, were surprised to be even asked who she is or where she comes from. Most, when pressed, would only venture that she is from "the Other Side, somewhere."

The men who hear her on the night in question do so without any inkling at first that a death is to follow. They are too busy trying to make a living during hard times. But as the very precise description of events shows, they quickly come to realize that the crying they have heard is something out of the ordinary. And the next night's events confirm this. But the fact that no one dies, though they recognize that it must be the banshee they have heard, mystifies them. It need not have, for when they discover, a few days later, that a family death has occurred some distance away it merely confirms what they and most Irish people know: that when the banshee "follows" (cries for) a family, her warning wail is heard not necessarily just at the place of death, but in the home, the ancestral property, also.

Two interesting points in this episode are that the voice seems to be disembodied (yet strong)—most accounts have her being only heard, though there are instances of her having been seen—and that she seems to be most at home during the small hours, though not all of those I questioned agreed with this, as we will shortly see.

"There were certain people that believed that the banshee used to follow their family, an' they weren't afraid of her at all. They liked to hear her."

BAREFIELD, APRIL 18, 1982

Banshee Comes for Dying Man

A FRIEND O' MINE, an uncle o' his was dying. At that time they'd be kept at home till they'd die. 'Twas very seldom people were put into hospital. And the better-off families'd have a nurse minding 'em. So, this family had a nurse for this old man, but they used to take turns over a couple o' weeks to stay up with him; they weren't expecting him to last too long. Every day they could see him going down.

My friend knew, from what experience he had, that the old man wouldn't last the night. They came home sometime that morning after being up all the night, and they were to go back again that evening. 'Twas a pony and trap they had, himself and his sister, and they hit away over about nine o'clock—a noble summer's evening. And just as he was coming out his own gate, he met an old man who had worked with the other family all his life. He came over to him and asked, "How's the old fellow?"

"Ah," says he, "we're not expecting him to put in the night."

So, they were talking away and the old man asked him, "Are you stopping beyond for the night?"

"Ah, we are," says he. "We're taking our turns looking after him."

"Well," he says, "if he's going to die tonight, don't be surprised at anything that happens over there."

This friend o' mine was a young man at the time and he paid no great heed.

He went over, and the old man was dying. The nurse and the family were above with him, saying the rosary. He stayed below in the kitchen with one o' the workmen, a man that was there all his life.

And he told me that he saw the latch on the back door lifting. The door opened. He sat up, and he was expecting someone to walk in out o' the yard. No one came in. So he went up and he closed it. The workman said nothing.

He told me the crying started outside around the yard, the very same as a woman crying. And the latch lifted, and it opened again. He looked at the workman, and the workman looked at him. So he went up and he closed it again. And it opened the third time.

And the workman said, "Leave it open. Don't close that door again."

The two of 'em sat down. The crying went off up the hill, and faded away. The door remained open, and the next thing, one o' the family came down and said, "Poor man is dead."

My friend got up—he told me this, now, himself. He walked

out around the yard. He said 'twas the grandest night you were ever out. There wasn't a breath of air. Nothing.

But whatever that old workman knew, he said to leave it open. Whether it had to be left open to let him pass through or not, I don't know.

It is obvious in this story, though we are not told it directly, that the banshee cries for the family of the old man who is dying. The two aged workmen, who have been there all their working lives, know that something odd is about to happen to accompany the old man's passing. Just how odd, the nephew finds out in due course—the door opening three times, the woman's voice crying in the yard, the warning to him not to close the door a third time.

The man who told me the tale is probably correct when he surmises that the two events—the door being open and the old man's spirit passing through—are connected. Equally connected to those is the banshee's crying, leading his spirit into the Other World.

*"She's the fairy woman, an' her business was warning you
of an oncoming disaster, a death in the family usually."*
DRUMLINE, OCTOBER 19, 2000

Banshee Alerts Family

THIS STORY about the banshee being only for the O's and
the Mac's* is *not* right. Not right. Because the Frosts had a banshee, and other families I know that came in with Cromwell,
too. Do you know that the Frosts came into Ireland in front
of the Cromwellian army, playing music? They were drummers.
There was an old lady up the road there, and anytime the
Frosts would annoy her, she'd read their pedigree and she'd
say, "Sure you only came here with Oliver Cromwell. You were
only drummers."

I knew another one o' those families, and the memory o'
what happened with the banshee'll never leave my mind. The
son o' the family, he was living over on the mountain and he was
a very quiet fellow. He had a number o' sisters—I knew 'em—as
nice girls as you'd meet anywhere. And when his father died, he
was on his own. He had no one to give him a hand to do anything. It was an isolated kind of a place, and his sisters were

---

*Irish families whose names begin with "O" or "Mac" (e.g., "O'Brien" or
"MacNamara").

married in the locality. He was a nice kind of a person, but a man that kept to himself, a very tasty, tidy farmer. Had his own horse and his own ancient machinery. And he cut the hay as they did fifty years before that.

But, 'twas grand fine weather in the summer, the month o' June, and he had the hay cut. And he was tramming it himself, making it into winds himself, and he died suddenly in the meadow.

There was a road going from where he lived down to where his sisters lived, and it ran along under the mountain. At about ten o'clock in the night the banshee started up at his farm, and the whole parish heard her. She *roared* like nobody's business and went straight down along the road, down into where the sisters lived. The alarm was rose, that there was something wrong. 'Twas known the following day that he was dead. But for the warning given, they wouldn't know he was dead. They went up and found him above in the meadow. And his horse was all tangled up in the chains. He was there all night.

This little account of the sudden death of a farmer in his meadow while saving hay would be no more than that, sad but local, were it not for two remarkable things. The man cried for by this banshee is not named "O" or "Mac"—the truest (i.e., Gaelic) Irish names—or even one of those of Anglo-Norman or Norse extraction (i.e., in Ireland long enough to be regarded as "genuine" Irish). He is one of the Cromwellians, "the enemy," "upstarts." Yet here is the banshee crying for him. Cromwellian or not, he and his people seem to have made themselves every bit as much at home in Ireland as the Vikings and Normans before them.

The second unusual fact is that the banshee in this case is heard by the whole parish. And she roars! Unfeminine, perhaps, but then she is no ordinary woman. Her business is to make certain that those who must hear her cry do so.

The end of this short story proves that she has succeeded—as always. And shows, too, that she is no creature to be feared. Far from it. Were it not for her intervention in this case, the discovery of the man's death might have been far more traumatic for his relatives.

"I know of a man who had to leave the country.
The banshee followed him night an' day. He could hear her
an' see her all over the place. She was a constant companion o' his.
He left the country, had to go to Australia to get away from her."
DRUMLINE, SEPTEMBER 19, 2001

Banshee Heard in Manhattan

RELATIONS O' MINE, they went to America—'twas the time the railways were being built in the States, and that's a few days ago! They were working on the railroads, and they never got married. They were very sensible men, and they accumulated a lot o' wealth. So, when my grandfather's family grew up, they inherited all the wealth, and they went to the States to claim the money.

At the end o' the day, anyway, my uncle, he was up in Manhattan. He lived there for a number o' years. He was at a funeral in Manhattan, an Irishman that was dead. And the day o' the funeral they were going on to the cemetery, in broad daylight, he told me. The banshee cried down by the side o' the Manhattan river,* at the other side o' the Manhattan river. I don't know what width it is. But she cried. He heard her at the other side o' the river. All the way down along with the funeral, he told me. And Lord save us, she terrorized the people at the funeral. 'Twas the most mournful wail that was ever heard. A lot o' people didn't know what it was. The Yanks didn't know what it was. It frightened the living life in 'em!

He told me that story a thousand times. And you know yourself that the banshee can't cross a stream. So, I put that to him years later.

"No," he said. "She traveled with us, down at the other side."

I said to him, "Did you see anything?"

"Not a thing," he said, "that was ever seen or known."

And remember, now, in the States that time 'twas only horses and buggies. There was no traffic, no cars. So, clearly and distinctly, he said, they heard her, at the other side o' the Manhattan river. Whatever width it was at that point I couldn't tell you.

---

*Presumably the teller means the Hudson River, East River, or Harlem River.

Though her crying was mostly heard in Ireland, it was not unknown for the banshee to be heard abroad also, particularly in closeknit communities from the old country.

In the case described here there are two things out of the ordinary. First, her lament is heard in broad daylight, whereas in the vast majority of cases her presence occurs in the dark or gray hours. Second, even those who had no knowledge of who or what she was (and there were many such present, it seems—"the Yanks") heard her and were frightened by the mournfulness of her wail.

We note, not for the first time, that she does not seem able to cross running water. And, of course, this begs a question: How could she be unable to cross the Manhattan river, and yet there she is in the New World, having presumably crossed a three-thousand-mile stretch of "running water"—the Atlantic Ocean—to be there? Once again, to put oneself in the cynic's chair, is she just a figment (though a necessary one) of Irish people's imagination regarding death, or a creature of fact? This account leads us to what could appear contradictory interpretations. Yet things spiritual have a habit of being like that: by no means as black and white, cut and dried, as we might like them to be.

A Prankster

LONG AGO, what they used to do—and 'twas the foundation of a lot o' the ghost stories and fairy stories—if there was a fellow that was kind o' frightened, lads used to take advantage and put on a bit of a show in the dark.

I had a cousin, and if he imitated the banshee at a distance there isn't a human being in the world 'd think but it *was* the banshee. He had the voice for it and he was expert at it, and he frightened many a one, I can tell you—including a crowd o' the archaeological society at a castle one night.

'Twas the fall o' the year, and 'twould be dark at six or seven o'clock. And there was a big lecture on, and a lot o' bullshit, and accents, and what haven't you—you wouldn't know what they'd be saying.

And I had this fellow primed, and he came down through the mountain, and he started off, "Ooouuu!"

I'm telling you that there was disappearance! There did ladies go in all directions, and they having accents. I tell you they had no accents . . . I'd say they wanted a new . . . few clothes.* And he went off laughing.

*They screamed and pissed themselves with fright.

Nightly pranks were by no means uncommon in the dark countryside and there are many accounts in which the joker turns victim of the very forces being mocked. Here, however, a similar prank succeeds and the grand ladies with their upper-class accents attending their fine archaeological lecture are scattered, their pompous accents reduced to screams.

In this story we see resentment (albeit good-natured) of castle, class, accent by the "ordinary" countryman—and a determination by the latter (the "owner" of the banshee tradition) to teach a lesson to those who merely talk about it. From his point of view the night is a great success. His opponents (the traditional enemy, anyway) are scattered in ignominy. Yet note that it is women he has defeated. Sadly, the only members of the perceived "upper class" who are interested enough to attend such a lecture are its women. The men, no doubt, would have been more interested in "huntin', shootin', ridin'," as was the hallmark of their class.

So, this joke, though successful in its immediate aim, fails at a deeper level, and gives, in the process, a glimpse into the chasm that divided the "real Irish" from the "upstarts," a divide that persists in many minds to this very day.

*"This fellow was coming home at night, an' she was at the side
o' the road an' she combing her hair. An' didn't he whip the
comb from her. An' went off, an' into bed. An' she came to the
room window, an' she told him to give out the comb. An' he gave it
out on a fork. If he gave out his hand, she had the hand an' all gone."*

TUBBER, NOVEMBER 30, 1984

The Barefield Banshee

YOU'D BE TALKING about strange things happening!

There was these three brothers in this parish one time, and
better men to dance a step, or play cards you wouldn't get from
here to Gort. Signs on, they were welcome anywhere they went.
But the mother, like every Irish mother, I s'pose, she was always
giving out to 'em: "Be home early, d'you hear me. Or you'll meet
the Bad Thing."

D'you think they took a blind bit o' notice of her? Indeed,
they didn't! Did you ever see a son to take any notice of his
mother in Ireland?

Anyway, they were out this night playing cards in a neighbor's house. Spoiled combs* they were playing. Three threes.

---

*A card game played by three teams of either two or three players. The aim of
each team is to make a comb (three tricks) and if unable to do so to prevent
the other teams from doing so (i.e., to spoil it).

That was the usual game in that house, so what they'd always do, if they could, was play in three different teams. That way, there was a good chance o' one of 'em, at least, winning a final. If the three of 'em played together on the one team, fine, they might win it out, but if they lost they'd all be put out together. So they'd usually play it safe and scatter out. The couple o' bob that one of 'em'd win was better than nothing at all. 'Twould keep 'em smoking for the week.

But this night, anyway, they were playing on, and the youngest of 'em, his team was the first to be put out. That was all right. Someone had to lose. They sat in by the fire and had a drop o' tea. Talked awhile. Then they watched the next round played.

The second brother was put out that round, played well but didn't get the cards. He joined the younger lad and they had nothing to do now, only hope that Seán, the oldest of 'em, might make the price o' smokes for the next couple o' days. That's how short o' money they were!

The game went on, and begod, Seán's team got into the semifinal. But 'twas a long one. Every trick was fought for and argued over—and you know the way some o' the old-timers could argue! And all about nothing. The less the better!

By the time the semifinal was over 'twas well after eleven o' clock, and the two lads were at Seán to hurry on or the mother'd be giving out to 'em.

"God blast it," says he, "what can I do! Walk out on my partners? If you want to go home, go. And tell her I'll be home when I'm able."

Well, they waited a while longer, but if the semifinal was slow, the final was worse again. No mercy. Every card argued over. Jeez, they nearly rose the row a couple o' times. Only for the man o' the house knew their form, there'd be someone hit. That same crowd, they'd be sitting down together an hour after like nothing happened! All forgotten.

The two lads, anyway, they'd wait no more. They hit off home, and when the game finished, maybe twenty minutes after, Seán's team won. Only just. Enough to keep the postmortems going another half hour.

'Twas the man o' the house put 'em out in the finish. They'd be there till morning if he didn't. They stopped outside the door arguing, playing this and that trick over and over again—"what *you* should have played here when *he* played the king o' clubs there," and all o' that.

I don't know how long they were there when the man inside came out.

"Ah, come on, boys! I don't know about you, but I have to be up in the morning. If you want to argue can't you do it down the road a bit."

They moved then, to the gate, and scattered, one man this way, another man that way, every man his own direction, until Seán was left there with the last couple of 'em.

He could go around by the road, o' course, but that'd be the best part o' two miles. He didn't. And didn't any night he was ever at that house before. He took the shortcut across the land. That'd be only half the journey, or less. Everyone was going the shortcuts in them times.

So he started, said good luck to the lads that were left, and off with him across the fields. It wasn't a dark night or anything, but even if 'twas, he knew his way well from all the times he went that way before, day and night. And he was in good form after winning the couple o' bob. Smokes for the week. What more could a man ask for?

But, he was gone more than halfway when he came to this small little hill—a rocky little place. 'Tis only down the road there, at this side o' the main road; you passed it on your left on your way up. All he had to do was cross over that, and he could see his own house from the top of it.

So, he came on, anyway. But he was only just at the bottom o' the hill—'tis only a small hill, now—and this crying started, lonesome, lonesome, *uuu-huu-huuu-huu!*

He stopped, and the minute he did, so did the crying. He looked around him. Not a stir. No one there. Or he could see no one, anyway. 'Twas a bright night. And the first thought that came to him was that some o' the prime boys were trying to frighten him, maybe. That was common in them times after a night out. Faith, he wouldn't give in to that. He kept going, on up the hill. And he was about halfway up when it started again, the same crying—*uuu-huu-huu-huw!*

He stopped, and the very minute he did, so did the crying. I tell you, he started to get a small bit afraid then, but he didn't show it.

"Come out," he said, "and face me."

No move.

He kept going, careful now, watching and listening, and just when he was nearly at the top o' the hill—he could see his own house!—it started again, the same noise. But this time, begod, he was ready. He had it! Where 'twas coming from! Even when it stopped like the other times. 'Twas coming from the top o' the hill.

"By the Lord," says he, "I'll find out once and for all who's blackguarding here."

He started making his way to the top of it—'twas only twenty feet away from him. But you know yourself the kind o' place 'tis, all cracks and rocks, just like the Burren.* You could break an ankle in it in daylight, not to mind in the middle o' the night. And worse again, 'tis all small blackthorn bushes. They'd tear you to pieces if you didn't step careful.

But, when he arrived above at the top, what did he see, only the woman, below inside in that bit of a . . . what would you call it? Would you call it a valley? Hardly. 'Tis too small. But 'tis over there, anyway. About twenty feet deep and the same wide. She was below in it, sitting down on a stone, long gray hair, and her back to him.

I don't know did he know 'twas a woman or not. I don't know what he knew. Maybe he thought 'twas some kind of a joke the boys were having on him. Anyway, he crept down behind her, and when he was a couple o' feet from her, he jumped, and caught her by the shoulder.

*A world-famous karst limestone area in County Clare where many unique species of plants are found.

But, by God, if he did 'twas all he did. She turned around and hit him a slap of her hand across the face and sent him flying. He was lucky he didn't split his head!

When he gathered himself up . . . oh, 'twasn't half a minute, there was no sign of her. But he felt the pain in his cheek and put up his hand. 'Twas then he saw the blood!

He let a screech out o' him and ran for the house, burst in the door, and there was the old mother, still up by the fire waiting for him.

As soon as she saw the state of his face, the misfortunate woman nearly died.

"What in the name o' God were you doing, Seán? Don't tell me 'twas fighting you were!"

Would you believe, but he wasn't able to talk to her, or even tell her one word o' what happened.

She poured a drop o' water out o' the kettle and bathed his face, and put some kind of a dressing or a bandage on it. Put him to bed then.

But the following morning he didn't get up at all for work—and it must be the first time ever that happened, 'cause he was a great worker, the same man. O' course, the father asked what was wrong before he went out. The mother gave some answer, I s'pose. And they all went off about their business.

But when they came in that evening Seán was still in the bed. No get up! Some kind of a fever he had. And 'twas worse the following day. He was twisting and turning in the bed and talking to himself, and rubbing his face. And his mother was trying to keep him from tearing off the bandage.

Three days he was like that, and no improvement. But the following day was a Sunday, and at Mass didn't the priest notice that Seán wasn't there at all. You know yourself how small Barefield church is. 'Twas easy for him see who was there and who wasn't. So, when the last blessing was given, and the prayers for the Poor Souls were said, he beckoned Seán's mother before she went, and asked her was anything wrong. And in fairness to the man, 'twasn't being nosey he was, at all, only anxious to know if there was anything wrong, or something he could do.

"Oh, Father," says she, "he's inside in the bed the last three days, and worse he's getting. Could you do anything for him, Father?"

"I'll try, anyway," says he.

And he did. Came to the house shortly after. But he only took one look at Seán in the bed and he said, "Get the doctor, and get him quick. Or that boy won't live."

So, the doctor came, and the first thing he did was to take off the bandage to see what was causing the bother.

When he did, "Lord God," says he, "what's this?"

Because there on Seán's cheek was the print o' four fingers, all blood. The banshee's fingers. He didn't know that, o' course. Only fixed him up with a proper dressing and said he'd be back again.

That was all right, but after about ten days or so, when the dressing was took off, he had the four scabs across his cheek. And when they healed up the four scars were there, the mark o' the four fingers. And they stayed with him for as long as he lived.

That boy went strange after. Turned in on himself entirely. Stopped going out playing cards and dancing and all the things he was good at. In the end, he wouldn't go out in the day at all, or talk to anyone, only walking the back roads, talking to himself in the evening and nighttime with his collar pulled up, for fear anyone'd see the marks on his face.

And, sure, 'twas pity people had on him, more than blaming him. But he did a bad night's work when he went next or near the banshee. He had right to leave her to go on with her own business and mind his own.

If, up to now, what we have seen of the banshee has been benign—she going about her business of death-warning and people accepting that respectfully and resignedly—we would do well to remember that there is another side to her, just as there is to the Good People. Interfere with any of them and they will retaliate. We might think that her punishment of Seán here for what, on the face of it, was a fairly harmless and unintended piece of aggression, is far too severe—permanent scarring, both physical and mental.

But at our peril we forget, in our dealings with the otherworldly, that its inhabitants do not accept insults lightly, just as their appreciation of favors done them can also be of a lasting nature.

PART THREE

"Their Own Way of Collecting"

GIFTS, PUNISHMENT, AND OTHER OUTCOMES OF FAIRY ENCOUNTERS

*"I knew these three or four brothers that done a dig
one night in a fort . . . an' they collected heaps o' gold.
An' they bought all around 'em—property.
An' anyone they gave the gold to, it melted. . . .
They throve. They prospered. But the gold melted."*

DRUMLINE, SEPTEMBER 24, 1999

A Transaction with the Other Crowd

THERE WAS several big horse fairs in Ireland long ago, like
Ballinasloe in Galway, Cahiramee in Cork, but the biggest of
'em all was here in Clare, in Spancilhill. 'Twas a three-day fair,
and the British Army even used to come to it buying horses.
That's how important 'twas. And 'tis still going on, but there's
only one day for it now. For a while there, about twenty years
ago, they thought 'twouldn't last at all, but it did, and 'tis going
strong again now.

But wait till I tell you about what happened to a man living
only about ten miles from here one time when he was going to
the same fair o' Spancilhill.

'Twas during the landlord times, and this man was from
above at the upper end o' Tulla Parish. Brian O'Rourke was
his name, a married man, a farmer—an honest man, too, trying
to make ends meet any way he could, like the rest o' the neighbors. And it wasn't easy to do that with the farm they had;
most of it was only rushes and bog. Whatever way they worked,

himself and his wife, they were always only one step ahead o' the hunger.

At that time the rent used to have to be paid twice a year, on the gale day—April and October, or June and December; it used to vary from place to place. But for Brian 'twas in June.

So, the gale day was coming up, anyway, and he says to his wife, Máire, "What'll we do?"

They hadn't the money. And if they faced the landlord's agent with their hands hanging to 'em, well, you know what'd happen. They could be thrown out on the road if he was in a bad humor the same day.

"We'll have to sell the horse," says he.

"Sure, that's no kind o' talk. If we sell the horse, how'll we manage?"

And 'twas true for her, o' course. If there was no horse, who was going to do the plowing and the rest o' the work? Himself? Or her?

"What'll we do, so?"

They argued it out and there was nothing to be done. 'Twas either the horse that had to go, or themselves.

So, he says to Máire, "Call me early in the morning and I'll get what I can for him below at Spancilhill. I can do no more than that."

So she did. Called him up at the break o' day, and he hit off. You know yourself, now, that 'tis about six miles from the upper end o' Tulla Parish down to Spancilhill. Well, he was making good time, going on along down below Tulla, there where the bit of a castle is at Lisofinn. 'Twas well day at this stage, when all of a sudden the horse reared up and nearly threw him. By God, he held on, somehow, and when he quietened him again and looked down to see what it was that made him shy—maybe a rat or a badger or something like that—he got the fright of his life. 'Cause there on the road, looking up at him, was a small little man, oh, maybe two foot high, and a look o' poison in his face.

"O'Rourke," says he, "get down off o' that horse! Were you trying to trample me, or what?"

Sure, Brian was looking at him, stupid, with his mouth open.

"Get down," says he. "Or I'll make you get down."

So Brian got off o' the horse and faced him on the road.

"I'm . . . I'm sorry," says he. "I never even saw you. I was half sleeping."

"All right," says the small lad, "but tell me this. Where are you going with that grand horse?"

"To the fair o' Spancilhill, sir," says Brian. "And I wouldn't be going there only I have to. The rent is due and we haven't the money to pay it. This horse is our only hope."

"And tell me, now, how much d'you expect to get for him at the fair?"

"Seven or eight pounds, I hope," says Brian, "if I'm lucky."

"Hah!" The small man laughed at him. "Why would you give away a fine horse the like o' that for eight pounds? I know someone that'll give you thirty pounds for him."

Lord God, thirty pounds was a fortune o' money in them days. A poor man wouldn't see the like of it together in his lifetime.

"Well, if you do, sir, I'd like to meet him," says Brian.

"Follow me, so," says the small lad. And he walked out in front o' Brian, off along that road, the main road between Ennis and Tulla.

They were only gone about a quarter of a mile when they came to this big old gateway, like the gate into a landlord's place. And the funny thing was, Brian didn't know it at all, even though he was walking that road all his life.

But the small man, he stepped in between the piers and says to Brian, "Come on. Your thirty pounds is ready."

So, Brian, he followed him in. He couldn't refuse that kind o' money, sure. And they went on, up along an avenue, until they came to the mouth of a tunnel. 'Twas dark, o' course, inside it, and he got afraid.

"I'll go no farther," says he.

"You won't?" says the small lad. "You'd rather eight pounds than thirty pounds? All right, so."

He turned, and off with him, into the tunnel.

And d'you think Brian didn't follow him? Indeed he did! Thirty pounds was a lot o' money.

But to follow him . . . that was the bother. 'Twas dark, you see, and Brian had the horse, leading him by the reins. He had to, even though he could see nothing in front of him, only hear the pitter-patter o' the small lad's feet. And he was getting more afraid, but he couldn't go back. The tunnel was too narrow. He'd never be able to turn the horse. So he had to keep going.

Then, after a lot o' walking, up ahead of him he saw this light, a green kind o' light, and when he came near it there was the small man standing in it beckoning him. The light was shining down out o' the roof o' the tunnel. There was no window there, or nothing. 'Twas just shining down through the stones o' the roof, and the small lad standing there calling him.

"Come on," says he. "This way."

They went on, down the tunnel, past the light, until they came to a crossroads.

"Now," says he, and he pointed to the left, "go down there and you'll come to a yard. You'll see three doors facing you. The one in the middle is the one you'll pick. Open that. 'Tis a stable. Put your horse in that stable. Take off the bridle and the reins, hang 'em on the peg on the wall, close the door after you, and come back here to me and I'll take you to where you'll get thirty pounds for your horse."

So Brian did as he was told, went down that passage until he came to the yard. And there was the three doors. So he put the horse in the middle stable, hung up the bridle and the reins on the peg on the wall, and came back to where the small lad was waiting for him.

"Now," says he to Brian, "come with me and you'll get your money."

Off they went, back to the tunnel again, and down along it in the dark until Brian saw more light up ahead. They came to another crossroads and turned left again. And the nearer they were getting, the brighter the light was getting, until they came to a second yard—a big, big yard this time. And there, at the far side of it, was a castle with lights in every window up to the top of it.

"Come on," says the small lad. "Thirty pounds, remember."

They crossed the yard and went up three steps to the door o' the castle. He knocked, and after a couple o' minutes the door was opened by this grand-looking girl in a long white dress. She smiled at 'em and welcomed 'em in. But what Brian was watching was her hands, 'cause she had a ring on every finger. He never saw the like before. His wife at home had no ring at all. Even when they were getting married they only got the loan o' one for the day.

She brought 'em into the hall, anyway, and there was a carpet in it. Brian was tripping over it, 'twas so high. But if he was, no one else was, even the small man. He couldn't understand it.

They came to this door.

"In here," says the small lad.

Brian was brought in.

"Now," says the lad. "How much for your horse?"

There was no one else there, only themselves. The girl was gone.

"Well," says Brian, "you said thirty pounds, sir."

"And thirty pounds it'll be. Sit down there, Brian, and I'll get it for you."

Brian sat in this comfortable chair—you wouldn't get the like of it in an old landlord's place—and the lad took a key out of his pocket, a small key, and went to the wall. Next thing, he opened up a door in the wall—'twas a safe, o' course, but, sure, Brian never saw the like in his life. 'Twas little use he had for safes!

He took out this box that was inside it, put it up on the table, and opened it up. 'Twas full up o' gold.

"Now," says he, "you'll get paid for your horse, Brian."

And he started counting. "One, two, three . . . nineteen . . . twenty-one . . . twenty-eight, twenty-nine, thirty. There you are, now. All yours."

You may say, Brian hadn't to be told twice. He stuck it down in his pockets as quick as he could, and he knew by the weight of it that 'twas the real thing, all right.

"Thanks very much," says he. "My wife'll be delighted to see me coming with this."

"I'm sure she will," says the lad. "Why wouldn't she! But, look, before you go, you'll have a bite to eat. You must be starved."

And 'twas true. 'Cause all Brian had that morning before he started out was a cup o' buttermilk and a crust o' bread. Anyway, after being treated like this, how could he refuse the hospitality o' the house?

"All right," says he. "I will. And thanks."

The small man led him out into the hall again, down along to another room.

When the door was opened and he looked in, he saw the like o' what he never saw before. There was a room—'twas very near as big as the field at the back o' his house at home—and a big long table down the middle of it, covered with food and drink in gold and silver plates and dishes and cups. There was chandeliers hanging off o' the ceiling. 'Twas all lit up beautiful. And people sitting down at the table. And behind every chair there was a young person standing to attention, with a kind of uniform on him—servants, I s'pose. And not a move out of anyone.

Brian stopped at the door, looking in.

"Go on," says the small lad. "There's your place," and he showed him where to sit. "I'll be back in a minute with your dinner."

One o' the lads with the uniforms pulled a chair for Brian and he sat down, and off went the small lad and shut the door.

By God, the more Brian was looking around him, the more he was thinking to himself, *There's something wrong here,* 'cause there was no sound, no move. No one was eating, or talking, or anything. And still, they were fine-looking people. But just when he was wondering what would he do, he heard the door opening behind him. He looked back, and there was the girl who opened the door o' the castle for 'em. She hurried over to him, and just when he was going to say something, she put up her finger.

"Shh," she says. "Listen to me. Whatever else you do, don't eat their food. If you do, you're doomed. You'll never again see your home."

Before he could even get up she was gone the same way, and the door closed behind her. Gave him something to be thinking about, I can tell you!

But he was only there a couple o' minutes when he smelt cooking. He didn't know what in the hell 'twas, but it smelt good—and getting better. Next thing, the door opened again and there was the small man, weighed down under a big heavy plate. 'Twas huge, nearly as big as himself. You could barely see him behind it.

He staggered across the floor with it, planked it up on the table in front o' Brian, and said, "Now, Brian, there's your dinner. You won't get better in Ireland."

And 'twas true. Brian had no doubt about that, even from the smell of it. But he remembered what the girl said, and bad and all as Tulla was, he'd rather be there than here for the rest of his time.

"Well, d'you know something, sir," says he. "I have so many strange things seen since I came in here that my appetite is gone. But thanks, anyway. I appreciate it."

The small lad's face changed.

"What d'you mean?"

"Ah, I'm not hungry no more."

"After all my trouble? Come on, Brian. Eat it up."

"Look, I won't bother," says he. "Thanks all the same, but won't I be able to eat whatever I like with this much money in my pocket."

The lad looked at him.

"I'd advise you," says he, "eat. Now." There was poison in his voice. "Or if you don't—"

Brian stood up and looked at him, straight in the eye. He was like a lot of Irishmen. He didn't like to be threatened.

"No," says he, "I won't."

And the very minute he refused the third time, everything inside that hall changed. The lights quenched; there was a crash o' thunder and a flash o' lightning and by the light of it Brian saw that the beautiful young servants down along the table were gone into ugly things like skeletons. And worse again, they were making for him—their bony hands reaching out to catch him.

He did what anyone'd do—jumped out o' the way and made for the door as fast as he could, down along the hall (and to hell with the carpet!), out the front door, jumped the steps, and ran across that yard like it wasn't there at all! He got as far as the tunnel. But behind him . . . he looked over his shoulder and there, out the door o' the castle, came the things like skeletons, after him, their bones rattling on the stones.

He turned to the tunnel, nearly frightened out o' his life, and tried to run. But he couldn't. He fainted. Fright, o' course. Would you blame him! But, just as he collapsed, he could feel strong arms catching him up. He knew no more until he found himself back at the first crossroads in the tunnel. And there beside him, holding him, was the girl dressed in white, the girl who opened the castle door, the girl with all the rings.

He looked up at her, stupid. "Uh, uh . . . what are you—?"

"Shh!" She put her finger up to her lips. "Say nothing. Only go in there, quick, quick, to where you left your horse. Leave him. He's paid for. But take the bridle and the reins and bring 'em back here. Hurry!"

And he did—in and out like that!

When he arrived back, "Come on," says she. "We haven't a minute to lose if you want to get out safe."

Poor Brian had no clue what was going on, but he ran. He knew by the look of her that she was in earnest. And when they came back to the crossroads and turned right they kept running, off into the darkness, and never stopped until they came to the mouth o' the tunnel.

That's where she says to him, "Listen to me, Brian, and listen well. D'you see that avenue there in front o' you? Go. Run. As fast as ever you can. Keep the reins and the bridle tight in your hand. And don't look back. Whatever you do, don't look back. If you do, they have you, and there's nothing more I can do for you. Remember that, will you? And don't stop until you're out below on the public road."

He looked at her, wondering who in the name o' God was she, o' course. Was she this world or the next? He said he would, except he couldn't go until she'd tell him who she was.

"Don't mind that," says she. "Only go, while you're still able."

You'd know by her voice that she was afraid o' something.

"I will, surely," says he, "only tell me, why did you help me, and I a complete stranger? How'll I ever rest easy if I don't know that?"

"Go, will you?! At once! They're coming. Listen!"

He did. And down along the tunnel in the darkness he could hear the sound, like bones rattling. 'Twas coming nearer and nearer all the time.

"No, I won't stir out o' this," says he, "until you tell me who you are and why did you help me." He was a stubborn man.

When she saw that he wouldn't stir, "All right," says she. "I'm your mother's grandaunt. I was carried by the Good People when I was sixteen years of age. But I had no one there to tell me not to eat their food. I ate it, inside that big room where you were tonight. I can never leave this place, but you can. But only if you go this very minute. Go on! I'll hold 'em back."

The noise was only a small bit away now, and she hadn't to tell him again. He ran, as fast as his two legs'd carry him. He didn't look back, either.

When he came to the two big gate piers he took one buck leap out between 'em, like the devils in hell were after him, out into the middle o' the road. Wasn't he the lucky man that there was no traffic in them times? Wouldn't it be a poor story to escape from the fairies and be run over by a truck or a car instead!

But when he gathered himself a bit, and looked out from under his elbow, he got the surprise of his life. Because . . . there was no gates, and no piers! He sat up and looked around him. Nothing, only the cows grazing in the fields.

'Twas then he noticed his horse was gone.

"Lord God," says he, "I'm robbed! Where's my horse?"

He jumped up, but if he did, his trousers very near fell down around his knees.

"What's this?" says he, and he put his hands in his pockets. What came out? Only fists o' gold!

He went home to his wife, anyway, and she was surprised to see him back so early.

"Did you sell?" says she.

"I don't know whether or which," says he. "All I know is this," and he emptied the money up on the table.

"Now," says he, "tell me am I dreaming, or what?"

He told her the whole story, from start to finish. And d'you know what that woman said? She said, "The best thing we could do now is go into the bank in Ennis and change it."

"Why?" says he. "Is it 'cause you think I got it wrong?"

"No, but I'd feel better about it, if the story you told me is true."

"Well, you can believe me. 'Tis true."

"We'll go to town, so, this very day," says she, "and change it."

And that's the very thing they did—into the main bank in the town of Ennis. I can tell you, 'tis very few times they were in a bank before that. And when they went in the door, they were stopped by one o' these lads with the uniforms.

"Who're you looking for?"

"Oh . . . the manager, sir," says Brian. He didn't know at all that he was only talking to the doorman. The man looked 'em up and down, just like he was God Almighty.

"And what's your business with the manager? Have you an appointment?"

"No, sir, but—"

"Well, then, he can't see you. He's an important man."

That's the time Brian's wife took out some o' the gold.

"That's a pity," says she. "We wanted to ask him about this. But, sure, we can always go somewhere else."

Wasn't she the brave woman!

But the old manager was watching all this from his office, behind a small window—oh, they're clever lads—and as soon as he saw the gold, he was out the door like a hare, full of old soft talk, like they were his nearest relations. "Oh, how are you?" and "You're welcome" and "Is there anything I can do for you?" and all that. They're terrible old hypocrites, them bank managers, you know.

So, he brought 'em into his office—no such thing as queuing up when he saw the money—and he sat 'em down.

"Now," says he, "you're here on business, are you?"

"We are, sir," says Brian's wife. 'Twas she did all the talking. And just as well, too.

"What'll you give us for that?" says she.

She took out the purse where she had the gold and counted it up on the table in front of him. "One, two . . . nine, ten . . . eighteen, nineteen . . . twenty-seven, twenty-eight, twenty-nine. There you are."

And Brian, the fool, he was just going to ask her what she did with the last one when she gave him a kick in the shin under the table and a dirty look. And d'you think the manager noticed that? Indeed he didn't! All he was interested in was the gold.

"Well?" says she. "What'll you give us for it?"

He weighed it and it nearly broke the scales, 'twas so heavy.

"Oh, 'tis worth . . . 'tis worth fifty pounds." That was a fortune o' money in them days.

She only laughed at him.

"Weren't we offered twice that across the street in the other bank!"

'Twas a pure lie for her, o' course, but he didn't know that.

"We'll go back there now, Brian," says she. "Come on."

"Hold on. Wait," says the manager. "Maybe I weighed it wrong."

Well he knew, the thief, that he was getting a great bargain even at twice what he was offering.

They settled for a hundred pounds, anyway. Sure, 'twas an unheard-of sum for poor people.

And when they came out on the street Brian says to her, "Why did you keep the last one?"

She only shook her head at him. "Your mother didn't teach you much, did she? Or maybe you weren't listening to her when she was talking. Don't everyone know that if the Good People pay you for something you should never give it all away. D'you want to insult 'em? Maybe you don't know that much. But I do."

'Twas true for her. Because after that, everything they put their hand to, it seemed to go right for 'em. As long as they had that piece o' fairy gold they were fine.

They built up into one o' the best-off families in the whole parish for a finish. Some of 'em are there yet, and decenter people you wouldn't meet in a long day's traveling.

In the most familiar of places the Good People can accost us, proving in the process that the reality we take for granted may not be as fixed as we think. Brian O'Rourke, a man bowed down by the brute facts of survival, little realizes that a simple journey to sell his horse, on a road that he has traveled all his life, will turn into an otherworldly nightmare. But so it happens.

He emerges safely from a sinister fairy netherworld only because of a relative of his who has previously been abducted by the Good People and can warn him not to make her mistakes. (An intriguing question must be: What fate befalls her for helping him thus?)

It could well be said about this story that though the main actor is male, it can really be seen as about women, their courage, self-sacrifice, and plain common sense.

And as regards the fate of fairy gold, it ends not in the usual way, but as having somewhat the best of both worlds: keeping it and spending it!

"There was a story, too, about women that used be up all night spinning an' a certain woman knocking at the door an' coming in—she was a fairy woman. Ah, she spun mad all night. She came to help 'em. I don't know why."
MILTOWN, JUNE 27, 1999

The Fairies Repay a Favor

I ALWAYS HEARD it said by the old people that 'tis bad to be bad. It'll only come back on yourself in the end. But to do the good act is no load to anyone. And there's plenty proof o' that.

There was a man living in the parish o' Ruan one time, a married man; his people are out there yet. He had a reputation o' being generous, and his father and grandfather before him were the same. Decent people, got on with everyone, and great neighbors. If you were in any kind o' bother you knew where to go for help. And if they could give it, you'd get it. No more about it.

There was this fort near the house, just outside the yard. Never interfered with, o' course. And this morning, early, his wife was gone on out before him to start the milking. He was washing something inside and he'd be out after her.

So he did, went out with his bucket. But as he was crossing the yard he heard a child crying, a young child. The first thing he thought was, "'Tis some tinker woman." There was a lot o' beggars and traveling people on the roads in them days, you know, so that'd be nothing strange.

He left down the bucket and went back, but there was no one there, or around the house at all.

He didn't know what was wrong, if he was imagining it or not. But when he was going back to where he left the bucket, he heard it again, the same crying. So he stood and listened. And 'twas there, all right—coming out o' the fort!

Begod, another man'd leave it, but he . . . he wanted to find out what was the crying. Didn't he steal over and look in between the bushes. And there was a woman inside, sitting down, feeding a small child. The child was crying, whatever was wrong. Maybe she had no milk for him.

He took one look, and ran to the cowshed.

"Have you any drop milked yet?" says he to his wife.

She had—maybe a jug full. He took whatever she had—quick! quick!—and back to the fort with him. He left it in ever so quiet between the bushes—never even spoke to that woman, or let her see him, I think. Then he went off and milked the cows.

But later on, when the breakfast was over—and I s'pose he had her told what was going on—they went out, and there was the jug, empty. And no sign o' the woman or the child.

If you had no belief at all in the fairies or any o' them things, you could say 'twas all a thing that happened naturally, except for one thing.

A while after, a dose o' TB came around there. Oh, 'twas desperate. I remember men nearly being broke with it. There was none o' the cures that's there today for it at that time, no antibiotics or nothing. If your cattle got it, you were in trouble. Many a man went to the wall because of it. 'Twas fierce around these parts for a while at that time.

But, wasn't it a strange thing, though? That man I'm telling you about, not a one of his cows died, or even got sick. And he was the only man for miles around that didn't lose some animal. That was well noticed.

Would you think had it something to do with the woman in the fort? If she was there, at all!

Wasn't it queer, all the same.

If a majority of accounts of encounters with the fairies seem to emphasize outcomes that are unpleasant for the humans involved, this story shows that this is by no means inevitably or necessarily the case. Which goes to prove that they also appreciate generosity, a helping hand in adversity, and repay a favor done, especially to the more helpless among them.

*"This man was at the fair o'Tubber an' when he came home he went off
to do his herding. . . . He sat on a stone, anyway, counting his money.
An' he left some of it on the stone, by his side, an' whatever else he
was doing, when he reached out his hand for the money, 'twas gone.
'Twas years before he got it back. He used always go to the stone
an' sit on it, an' this day, after a long time, he went to the stone
an' the money was there for him. They left it back again."*

BALLINRUAN, AUGUST 17, 1999

Fairy Races Horse to Repay a Favor

FAIRIES AND MILK, yes. There was a lot between them, all
right. I heard stories about fairy women milking cows. I'll tell
you one of 'em.

This man was a big farmer, but he had a terrible shine for
racing. Between gambling and racing, 'tis a risky business and he
got into trouble. He was breeding great horses. They were as fine
as you could look at, but they were missing the turn o' speed.

He was going down, down, down, anyway. He had only nine
or ten cows in the finish, and they used to keep forty cows there
at one time. But one morning his wife told him that there was a
certain cow milked, milked dry. And she was a good cow. He
made nothing of it, but the next morning she was milked again.

After about a week, 'twas getting serious, and he brought out the shotgun one morning before daylight. He thought 'twas some live person, now, milking this cow.

This cow was missing from the rest o' the cows and she was inside a fort near the house with a woman sitting down milking her.

He confronted her, anyway.

"Well," she said, "we're in trouble. I'm a fairy and my husband was killed. The fairies had a battle. My husband got killed. And d'you see that little boy there?" He was sitting down on the ground; he was about three or four or five years old at the time. "I'm milking your cow—"

"Oh, you're welcome," says he. "Milk her away." He got frightened.

"That little boy'll do you a turn yet," she said.

That was all right. Years went by, but, sure, 'tis hard to come back when you're broke. And even though they had a very big farm, farmers had to pay rent and rates at that time. 'Tisn't like now. But he had this three-year-old horse. She was out of a very good racing mare, but anything she bred up to then was missing the turn o' speed. But 'twas only an ordinary horse that he gave to her; someone like himself had an old broken-down thoroughbred that he brought her to. And he was thinking o' flapping the horse. You know, flapper races* were in every town at the time, small stakes, nine or ten pound. He'd make a few pound that way.

*Small-time races in which the horses weren't affiliated with any national governing or regulatory body and so didn't have to comply with strict rules.

This was years after—maybe ten or twelve years after.

He was out one morning, early, to gallop the horse. The course he had for galloping him was around the fort. And this young fellow, about sixteen or seventeen years, came up to him and stopped him. He put up his hand and stopped the horse.

"You're going flapping that horse," he said to him.

"I am," says the man. "I must make a few pounds some way or another."

"Don't," he said. "There's a big race above in the Curragh o' Kildare, a hundred sovereigns and a gold cup. I'll ride that horse for you," he said. "Train him as good as you can now, but I'll be there. You won't see me now, till before the race starts. But I'll be there on the Curragh o' Kildare."

The man trained the horse. He had no money to send him, so he had to walk him from Clare to Kildare. He started off, and he knew these racing people along the road here and there that gave him a night's lodging and put up the horse. He landed at the Curragh o' Kildare, anyway, and 'twas all English landlords and big people there. He had the horse entered beforehand for this big race, but, by God, there was no trace o' the jockey coming up. The bell was ringing for the race and there was no trace of him.

But all of a sudden he saw this young fellow dressed in grand colors—the jockey—walking across the course, a riding whip in his hand.

He gave a slap to the horse behind the saddle, and the horse went wild. Only for he was a right good man he wouldn't be able to hold him.

He spoke then and said, "Things aren't as rosy as I thought. There's a Freemason* jockey from Wales riding in this race and it'll be touch and go between the two of us."

"Well," says the owner o' the horse, "racing is always like that. 'Tis always dicey like that. That's what makes it good," says he. "'Tis known as the sport o' kings, but I'm in no humor for that now. I'm too broken. Do your best anyway."

"But have you money?" the fairy jockey said to the poor man.

"I have nothing," says he, "but a fiver."

"Well, that horse, he's a rank outsider. He's forty to one. If you get a bookie to take you on, do. But I must go a furlong first," he said. "I'll have the Freemason's measure taken then, and I'll take a red handkerchief out o' my pocket and wave it back three times. If I don't do that, don't put on the fiver."

The race started, anyway. This fairy mounted the horse and when the signal gave that they were off, the man was watching.

When the fairy jockey passed the furlong mark he put back the handkerchief. The man went to a bookie. He was well known, but they seldom take a bet after the start. But this bookie took the fiver from him; he was forty to one.

*Freemasonry dates back to the Middle Ages at least and was originally a craft association. By the mid to late nineteenth century in Ireland, Masonry had become anathema to most Catholics, partly because of papal condemnation, partly because of Irish political conditions. Even today the very name is synonymous, whether justifiably or not, with secrecy, sinister practices, and exclusiveness.

They rode on, anyway, and 'twas hell for leather, but the Freemason jockey didn't put his horse to the front for a long time. There was fifteen great horses in this race. And every time the fairy jockey'd make a move, the Freemason jockey'd make it after him.

They went on and on, anyway, and they was fifth; then they was fourth. This was a long race; 'twas a three-mile race, with no jumps.

But in the finish, the Freemason and the fairy, they were riding very close.

The Freemason said, "You're a fairy."

"Well, if I am," he said, "you're a limb from the Devil. We'll have it out now."

They went on, anyway, and they were second, and for a finish they were first, the two of 'em. They were locked in each other. They could get no more to make the horses faster. They had everything tried, the spur and whip and everything. But the fairy jockey thought of a plan. 'Tis a big tape they'd have across the course at that time. There was none o' these photo finishes, no electricity, o' course. And the fairy took his leg out o' the stirrup and he kicked the horse under the jaw. He hit the tape first, and he beat the Freemason jockey.

That story was told a thousand times. 'Tis way longer than that, but that's the main part of it.

And the money? Well, that's the best of it, entirely. The man drew his money from the bookie. He got two hundred pounds and he got the gold cup. But the next thing, the newsmen surrounded him to know who was riding the horse and know all about him.

The fairy jockey went another way, but he whispered to the man before he went, "Sell that horse. He'll never again win a race."

The man, being a man o' horses, he wouldn't sell the horse for anything. He brought the horse home, and the horse died when he came into his own land. But he was a rich man ever after.

He discouraged his sons from racing. One of 'em went at it, though. I s'pose 'twas in the blood.

But that was a fairy, the woman who was milking the cow for to rear her son.

They have their own troubles, you know.

Here we see once more the fairies not as inhabiting an ideal world, distant from ours, but very near us, sometimes even dependent on our good offices in their time of misfortune. And for those humans who respond kindly, their response is no less benign.

In this story are paralleled two worlds, ours and that of the Good People, mediated by familiar animals—in this case cows, horses. But there are other details also which increase the sense of drama—the introduction of Freemasonry (for most older Irish people, synonymous with sinister deeds), the competition between the Freemason and fairy jockey, and the manner in which the fairy scorns the Freemason as a "limb of the Devil." They, too, have their priorities, obviously.

But the mystery continues: Despite the fairy jockey's warning to its owner to sell the winning horse, he refuses and pays for his sentimentality. The horse dies as soon as it returns home to the man's own land. But why there? We are not told.

"There was a man above here across,
he had a horse that used be sweating in the stable
in the morning an' the print o' the saddle on him.
In the wintertime, now! Found in the morning sweating
different times. He used be gone with the fairies."

MILTOWN, JUNE 27, 1999

Mare Taken for Fairy Battle

AN ANCESTOR O' MINE, he lived between here and Ballinruan, up the hills. He was in bed this night and he got a call. He thought he knew the voice. And they asked him if they could get his mare. Now, his mare was a *fíor-lár*, a fairy horse, and in the night, if she was coming home from Tulla, she'd nearly throw him out o' the saddle at any haunted spot—like Tyredagh Gate.

Anyway, they asked for the mare. He said he'd get up and they told him, "There's no need. Can we take her?"

I don't know if the saddle was in the stable, but they took away the mare, and he didn't get up.

Around daybreak, four o'clock, the voice came again, the very same voice. They told him they brought back the mare, but that she was wounded. They said he'd get a bottle in a hole in the stable, and to rub what was in it on her, and that she'd be all right in a short time.

He questioned 'em, "What were you doing with her?"

"Ah," says the voice outside, "we had a big fight between Galway and Clare, and if not for your mare we'd never win it. With your mare, we won the day."

That was all right. The mare was cured and the old lad stuck the bottle in a hole in the stable. And he stayed . . . in awe of it, if you like to put it that way.

But his son, or his grandson, went out to America, to a city or town called Danbury. And when he came home, he was knocking down this old house, and didn't the bottle fall out o' the wall.

"Oh, great God," he says, "that's the bottle my father got from the fairies. By God, there's an old bullock outside and he's dying. I'll try him with it."

So he brought out the bottle and, whatever stuff was in it, he poured it into the bullock, and the bullock got up and walked away. It got to be a great beast after.

I knew the old lad that happened to. Admittedly, those *fíor-lárs* are there, but they're very rare.

This short narration shows us (as does the Latoon bush story) that the Irish fairies are a belligerent, territorial race, often at war for the honor of their county or province.

We also see once again that a fíor-lár *is far more sensitive to things other-worldly than an ordinary horse.*

And, lest we forget, the Good People are more likely to succeed in their enterprises if they have help from our earthly world, even though in this case it is animal rather than human assistance.

The bottle in question here is reminiscent of the bottles of herbal mixtures or spring water that the famous healing woman Biddy Early dispensed to the thousands who came to her seeking cures. The fact that she herself possessed a mysterious dark-colored bottle, from which her power was believed by many to come, probably influenced stories like this one, though the factual details described make it seem an actual part of a family history. If it is that, what a tragic waste on a sick bullock of, literally, the elixir of life—a cure for any of the worst diseases (cancer, for example) that the human condition is subject to.

"There was a man one time an' he was brought off with the fairies, hurling. . . . He won the match, anyway, an' they gave him a hurley coming home of him. An' they told him wherever he'd hurl he'd win. An' everyplace he hurled he won. But I suppose when he got old, too old for hurling, he told it. But as soon as he did, the hurley won no other match after, only lost everything after. If he kept his mouth shut he was all right."

BALLINRUAN, AUGUST 17, 1999

Hurler's Bravery Rewarded

BEYOND AT DOON, now, where Whitehead lived—the house is knocked down now—there was a castle there before there was a Big House* in it. And this fellow called McMahon, he was a herdsman there. At that time, when the sheep would be having lambs, the herdsman would often have to stay up all night watching 'em, to keep 'em from foxes and things like that.

There was a big level field out in front o' Doon House, and he was sitting down this moonlight night, watching his sheep. You could see for miles. The next thing, it went very late, and these two teams landed out on the field with hurleys.

---

*A landlord house.

He was watching 'em, anyway. They lined up. And Mc-Mahon was a noted hurler. The captain o' one o' the teams looked around and he said, "We're short one."

So he walked over and he said to McMahon, "Will you stand in? We're short a player. And you're a good hurler."

"I will," he said, "but I have no hurley."

"That's no problem," says the captain. "I'll get you a hurley."

He handed him a hurley and the ball was thrown in and the match started. There was fierce hurling and, begod, he was holding his own. But the lad he was on was tough. And at that time there'd be kind o' wrestling in the hurling and they'd be testing each other's strength.

But, by God, the lad that he was on knocked him twice, and he knocked the lad twice. So the captain walked over to him, when a bit of a lull came, when the ball went wide, and he said, "If he knocks you a third time, you're finished. Don't let him knock you a third time."

"Begod," says McMahon, "I'll be prepared for him."

So the next ball that came in, he was prepared, and he knocked the lad a third time. He got the ball, and he went down through the field and he scored a goal.

The very minute the goal was scored, the match ended. They all gathered around him, and he was chaired off o' the field.

The captain came over and congratulated him and he said, "We're meeting here for three hundred years and you're the first man that scored a goal. We needn't come here, now, anymore. The match is decided." And he said, "As a reward I'll give you that hurley. And no matter where you go or what you do, if you have that hurley with you, no harm will befall you. You're only a herdsman, isn't that right?"

"That's all," says McMahon.

"Well, I won't be meeting you anymore," he said, "but if you want to get your fortune, go into Limerick next Monday and stand up at a certain corner at a certain time, and there'll a man approach you. If he asks you to go to work for him, go with him. But take the hurley with you wherever you go."

He was only a poor man, and there wasn't much wages out o' being a herdsman. So, the following Monday, he struck the road for Limerick, stood up at a corner, and the clock struck three o'clock. He was looking around him till the next thing, he got a tap on the shoulder. He looked around. And this man—a well-dressed man—was standing behind him.

"You're like a man that's looking for a job," he said.

"I am," says your man.

"I'm looking for a good man to come working for me," he said. "I have a big farm out in County Limerick. Would you come and work for me?"

Begod, they made the deal and they went out. The man had a big house and a fine farm. And after about a month McMahon was getting on great. Everything the man gave him to do, he did it, and the farmer made him the manager over his farm. But he still had the hurley. He never hardly went any-where without it.

Now, about a mile away from the house they were living in, there was another house, a bigger house again, and a newer house.

So one day he said to the farmer, "How is it that you never lived in the new house? 'Tis a finer house altogether than the one you're in."

"Well," says the farmer, "there's a story attached to that. There's a story that if any man can spend three nights in it, he can live there for the rest of his life. But it has failed everyone that has tried to live in it for the three nights."

So McMahon said, "I'll chance it."

"Well," he said, "if you can live the three nights in it, the house'll be yours, because 'tis no good to me standing the way it is."

So, McMahon went there, put on a roaring fire and sat down beside it. He had the hurley alongside him. Everything went grand and he was getting sleepy and the clock struck twelve. The next thing, the door was thrown open and this huge man tore in.

Begod, McMahon got up and he grabbed the hurley and the two of 'em fought and wrestled around the floor until the cock crew. And when the cock crew the man disappeared.

So they came in the morning and when they saw he had survived the night, they said, "Will you chance the next night in it?"

He said, "I will."

Begod, the same thing happened the next night. They wrestled and they fought around the place. But anytime he was being bested, the hurley was saving him the whole time. The cock crew, and the man disappeared again.

The third night the same thing happened. And he bested the man after a hard battle.

"Who are you?" says McMahon. "Or what are you? Or what did I do to you, that you're attacking me?"

Begod, the man stood up that minute.

"Why didn't you ask me that the first night? Or no one ever asked it to me," he said. "If they did, everything would be all right. I'd have answered it. Do you recognize me at all?" he said.

"No," says McMahon.

"I'm the man," says he, "that was your opponent the night o' the hurling match in Doon."

They sat down, anyway, and they got chatting. He was a fairy, or a spirit.

After a while talking he said, "Come on," and he took McMahon down a big long corridor and through a big long cellar.

The way it turned out was that there was three rooms. 'Twas a secret part o' the house. There was one room with a box o' gold in it. There was another room with a box o' silver, and there was another room with a box o' copper.

But whatever had happened, anyway, when the house was built, the money had been got wrong and the people that built the house were never paid. He instructed McMahon what to do, and who was to be paid, and how the money was to be spent.

"And when 'tis all done," he said, "the third box, o' copper, is yours. Good-bye now," he said. "I have been released from my task. I'm coming here for the last hundred years, and I have been released by you. You done me a great service. I'll never trouble you again. Or anyone."

McMahon went up and met the farmer, and told him. The farmer did what he was instructed to do and moved into the big house himself and gave McMahon the smaller house. After a few years, he was such a good workman he married one o' the man's daughters and, as they say, lived happily ever after.

Well, the man that told me that, he was Jimmy Ned Doyle beyond. He was a van man in the county council that time. They used to go around with the steamrollers. And Jimmy was up in west Clare, up far in west Clare, and a man used to come in the night, an old man. You know, they'd be living in the council van and people used to come in for a chat in the night, for company. And when the old man heard he was from Broadford he said, "Is there any place down there called Doon? With a lake and a Big House in it?"

Jimmy said that there was. And that's the story he told him, now. Wherever he picked it up, I don't know. 'Twas a story that was never told around here, as far as I know. It came in from the outside.

I have stood in this field in front of where Doon House once lorded it, the field in which the fairy hurling match took place—if it was a fairy contest, that is. Because here is one of those stories where the teller makes little distinction between fairies and spirits.

There are several inconsistencies in the story, as any alert reader will notice, but these are not, perhaps, as important as those points that link it to the genuine tradition of Irish fairy lore, e.g., the special power of articles bestowed by the Good People, the fairies' love of sport, their sense of fair play, and the recurrence of events in groups of three.

Yet, the character who hurls against McMahon and later attacks him in the "haunted" house, what is he? Spirit, fairy, or walking dead? A combination of all three, it would seem. Inconsistent, yes, but unusual, no. That is the way the stories are, for better or worse.

"They taught him a tune, an' it made twenty tunes.
The power o' the fairy."
MULLAGH, FEBRUARY 5, 1988

How the Sextons Got the Gift of Bonesetting

THIS WAS TOLD to me as a true thing, and I have no doubt that it was. There was a family in West Clare; they were famous bonesetters—Sextons. You often heard tell of 'em.

I knew one of 'em well and he told me that 'twas his great-grandfather that first got the gift of setting bones. And he told me how 'twas.

His great-grandfather used to stay out a lot at night, and generally go into Miltown village and have a few drinks there and come home rather late. He was coming from it one night—

'twas a grand moonlight night—and he saw two sets o' people hurling. He stood up to see 'em at the game and was enjoying it. And one o' the hurlers got a blow of a hurley. Broke his leg.

One o' his companions said, "Who's going to set the man's leg?"

Another of 'em spoke up an' said, "Sexton will!"

Out they came, told Sexton to come in and set the leg. He said he never did the like in his life. They said to come in and do it and no more about it. He went in and he set the bone as best he could, and tied it up with what things they gave him. And the very minute he had the last knot tied, the man sprang up, caught his hurley, and started up the field again hurling as good as ever.

So, some few days after, someone broke his leg around, and Sexton thought about what he did that night and why shouldn't he do it again? He went and set the bone, and from that time out the Sextons were setting bones.

In an age when belief in the fairies was, for many, as vivid as religious faith, people with unusual natural gifts—of healing, memory, music, etc.—were presumed to have acquired those gifts from sources outside the everyday. (Biddy Early was a prime example.) Not surprisingly so, in a relatively static community, where relations and ancestors could be traced back for many generations. These gifts could only come from God, the Devil, or the fairies. The problem was to distinguish among them. But people's attitude was very much "by their fruits shall you know them."

In the case of Tom Burke, another well-known bonesetter from west Clare, there was no doubt in the public mind: He was even elected to the Dáil (the Irish national parliament) in the 1940s.

*"The first sheaf of oats they'd bind used be given to the fairies
in some places. It wouldn't be collected up with the rest
o' the oats at all, only left there for 'em.
That was to keep in with 'em."*
MILTOWN, JUNE 27, 1999

Man "in the Fairies" Moves Hay

I HEARD TELL of a man around here one time that was supposed to be "in the fairies"—oh, that'd be a long time back. But
I heard the old people talking about him.

He was living just there up the side o' the main road, a hundred yards up from where you turned in here. There's no sign of
anything there now, but I saw the print o' the house there myself.
I was in there fencing, and I was building a bit of a wall in part
of it and I came on the whitewash.

But this fellow lived there. His wife was there, too. He seemingly used to keep a pig and a small vegetable garden in it. He
went over to a cousin o' his that lived beyond the lake here, Cullane Lake, for a bundle o' straw—a place called Ráth Lúb, near
Craggaunowen. He brought a rope about twenty yards long with
him. Met his cousin.

"Where are you going with the long rope?" says the cousin.

"Have you the straw?" says he.

"I have, tons o' straw," says the cousin, "but if you fill that rope what's going to bring it?"

"Ask no questions," he said. "Will you gimme the rope o' straw?"

"I will," he says.

They filled and filled and filled the rope. The rope was a hundred yards long now.

And the lad was looking at him all the time, you know.

"Fill away," he says. "Fill away. Don't worry." So they filled away.

"What's going to bring it?" the lad said.

"Don't bother. It'll be brought, don't worry," says he.

So, they filled it, and 'twould take a good ass to bring it in a cart, not to mention a man bringing it on his back.

"Tie it up, now," says he.

The man did.

"Would you be able to lift it any couple of inches off the ground, now," says he, "with me."

"I'll try," says the poor man.

So they rose it a half foot off the ground only. Then, it came across the lake and it landed above at the garden, there above on the side o' the road!

'Twas supposed by the old people when it came across the lake that he was in with the Good People. How else could it happen?

They used to be gambling there, too. And one night this fellow had a lot o' talk. You know, he was at him—"You're in the fairies," and all o' that.

"Listen," he says, "you were coming down Moymore the other night last week"—Moymore is there as you go in the Ennis road—"and you had a tight call, my boy. Only for me you wouldn't be here tonight. So shut your mouth."

I heard that told by the old people.

That house is gone a hundred years, at least. Ah, 'twould be more. 'Twould be a hundred and fifty at least. For other people got it after, and they left it, and other people have got it since. One hundred and fifty years, anyway.

The belief that some people were "in" the fairies was widespread in Ireland, and such people were regarded with suspicion and fear, for they could know the unknown, do the undoable. How these people came to make their compact with the fairy world is never—so far as I know—revealed. Though people might guess at it. But occasionally the end results become all too clear. And they are not, by and large (as in the case of witches and the Devil), positive for the human actors.

Tom of the Fairies

THIS MAN was a neighbor of ours in Kerry, near Ballyferriter, and he was known locally as Tomás na bPúcaí, Tom of the Fairies, and he was supposed to go every night all over the country with the fairies. They'd get a horse for him, an old plough or something like that; they'd touch it and turn it into a horse. They had the power to change things like that.

They made a horse for him, and he'd go off with them all over the place every night. And when his wife would wake up during the night she'd find a block of oak in the bed with her.

Anyway, one day he was in Dingle and he met a cousin of his from Ventry. They stopped and had a chat.

"By the way," he said, "we called to your house the other night"—and he mentioned which night—"and it was in a bit of a mess. We wanted to have a dance and the place wasn't clear for us. There was no clean water there and there was no clean cup that we could take a drink o' water. And they weren't very happy about it," he said, "but because I was your cousin I spoke to them about it, and they let it pass. But they weren't too happy. I was surprised myself that you'd have your kitchen in such a mess."

"Well," she said, "it was Tuesday night, wasn't it?"

"'Twas," he said.

"I know," she said, "because I was out working all day. I was out in the field binding sheaves and if you remember 'twas a fine day and I was the whole day at it. When I came home I was exhausted. And I couldn't do a thing. I had to go to bed. And that's why the place was in a mess. But if they came any other night it'd be nice and tidy and they'd be welcome to have their dance, and there'd be water there, and there'd be clean cups there."

"Ah," he said, "it's all right now, but only that I was your cousin and that I spoke up for you, they wouldn't be too happy, and they might . . . well, I don't know what they might do."

It might seem strange that the fairies made a horse out of a plough, 'cause they're afraid of steel. But maybe 'twas a timber plough or maybe 'twas only a bit of a plough, a wooden part, or something. Because they brought somebody else off like that and he was surprised when they were able to make a horse out of the plough. And when the plough jumped at a big jump he said, *"mo ghrá do léim, a shean-bhéim céachta"*—a fine jump for an old plough. And suddenly he fell off it.

They didn't like that kind of talk. And they let him go. He shouldn't have made comments, you see. He should have accepted his horse, not be looking a gift horse in the mouth. He was only congratulating the horse on the fine jump he did, but they didn't like that.

This story, from Irish-speaking west Kerry, shows us some more details of what it was like to accompany the fairies on their nightly travels: their power to transform things at will (in this case to make a horse for the man accompanying them); what was left at home in his place while he was gone—an interesting point here is that it is a block of oak and there would have been no oak occurring naturally in that treeless part of Kerry; their pastimes—dancing—as well as their cleanliness.

But there is also the veiled threat of what might have happened to the woman whose house was not tidy for the fairies' nighttime revels were it not for the intervention of her cousin "in the fairies." And their mercurial nature and the great care needed when dealing with them is further shown in the final episode, when what should have been a wonderful adventure—"a gift horse"—for the man in question, turns into a sudden upset, and probably a long walk home, and all because of an ill-timed, though innocent, comment made in the excitement of the moment.

In the light of this kind of sensitivity on their part, is it any wonder that humans should find it difficult to tread unscathed among the sidhe?

*"They maintained that they used take the children. But there
was no question of violence, or anything. The child would,
maybe, develop a hump on his back, or he'd be a hunchback
or something like that, an' eventually he'd die."*

DRUMLINE, OCTOBER 17, 1992

Hurler with a Humpback

'TWAS ALWAYS KNOWN that there was certain people more
in touch with the fairies than others. There was a man like that
in this parish one time. They always made out that he was in
the fairies.

There's a story told that the Broadford team was hurling one
day—above in Tulla 'twas—and this man o' the McMahons was
in the goals. He was a good hurler, too, the same man. During
the first half, the man that was in the fairies was standing behind
the goals. And no matter what way the other team hit a ball at
McMahon, he'd block it.

But at halftime the man said, "I'm going away now. You're on
your own after this."

Whatever way it came during the second half, the other
team scored—several times.

What people used to make out was that the man wasn't
on his own. He'd have five or six of 'em with him that no one
could see.

That man, when I remember him, he had a hump on his back. But he hadn't always that hump. Everyone will tell you how he got it. He was a terrible man for being out late when he was young, at dances, and playing cards especially. And he had a good distance to go home, at least two miles off o' the main road. And 'twas up a very lonesome old road. He was going home one night, and someone found him in the morning flung on the side o' the road, nearly unconscious. He was taken home and put into bed. And he didn't leave the bed for the best part o' six months. When he got up he had a hump on his back. 'Twas the fairies attacked him and beat him, they said, and put a hump on his back. And he was no small man. That's a fact.

If this story confirms anything it would seem to be that being in the fairies can be a dangerous business, with its perils as well as its rewards. But the teller is, perhaps, doubtful as to what really befell the man on that dark lonely road home. There were no witnesses to what occurred. He does not say the fairies attacked and beat the man, only that others said so. Yet he was attacked and ended up with a hunchback, so everyone drew the conclusion that it must be the fairies, since there was no mention of robbery and he was known to be "in" them. And the detail "and he was no small man" seems to be added as an after-thought, as if to say, "What use would mere human strength have been against opponents like the fairies, anyway?"

Biddy Early "Strange" as a Child

BIDDY EARLY was always the type that was going off on her own, when she was a child, and talking to herself.

Her mother had a hatching hen, anyway. She wanted to get eggs from some woman. And she sent Biddy for the eggs to put under the hen—to bring out the chickens. But in three hours, she wasn't back, so her mother went looking for her. And she found her above, under whitethorns, chatting and talking away. She didn't even know her mother was talking to her when she met her, she was so engrossed in it.

She could see things another couldn't see.

Then, she was hired out when she was fourteen years. Poor people used to hire out their children to work; there'd be a fair in Ennis and they'd be looking for servant girls in it. Someone in Tulla hired her. His wife was dead and he had two or three children. He had a baby in the cot, even. He brought Biddy home, anyway, and she was a great little housekeeper.

He was out saving hay one day. There was no one there but herself and the baby in the cot. And the baby spoke to her and asked her to take down that fiddle there and he'd play a tune for her.

She gave it to him. 'Tis up under the rafters they'd have things hanging at that time. The baby played the tune, anyway, the nicest music you ever heard. The fiddle was left on the table, and when the man o' the house came in for his dinner he asked her was she able to play. She said no.

And he said, "What was you doing with the fiddle, so? You *are* able to play."

And she said, "No."

But she handed it over to the baby and he played this tune again, for the father.

Mystery, and therefore curiosity, has always surrounded Biddy Early's early years and how she acquired her power as a healer and intermediary. Here we get a glimpse of her as a child "under the whitethorns"—in a fort, probably— "chatting and talking," presumably with the fairies, so engrossed that she is oblivious of all else around her.

In the second part of the story, if ordinary standards of proof were applied it would be dismissed as at least incomplete, perhaps even childishly simple. For example, is the father not surprised at the baby in the cradle's speaking like an adult and playing the fiddle? Or maybe the usual part of such a tale, where the changeling in the cot is banished and the real child restored, is missing.

Yet, I think not. Far more likely the focus here is on Biddy, how she was from a very young age a convergence point for the otherworldly and our world. The inconsistencies are incidental and in a telling of the tale would probably pass quite unnoticed.

"Definitely she had the power.
There's no question about that.
She could foretell."

DRUMLINE, MARCH 14, 1990

Biddy Early Helps, but a Price Paid

BELOW, at the Point, at Shannon Airport, there was a family living. They had a son and he wasn't well. So the father went on the horse and saddle over to Biddy.

"I know," says she, when he arrived in the yard, "I know what brought you. Your son is not well."

"That's right," he said.

"Well, come in," says she. She told him that his house was built at the end of a fort, and one room of it was in the fort, and that he'd have to cut that away from the rest o' the house.

She gave him a bottle and told him to give the son so much of it morning and evening, or three times a day—I can't remember.

"You'll break that bottle," says she, "before you reach Quin,"—which he did. He was coming in at the back gate o' Quinville and the bottle fell out of his pocket, down on the road, and smashed. He had to go back to Biddy again, and she gave him another bottle.

"I knew you'd break it," says she. "So be careful now, that nothing'll happen to you this time. Go straight home,"—which he did.

So he did what Biddy told him: He built up the room door, discarded that room. And he gave the bottle to his young son. The son got better.

Now, he had three pigs out in the shed. One evening, as soon as the son was better, a storm came up the Shannon river and swept the roof and the door off o' the cabin. Out went the three pigs, into the river, and was never seen again.

Here we see that Biddy can save a person from the Good People, but that they may become very angry at being deprived of their chosen prey and take some-thing else valuable instead. It is said that Biddy suffered many beatings from them because she had, by her power, helped keep "dying" people alive (i.e., people who were being carried by the Good People), thus depriving them of their chosen victims. Some stories of "curing" priests have the same theme: the priest cured at great expense to himself, and most such priests were short-lived.

A Clash of Power: Biddy Early Versus the Clergy

ONE TIME she told 'em how to resurrect a fellow, but the Church moved in.

When they went to her to cure this fellow she said, "Ah, you're coming now. Pat is down. He wouldn't let the magpies alone. He went down on his knee to shoot a magpie, and he wouldn't let the old bloody magpies alone. They weren't doing any harm to anyone. But when the Fool* got him on his knee, he hit Pat a clip. But go home and mind him for two weeks. Don't leave his bedside day or night, for two weeks!"

Jeez, he was grand. Everything was going fine. The other brother came into the yard one day, and he had two horses out in the garden. He was plowing and he fed the horses and they started a kicking match outside over the oats.

The sister that was minding him inside in the bed—and he was inside singing a song!—she ran out to separate the horses. The very minute she did—spell broken!

---

*The Fool of the Fairies.

So they went to Biddy again and she said, "Ah, the red-haired sister went out in the yard to separate the horses that were kicking."

She told 'em what to do then: Place black-handled knives at the four corners o' the coffin, get the four strongest men in the parish to carry it, and let the coffin down at the crossroads and he'd be all right. But the coffin got so heavy on the way to the crossroads that it bent 'em to the ground. But they got it there, anyway.

But, sure, the priests moved in and they whipped 'em, whipped the crowd out of it with their whips and horses. They whipped 'em out of it—before anyone knew if he was alive or not! So, they had to take the fellow away and bury him.

Sure, if the priests didn't come, they'd have succeeded in bringing him back. Oh, definitely. Definitely.

There are differing versions of this story. In some of them the man being "brought back" by Biddy is one who has been carried by the Good People, but here we have him being resurrected, so it is hardly surprising that the Church moves in. Someone as untutored as Biddy performing such a miracle could hardly be tolerated. It would show the clergy in a very poor light.

Yet we see that it was the fairies who punished the man, the Fool of the Fairies (Amadán na Bruíne), in fact—whose stroke was usually fatal. And so it proves to be, even though in a roundabout way.

This story leaves us in no doubt as to why Biddy is remembered so vividly (and affectionately, for the most part) even today: Hers was a helping mission, whereas too often the clergy were more concerned about the power of the Church as an institution than about the individuals who made up that same church— as is obvious here from the way they whip them like animals.

"There are so many stories, they can't all be apocryphal.
And even though some of them can be taken with a grain of salt,
there are others that make you think. I wouldn't like to be thought
of as somebody who believed everything, or somebody who's
laughing at the idea, either—which I'm not."
A PRIEST'S OPINION, LISCANNOR, AUGUST 28, 1999

Three Stories of Priests Who Can See the Other Crowd

THIS PRIEST in the parish of Killanin was given all kinds of credentials by the people. They said he could cure people and read souls. And there was an old man called John Joyce, and John was telling him that as he came home to a place called Aur, which isn't too far from Moycullen, he saw people playing hurling in the moonlight. He was looking down over them and there they were. He didn't recognize any of them. And one o' them spotted him and in Irish said, *"féach an fear ag faire orainn"*—"Look at the man; he's watching us." And they disappeared.

They were up on horseback, and he was riding behind the priest. So, the priest said to him then, "Would you like to see the fairies again, the *siógaí*?"

"Why?"

"Well," he said, "if you put your foot up on mine,"—which was in the stirrup—"you'll be able to."

But John Joyce refrained. He didn't want to do it.

I KNEW AN INSTANCE of where there was an old sports field out in the country, and the priest used to come there every evening. He was a great man for sport, a great man for the youth, and a great man for the parish. Great man! He had all the lads hurling and footballing, hundred yards and long jump and weight-throwing and tug-o-war and everything. He had the youth o' the parish interested. They weren't going deviling.

When the chat'd be getting serious in the night, you see, when the old bit o' sport'd be over, there'd be a crowd o' young lads around and they'd have an ear on 'em to hear what the older lads'd be talking about. And, o' course, they didn't want the young lads to be getting the gossip. So they'd frighten 'em to send 'em home, you see: "Oh, the fairies'll catch you. Go home now. 'Tis getting dark. Be home before the fairies'll catch you."

You know, the usual old thing.

So, the young lads'd run, o' course, fly for their lives. And the boys could talk away then and there was no one with their ear cocked.

Begod, one fellow said to the priest this night, "I wonder are they there, Father?" he said. "I wonder is there such a thing as fairies,"—just in the course of events, casual.

"Oh," he said, "are they what! Anyone care to look out under my arm?"

Jeez, there wasn't a man in the crowd did.

"Look," he said, "d'you see that valley down there? They're as thick there as the hairs on your head. As thick as the hairs on your head."

If I was there I wouldn't look, either. He might show me one, what I didn't want to see. Them things are best left alone, nearly.

Them fellows'd put you thinking very quick! And d'you know there's an exorcist priest in every diocese? The clergy have power over certain ones of 'em. But not all, not all.

A PRIEST from Liscannor used to go in to Lahinch in the Sunday nights. He had some friends he used to call to and this other bloke from Liscannor used to be going in playing cards. They'd walk in together. But the priest'd tell him on no account to go home when he'd be finishing up at the card game, or wherever he'd be, without calling to the house where the priest'd be, to go home with him.

So, when they were coming up the Liscannor road—they were walking—the priest took off his hat and he put it on the man. He had to go up to the parochial gate with the priest.

And when the man gave back his hat, the priest said to him, "Did you see anything?"

"No," says he.

"The road was black with 'em," says the priest. That's what he said.

It might be on account of putting his hat on the other bloke that the man didn't see 'em.

It might seem to us nowadays that Christian clergy (priests in particular) would give little or no credence to the fairies; that in fact they should be actively discouraging their flocks from belief in such "pagan nonsense," such superstition. But the reality was often very different from the theory. The clergy had, after all, to live in the real world with people who felt no contradiction between their fairy beliefs and their religious practice. And a great many people credited the priest with power to see the fairies, if not always to control them—as these stories show. The notion that a priest could make a kind of window through which the world of the Good People could be seen by making a circle with his arm and touching his fingers to his hip was very widespread—in the process often confounding and terrifying skeptics.

If (as these three stories hint) priests were vividly aware of the presence of the fairies, is it any wonder that so many of them were reluctant to condemn them publicly, whatever the official Church position might have required? They knew, far more clearly than ordinary people, if we are to credit popular accounts, the results such condemnation might bring on themselves, despite all their power.

*"What I'd like to know is, how did they quieten down, that
they aren't appearing now to the people of today? Well, I
was doing that questioning in people, an' d'you know what the
people told me? They said all the Masses that's said now, day
an' night, that quietened 'em down, that they can't appear
like they were appearing years ago."*
LISCANNOR, SEPTEMBER 2, 1999

Holy Water Given As Protection

"ALWAYS MAKE THE CROSS over the grave when you have it
opened," an old man told us here one time, and 'tis always
done—to stop them carrying the dead person. I'll tell you a
story about that.

One Sunday at Mass a man stood up at the elevation, and he
shouted, "Will the fallen angels be saved?"

The priest looked back, said nothing.

But, before Mass was over, he asked, "The person who asked
the question during the elevation, I want to see him in the sacristy after Mass."

The man didn't want to go, but the people said, "Go on in.
Do what he told you."

So he went in.

"Why did you inquire?" says he.

"I was told," says he.

"By whom?"

"I won't give any names," he says. 'Twas someone that never went to Mass or had the black art, or something, you know.

"You have put yourself in an awful predicament," says he. "They'll come tonight for you."

"Indeed, they won't."

"They will," says the priest. "I'd advise you now, go and dig your grave. I'll bless a bottle o' holy water for you, and when you have the grave dug, put a cross over the grave, and keep the bottle o' holy water."

He was there that night, and they came in flocks, thousands of 'em, and they were grabbing for him. But he shook the holy water, and they couldn't touch him. When daybreak came he was all right. They came no more, then, and he went home. So, he went to the priest again and the priest gave him a blessing.

"Never again," he said, "do anything o' the like. I saved you. If you didn't come to me, you were gone with 'em."

Several interesting points are raised by this story: Do the fairies (and note, they are never once mentioned directly by name throughout the telling) take the dead, as well as the living? If so, for what purpose?

The priest is seen to be the chief counselor in this society, whose word is the last word and whose power is the ultimate protection against the forces of the unseen. (Note that the bottle of holy water he gives the man to safeguard him has echoes of Biddy Early's bottles of spring water which she so often dispensed, together with exact instructions as to their use.)

We see also that the power of the creatures that threaten to "carry" the man extends only as far as daylight—a strong hint that it is the fairies who are here rather than the fallen angels, though either might be understood from the text.

Finally, the priest's parting comment to the foolish man, as said previously, shows the belief of many clergy in the Other Crowd. And however it may be understood by him theologically to mean the fallen angels (though he is careful not to distinguish), in his parishioners' minds no doubt it is the fairies that would have been understood by that final word "'em."

"'Twas known that children would disappear. They might be seen at the fairy fort in a week after, going into the bushes."
DRUMLINE, OCTOBER 17, 1992

Girl Carried by the Fairies

I HEARD A STORY from a man over in Lissane about one of his own family a couple o' generations back. She was a lovely young girl and she died.

But after about twelve months a brother o' hers started dreaming of her. He had this recurring dream that she'd be passing through the yard on a horse in the middle of a crowd of horsemen.

The dream changed, then, and she spoke to him. She told him she'd be coming on a certain night and if he was there, and if he pulled her off o' the horse, when her feet'd touch the ground she'd be able to come back. Once her feet touched the ground, that was the thing.

He was worried over it and the night that was fixed was coming near. So, he went to the priest. And he told his story to the priest.

The priest said, "Look, it can happen all right. But for everyone's good, it can't be allowed to happen. How can you bring back a person that's dead twelve months? Wouldn't it frighten the life out o' the people in the parish? Look," he said, "I'll do something. I'll say a few prayers, and I'll guarantee you, she's better off where she is."

So, he left it at that. He never dreamt again.

Here we see what today still exercises people most violently: the death of the young, the beautiful. This storyteller's approach to it leaves us in no doubt that he is part of a tradition that has come to terms in its own way with such an enormity.

The brother's dream of his dead sister, the supremely important point of her wanting to touch the ground, our physical earth, again if she is to be freed from those who have abducted her, the traditional priest's admission that such things can happen, all these reactions are normal in their context.

But then, a jarring, foreign note is introduced: the rational voice of modernity: "It can't be allowed to happen." The amazing thing is that the priest does not believe that the dead can be allowed to rise! Yet his intentions are well meant.

His solution seems somehow tawdry, though: "I'll say a few prayers." And the "better off" place where the girl is? We are never told where that place is, whether Heaven, Tír na nÓg (The Land of Youth), or somewhere else. Perhaps, ultimately, it matters not at all.

The Girl Saved from the Good People

ISN'T IT A FUNNY thing how there's some forts and we know nothing at all about 'em. They're there, and that's all. Maybe there was stories about 'em one time, but the people that knew 'em are all dead and gone. I often thought about that, once a story is gone from a place, how it'll never again come back. And that's wronging that place. 'Tis taking away a part of it. That's why I always liked to listen to old people talking about history, especially when they'd be talking about places I knew. I could go to them places myself and see if they were right in the way they described 'em. And once I'd see the place o' the story I'd always remember the story then.

One story I heard I could never forget it 'cause I went after to the place, and nearly everything was the way he described it, except for one thing.

I'll tell you about it.

The place I'm talking about is Corbally fort, on the road down to Quin. You couldn't miss it. 'Tis up on a small hill there on your right-hand side down from the main road to Ennis, about a field in.

All that place, in the old days, belonged to the Mahons. They weren't big landlords at all. More like gentlemen farmers. But they were well-liked people.

Now, there was a young fellow, John O' Brien was his name, working for Mr. Mahon—a yard hand you'd call him, I s'pose, a kind of a general laborer. This November Eve, he had all done and the supper ate, and he was just smoking his pipe before he went to bed. But when he looked over towards Corbally fort, he saw a light, about halfway up the hill.

"By the Lord," says he, "that's strange. Who's up there at this hour?"

He thought 'twas someone with a lamp, you see.

He watched it, anyway, for a while, but there was no stir. He didn't know what to do. But at the same time, if something was gone wrong in the morning . . . well, he didn't like *not* to go, just in case. So he said to himself that he might as well investigate it.

Off with him—out along the avenue, across the road, in the field, and up the hill. But he wasn't gone far when he saw that there was no one there with any lamp. What was there above him was a kind of a door in the hill. 'Twas open, and the light was shining out of it.

Begod, that put him thinking a bit. But he was a plucky young lad, and he said once he came that far he might as well go farther. So he went up and put in his head. No one there—only a kind of a passageway going in under the hill, and that's where the light was coming from.

"Begod, since I'm here I'll go in. You'd never know what'd be inside."

So he did, went in along, until he came to this doorway. And the light was coming from beyond it. He crept up to the door and peeped in. There inside was a big room with a table in the middle of it. At the two ends o' the table there was two old hags, gray hair and whiskers on 'em, and they were talking.

"Oh, she's coming, and when they bring her, that's the time we'll have the dancing! And 'tis about time, too, for 'em to get someone. I'm crippled here sitting down doing nothing."

"True for you," says the other one. "And which horse are they bringing her on this time?"

"The white one, o' course."

"And the same way in, I s'pose."

"The very same. The southern side o' the hill. Like every one before her." And she took a slug out of a jug that was there on the table—*poitín*, maybe, or something stronger.

Begod, John was listening to this, taking it all in. O' course, he often heard o' people being carried but he never believed it until now.

So he says to himself, "We'll see about that. You'll wait a while longer for the dance if I can help it."

He crept out again, out along, and there was no sign of anyone coming. Nothing moving, only a grand moonlight night. He made his way down to the southern side o' the hill, to a gap there, and kept watch. And he was only there a small while when he saw the crowd o' horsemen coming. And when they came nearer he saw that all of 'em were on black horses, all except one. There was one white horse and on that horse was the girl.

He hid down behind the bushes and didn't stir while they went in the gap only a couple o' feet from where he was. One by one they passed, and the girl was the last to cross in. And just as she passed, John jumped up and pulled her out o' the saddle. The minute he did it, the rest o' the crowd stopped. Oh, he thought he was dead, that they'd attack him, for sure. But all they did was to turn around slowly and stare at him. They went on up towards the fort then and he saw 'em no more.

Anyway, he had enough to be thinking about now.

"Come on," says he to the girl. "Come out o' this place, quick."

He brought her on down along and across the road to Mr. Mahon's place, and took her in. They were all gone to bed, o' course. All he could do was give her something to eat—but not a word o' talk could he knock out o' her.

'Twas the same the following day—no talk! She hadn't a word, whatever was wrong. He asked Mr. Mahon could she stay and help around the house, a kind of a maid, and he said she could.

She was a grand girl in every way, except for the one thing: that she had no word. No matter what they did they could get no talk out o' her.

So, all that year John was thinking about this, that a fine girl like her couldn't explain herself.

And when 'twas coming up to November Eve again he said to himself, "If that light is above there again at the fort tonight, I'll find out once and for all what's going on here."

The night came, anyway, and he kept a lookout. Sure enough, close to the time, he saw the light above on the side o' the hill.

Out with him, and off up, until he came to the same place where the passage was. He looked in. 'Twas the very same. He went in, as quiet as a mouse, until he came to the door where the light was coming out.

When he peeped in, the same room was there, and the same table, with the same two old hags. He knew by the way they were talking, though, that there was something wrong. So he listened.

"Oh, that thief, John O'Brien," says one of 'em. "That he may rot alive."

"True for you," says the other one. "Only for him we'd have a fine dance last November Eve."

"What right had he to steal our grand girl, anyway? What business of his was she?"

The other old lady laughed—if you could call it a laugh! "Sure, what good is she to him? She'll be like she is the rest o' her days—as dumb as a stick o' timber. Ha-hah!"

"True for you. Just as well they don't know that this is the stuff that'd give her talk enough for twenty—ha-haaaa!"

And she took a slug out o' the jug that was on the table.

As soon as John heard that, he didn't wait one second, only jumped in the door, snapped the jug off o' the table before they hardly knew he was there, and off with him, out, and down the hill holding on to that jug like 'twas gold.

When they got up in the morning, he told Mr. Mahon about where he was and what happened.

"You better call her in," says he.

They did, and gave her a drink out o' the jug. She smiled at 'em. But she had no talk. They gave her a second sup out of it. She laughed. But still no talk. So they gave her a third drop out o' the jug. And that was the time she found her tongue. 'Twas like a waterfall! She couldn't stop, maybe even if she wanted to. But I s'pose after a whole year with no word she was entitled!

Anyway, when she had enough said about whatever she was talking about, she says to John, "What you have done for me, I can't repay you for or thank you enough for. But there's one other thing I'll ask of you, if you'll do it for me."

"Why wouldn't I?" says he. "If I can, I will. What is it?"

"'Tis this. I want to go home, but I can't."

"Why can't you?" says he.

"How could I? Below, in Castleconnell in County Limerick where I come from, all my people think I'm dead. 'Tis so I was carried by the Good People last November Eve, up to that fort over there, where you saved me. But when they carried me they left a thing instead o' me at home that looked like me, and that thing died away and away and was buried. If you go back there now and tell 'em I'm here alive and that you saved me, they'll think you're cracked, fit for the madhouse."

"What'll I do, so?" says John.

"If you'll follow my advice, now," says she, "everything might end well yet. When I was at home, my father bought a pony for me so I could ride out with him on the hunt. We went everywhere together, me and that pony. Now that he thinks I'm dead, he wouldn't part with that animal for any money. But if you'll go down to my father's place, get a job there, and bring back my pony here, he'll follow you sooner or later. When he finds me here, safe and sound, everything'll be fine. Will you do that for me?"

"O' course I will," says he.

The following morning he got permission from Mr. Mahon and set out for Castleconnell. She gave him directions and he made out the place easy enough. He got a job, too, in the stables, and he was working away there for a week or two. The little pony was there, getting the very same attention as a person would—maybe even better. And 'twas no time before the father was telling him all about his daughter that was dead and gone, how he used to come out several times in the day to talk to that pony, and every time he looked at him, he thought of her.

"All the better," says John to himself. "He's sure to follow me if I take him."

And that's just what he did, a few mornings after, early, before anyone was stirring. Tackled up and headed off for Corbally, and was gone a good few miles before anyone noticed he was missing.

But when they did, there was murder! The father was fit to be tied. His daughter's pony gone!

"I'll kill him! He's a dead man when I get up to him. After I trusting him, and all."

John brought the pony back to Corbally, anyway, and 'twas only a short time after when her father came in the avenue, still in a temper. Oh, for sure, he was going to do damage! He was savage, man.

But he was just passing the front room window when he looked in and saw his daughter looking out at him.

The poor man collapsed. Fell off o' his horse there in the yard, with shock.

There was fierce commotion! They brought him in and revived him. But, sure, he nearly passed out again when he saw his daughter standing in front o' him. They talked to him, anyway, and told him as much as they knew. The poor man was listening and half listening. You wouldn't know if he understood half of what they were saying. But when he came around right, and Mr. Mahon told him 'twas all true, he had to believe it. Moreover, when his own daughter was holding his hand, the girl he thought was dead.

When things settled down, anyway, and they had a bite to eat, the father says to John, "You have done me a great service, John O'Brien. But for you, my daughter was gone. The least I can do is put no obstacle in front o' her if she wants to marry you."

Want to! Anyone'd know by the way they were looking at each other that they were made for each other.

Mr. Mahon didn't stand in John's way, either. He did not, only gave him a good send-off, something he wasn't the worse of, anyway, when he settled in at Castleconnell.

And he *did* settle in there. And got on fine. And their people are there yet, for all I know.

But, one thing, when I visited that fort after, I couldn't find any sign or trace of a hole or passageway on the side o' the hill facing Corbally House, or anywhere around that hill. 'Cause, you know, a lot o' forts have a room undergrowd and a passage leading into it.

On November Eve, as well as May Eve, it was regarded as very dangerous to be outdoors come darkness, for on those nights above all others the fairies were on the move and anything might happen to a person who met them. So, when John O'Brien saw the light on Corbally hill, the fact that there was a fort there should have given him pause.

Luckily for us, and for a certain girl carried by the Good People, curiosity got the better of his fear, and his subsequent investigation and display of courage changes his life forever.

This very detailed account was given to me in 1980 by one of the last and best traditional storytellers from that part of County Clare, a man with a memory for the details that other people pass over. And here is the result, one of the few "happy ever after" endings in this book—deservedly so for a hero who dared the fairies on their own ground for the hand of the beautiful maiden. Even they seemed to respect his bravery, for they did not interfere when he risked all by snatching her from them, she who was necessary for their annual celebration in Corbally fort and whose absence spoiled it.

"If I was involved in a thing like that I'd very,
very well let sleeping dogs lie."
DRUMLINE, MARCH 13, 1997

Woman Carried Asks for Rescue

THIS WOMAN DIED having a baby, and in a case like that they usually said, *"Oh, is amhlaidh a sciobadh í."* She was carried. She didn't really die. She was carried by the fairies.

But, down in County Limerick, in this farmer's house, there was a servant boy and he used to go out playing cards at night. And when he'd come home, the farmer used to always leave some food for him ready, milk and bread, so that he could eat a bit before he went to bed.

But this night, there was nothing left. And the next night there was nothing left. And he said it to the farmer. "By the way . . ." and he told him.

And the farmer said, "But I did leave it."

"Well," he said, "it wasn't there when I came home."

So, the next night, the farmer himself sat up waiting, with the door open in the room, and he was listening. And he saw this woman coming in and eating the food. He went up and spoke to her. And she told him that she was such and such a woman from Ventry in Kerry, and that the fairies took her. She said she was married, had a baby, and the fairies took her on a certain night. But she didn't eat their food. They carried her away, but she didn't eat their food. And while she wasn't eating their food, she was safe. But her husband would have to come and get her away. She told him what to do. She told him her husband's name, everything about him, where he lived, and so on, and how he was to take her out.

So the farmer wrote to the man and he told him what had happened and how he met the man's wife. But the man had re-married in the meantime, because they married very quickly then.

He went to the priest and asked the priest, "What should I do?"

And the priest said, "Look, leave things as they are. That's the best thing to do."

So he did. She never came back and that was the end of it. He carried on with the other wife.

That happened the last century.

In this poignant little story one may imagine the feelings of the priest, if he was a man of any conscience, to have to give the advice he does to the husband of the woman who has been carried in childbirth by the fairies (since there was no such thing as divorce in that society). Where does that leave her? In a limbo, neither lost to them nor at rest in a Christian sense. In fact, no one should be happy at the end of this tale, where people are less important than social conventions and all that seems to matter is that the surface calm of society be preserved, whatever the hidden cost to the individuals involved.

(The servant-boy system, by which young men and women from poverty-stricken west Kerry spent part of the year working for farmers in the rich dairy lands of the Golden Vale—counties Limerick and Tipperary—lasted well into the 1940s.)

"Any man or woman or girl that'd die that'd be good an' healthy-looking, the fairies that'd have 'em taken. That's what the old people believed, anyway."
MOYREE, MARCH 10, 1985

A Tragic Loss of Nerve

THE FAIRIES used to move from place to place. In fact, I heard a story about it.

These two brothers, they were farmers, they lived together in one house. One of 'em was married; he had three or four children. And the girl that came into the house brought in a dowry. The other boy, he got that fortune and more money that they had made, and he was going to marry a farmer's daughter after a while. But when the man's wife died, he didn't marry. He stayed on to help the brother. She died very quick; she was only sick four or five days. A lot o' people had an idea that she was swept.

The man that was married had a lot o' work to do around the house, you know—milking cows, and had to keep the place going, and ready the children for school.

Everything was going according to plan, anyway. Now, the married man wouldn't go on *ragairne** on winter nights, but the single man did. He used to go to a place where they'd be playing cards. But the married man always left roasted spuds by the fire for him, and butter if they had it, and a cup o' sour milk, butter-milk. And he'd have them when he'd come home.

He came in one night, anyway, and the plate was empty and the buttermilk was drank. That carried on for four or five nights, and he didn't know what in the world was wrong.

They were abroad digging spuds a while after, himself and the brother, and he said to him, "Am I not working as good as ever for you? Why don't you leave up my supper for me?"

"I beg your pardon," says the brother, "I leave up your sup-per every night."

So that was all right. He went on *ragairne* the next night and he went to a place where there was a couple o' more people. They were talking away until about half past nine o'clock, and he said he didn't know if his brother was leaving up the supper for him.

He went off early and when he came to the house, he looked in through the window. And the brother had the supper up

*Night visiting.

on the fireplace for him. He used to eat this before he'd go to bed.

When he looked in through the window, didn't he see the man's wife eating the spuds—the woman that was dead! He took the latch from the door as easy as he could, and he came in and he spoke to her.

"I'm eating your supper," says she.

"I don't begrudge it to you," says he. "Even if 'twas beef, I wouldn't begrudge it to you."

"Well, I'm eating that for the last four or five nights and the reason I came here tonight is to make contact with you," she said. "We'll be leaving this fort below"—there was a fort below, about a half mile from the house—"such a night," she said, "and I'll be above on the fifth horse in front of a fairy man, the fifth horse that'll come out o' that fort. We're changing. We're going to a different fort."

"Okay," says he.

"Tell my husband to be there. And if he'll whip me off o' the saddle when the fifth horse'll come out, I'll get to come back," says she.

"Or if he don't, I will," says the fellow.

"No good! You have no claim over me," says the fairy woman. "It must be my husband."

On the night, the brother went with him and they stayed outside the fairy fort. The first horse came out, and the second horse. They were grand-looking people. Then the fifth horse came out, and when he saw his wife in front o' this—he wasn't too fairy-looking entirely; he was a fairly good-looking man—he dropped in a dead weakness, and he failed to whip her off the saddle.

And people that was out that same night, the crying was heard all over the country, the woman crying as they went to whatever fort they were going to.

She was never again seen, nor heard of. That's a true story.

What makes this story particularly interesting is the glimpse it gives us into what it may be like in the Other Place for a victim of fairy abduction. Obviously the woman wants to return home permanently and it is still possible for her to appear to her relatives and give instructions as to how she may be saved—but only for as long as she is in the fort to which she has been first taken. On the vital night on which she is moved to another fort her single opportunity of salvation presents itself. The fact that it is not taken obviously consigns her to some awful fate in her new place of abode, if we are to believe the teller that her weeping was heard all over the country. And the statement that "she was never seen again, nor heard of" suggests that after this one window of escape from the Other People there was no second.

"A man went to the fair o'Tulla, sure, an' he
disappeared. He vanished with a cow. No one knew
where he went. That was in the month of April, or May.
An' that day twelve months later he showed up at the fair,
with the cow. An' no one could ever know where he was,
nor he never knew himself where he was. Jeez, the people ran
from him at the fair. . . . He was carried, o' course."

DRUMLINE, MARCH 14, 1990

A Woman Dies . . . and Remarries

THERE WAS THIS MAN; he got married. He was married for a
bit, and his wife died. She was buried and all, and there was no
more about her for a good bit after.

So, there was a neighbor o' this man, then, he was a cattle
dealer and he went to the fair one day. And he saw her walking
down the street, that same woman, now. And, by Jeez, he knew
her, but he didn't want to go talking to her, for I s'pose he got so
stunned and surprised. How would it be that she'd be there in
the street when she was dead and buried?!

He left that day go. He didn't go to talk to her at all.

So he came on home that evening, and he went to this man's
house and told him his story.

"By God," says he, "I met your wife today in the street."

"God, don't be joking me," says the lad.

He was talking away about it, and in the finish the man believed him. He knew then that he was telling the truth.

So, the man asked then if he'd be going to that place again.

"Oh, I will," says he. "The next fair day I'll be going there again."

"I'll go with you," says he.

"Oh, all right," says the neighbor, "we will. The two of us'll go."

The two of 'em struck on to the fair, and they were there for a bit. They were going up and down the street, and didn't they see her again, walking down the street. The two of 'em knew her, and she knew them.

They went talking to her, and she was talking to them.

So then, they went into the house where she was living. She was married again. And there was the two husbands then: the first man and the man she married the second time.

The first husband asked her if she'd come home with him and she said she would. But the second husband, he wouldn't agree to that at all. So the cattle dealer came between 'em and he said to have one o' the husbands go out the back door and the other man to go out the front door, and whichever one of 'em she'd follow, she could go with that one.

By Jeez, when they went out the two doors, one of 'em out each door, didn't she follow her first husband. But when she did, a child inside in the cot had every yell and bawl and roar.

"Oh," says she, "I can't go from the child." She had to turn back in again and stay there.

'Tis the way she was carried, by the Good People. There was them kind o' things there long ago, man.

But how is it that she was carried, and dead and buried, and then, wherever she was carried, that she was married there again?

Christ, there was awful strange things there long ago.

I knew the man who told me this story for the last ten years of his long life (ninety-three years). He was tough-minded, levelheaded, the kind of farmer who would drive a hard (but equitable) bargain at fair or market. He was not by nature a dreamer, yet he had a healthy respect for the Other Crowd.

If I had to choose a sentence from this episode that sums him up—and his thought processes, too—it would be, "But how is it that she was carried, and dead and buried, and wherever she was carried, that she was married there again?"

I can see him still, that so-called simple man, stroking his stubbled chin, trying to come to grips with what for most people, no matter what they profess to the contrary, is the unthinkable: that there really are two worlds, ours and another one that parallels it, and that we may, for no logical reason, be transferred from one to the other with consequences that are sometimes heartbreaking, as for the woman here.

"Boys they used be more after than girls.
That's why they'd have petticoats on 'em till
they'd be five or six years, ducking the fairies."
MILTOWN, JUNE 27, 1999

Garret Barry and the Changeling

A GOOD-LOOKING PERSON, it seemed, they had some great set on 'em. They wanted 'em. And they carried women more than men. And children. Sure, we heard the one about Garret Barry. Garret used go round to all the houses, and he'd be kept for a week, maybe, playing music for 'em.

He was in this house, anyway, and they told him keep an eye on the cradle till they'd come in. They were gone out picking spuds or something.

Garret was there, and he was playing away nice and easy on the pipes. The child was hardly two years old, and he sat up.

"Garret," says he, "you're a good player, but I heard a lot better than you."

When they came in he told 'em about what the child said, and it seems they reddened the shovel* and made for the cradle. Whatever was there vanished and the right child was left back.

*Heated the shovel until it was red hot.

Stories of babies that appear to be human but which, in reality, are changelings are legion in Ireland. This one is reasonably typical.

The applying of fire as an antidote to fairy "possession" could have tragic consequences, as was illustrated in the well-known case of the burning of Bridget Cleary in County Tipperary in 1895. She was believed by her husband and relatives to have been carried by the fairies, was held over a fire to drive them out, but died as a result. The subsequent trial and convictions made international headlines.

Garret Barry was a famous blind piper who died in 1900. Many stories of his extraordinary music and sense of hearing are yet told in west Clare.

"Why would the fairies want to take a human child?
I s'pose to make the fairy crowd stronger. They used take 'em
anyway. As time goes by, the fairy child that's left
don't ever develop right, only decline away."
MILTOWN, JUNE 27, 1999

Two Changeling Stories

MY MOTHER'S FATHER used to have great stories. One of 'em concerned a young man coming home at nighttime, passing a ruin of a house, seeing a lady in white coming out the door. Then she spotted him. She had been at the open window and she came out the door and she ran. Then another lady inside handed out a baby—which he took, 'cause he'd arrived at the door at this point. The house was on the side o' the road.

He brought the baby home and the mother was waiting up for him. "Where on earth did you get the child?" she asked, and more like that.

They made the baby as comfortable as possible and, "Well, 'tis twelve o'clock at night now so we'll wait till morning."

They didn't know where or how the baby came to be there, if it was being kidnapped, or what.

But next morning, anyway, there was great crying and weeping in a neighboring house because the baby there was found to have died. He went in to sympathize and he saw this wizened little baby.

So he said, "Put down a good fire there, now. I'm going to burn this baby. This is not your baby."

And, as soon as he said that, the wizened baby quivered and, according to my grandfather, jumped out o' the cradle and up the chimney he goes. Then the man went home and brought the real baby back to them.

Now, my grandfather went further and said that baby lived, grew up in that village and she went to America when she was about twenty or twenty-two. I didn't get her name or, if I did, I've forgotten.

THE SECOND STORY had to do with a family in the same area who had a handicapped baby. But they were beginning to realize that the baby wasn't as handicapped as they thought, or as he let on. And once or twice, when they came in suddenly, they found that he was out o' the cradle but managed to kind o' scramble back in. But he wasn't supposed to be able to walk. Next thing, he was demanding more milk than he was getting.

They had tried the priest, and they had tried praying, and they decided they would take him to the doctor. The nearest doctor was in Tuam, Dr. Bodkin. So, the father carried the baby on his back, and as he was passing Knockma, beyond Caherlistrane, the baby, the handicapped baby, began to get free of him, spoke for the first time and said, *"Tá mo bhean is mo chlann thuas ansin"*—"My wife and my family are up there."

And the father said to him, "Well, in that case, off you go with them," and let him down, and he ran off.

They knew 'twas a changeling then. But where the real baby was isn't answered in that story.

Now, my grandfather would *really* swear to this, because I remember putting the questions to him.

In a society where child mortality was very high and belief in the otherworldly was strong, it was only to be expected that people would account for many of the sudden deaths or wasting diseases of children through fairy abductions.

But were the resulting stories all just the product of vivid imagination?

We will probably never know for certain. All we can do is note the details and estimate the probability (or lack of it) for ourselves.

In the second story above, note that the changeling speaks Irish. This was commonly believed of the fairies, that Irish was—and is—their native language; and that he should run off to join his family on Knockma would hardly be surprising, for it is reputedly the burial place of Maeve, mythical queen of Connacht (from which it derives its name) and the seat of Finnbheara, leader of the Connacht fairies.

"This woman, she had a sister, an' didn't the sister die—a girl of seven or eight years of age, in her health. An' it wasn't an ordinary death, at all. She started to wither, an' she was left with a little, withered thing, oh, a real little witchy thing inside in the bed."
DRUMLINE, MARCH 13, 1997

A Tailor Saves a Baby

THERE WAS A TAILOR and his mother that was doing a lot o' chauffeuring around and catering when a baby was going to be born in the house next door.

Eventually the parents o' the baby said that since the tailor and his mother done such a lot o' work for them, 'twas right for 'em to ask 'em to be sponsors for the little baby. So they asked 'em, anyway, and the two—the mother and the tailor—was delighted when they were asked.

Anyway, the tailor was an awful man for gambling, and he'd go far and near for a game o' cards. But this night, anyway, when he was coming back 'twas very late. He had to pass near the house where the little baby was that he stood for, and when he was coming back he heard the child crying.

He stood and thought to himself, "Why's the child crying at this hour o' the night?"

There was no light in the house, and no commotion. Curiosity overpowered him. He said he wouldn't go home until he'd see what was wrong. So he came up to the house. And when he was coming in around the corner o' the house, he seen a fairly tall woman standing by the kitchen window. And when she saw him she vanished away. He couldn't see her at all then. But he went over to the window, to see what she was doing at the window. And the kitchen window was wide open. There was another one inside and she had the child, and she was handing him out, as she thought, to the woman outside. But when she handed him out 'twas the tailor standing there. The tailor took the child, put him under his coat, and away he went home. He went in, told his mother what had happened, and asked would she nurse the child along with him until morning.

"God," she says, "why wouldn't we? Is it the little baby we stood for a month ago?"

So they put down a big fire, she warmed milk for him and gave him a great old feed. And the two of 'em sat down by the fire and minded him until morning.

But when the morning came, and the day broke, the tailor said to the mother, "I'll go back over, now, to the house, until I see what's going on."

So he did. And when he was coming very near the house, he

heard the hullabaloo and the crying, and the first thing that he heard was, "How the hell would we have any luck with our little child when we put a little bastard of a tailor standing for him?"

So, begod, in the tailor walked and he asked what was the commotion.

"Oh, what is it," she says, "only look at our little baby there in the cot and he's stone dead."

"That's not your baby at all. I have your baby high and dry beyond. My mother is minding him, and he's well fed and well looked after. That's not your baby at all," he said.

They sent for the priest. And the priest came and read over the cot. And what appeared after a few minutes when he was reading? Only a broom o' heather.* The priest got the tongs, fixed up the fire, caught the broom o' heather, and shoved it into the fire. And up it went, up the chimney in flames.

And the priest said, "You'll never get any trouble from that again. That'll never come around this village again."

And they went over to the tailor's house and brought home their child. He grew up to be a big strong man after.

I got that from my mother. She was from Ballyhogan in Barefield.

But, children being taken that way, I believe 'twas a common thing at that time. There was a lot about fairy business going on at that time. There was. But, sure, they had to believe it when they seen it.

---

*So, the broom o' heather is all that was ever there; the fairies made it appear like a baby.

Even though this story comes from seventy miles away from where the changeling story on the previous page occurred, the details are remarkably similar, e.g., the handing out of the child by a woman to a woman in each case, the threat of burning, the flight up the chimney.

But in this version, we have the added detail of how the fairies can change the shape of ordinary things for their own purposes. The priest is not fooled, though, and uses his (in this case) superior power to make certain that the banishment of the changeling is permanent.

"Will the fairies be saved the Last Day, do you think, will they?
Well, if they do, all them people they brought'll be saved,
too, won't they? So, I hope they will."
LISCANNOR, JULY 17, 1999

The Fairies Get Set
on a Whole Family

I DO PRAY for my own two people that the fairies brought. And when I have prayed for 'em—I don't know if I'm doing right or wrong—I'm offering up the prayers also to save the fairies that brought my people. The Last Day. By saying that, d'you see, they could be saved.

My uncle was working in Doonagore quarries above, just a mile up from here. You can go no farther. Doonagore quarries was working at full swing over a hundred years ago. The United Stone Firm Company Limited, George Watson and Company Limited—they was working there over twenty years. They was transporting the flagstones for floors and footpaths, sending 'em out to Liverpool and Manchester from Liscannor dock below.

So, this man, my uncle, was working in it. He was working inside in a forge. Where you have a quarry working like that, you have to have chisels and pickaxes, and bars—sharpening, you see. Because the stone does blunt 'em. And 'tisn't every man that's able to sharpen 'em, you see. He can sharpen 'em, all right, but the bother is to temper 'em.

So, this man came in one day and he said, "John, you're getting so big and so strong and such a fine man, they'll have to knock the door o' the forge for you soon,"—that he was getting big, and good-looking, and heavy, you know.

But, 'twas his last day working in the quarry. He got sick the day after. He never put "God bless" on the man. No, never put "God bless" on him. No.

He was sick the following day, and they didn't know. They thought 'twas flu or something he had. He was there for days upon days, and they had two or three doctors at him, and they couldn't find what was wrong.

Eventually, a woman came up there from Liscannor. She had

an ass and baskets and she was selling fish. She was around a few weeks before that, and she had heard about his sickness.

"How's the patient today?" says she.

"If 'tis anything," says the father, "'tis worse he is since you was here last."

"Why don't you go down to Liscannor?" she said. "There's a great priest there. He has great power. He can cure people."

"Begod," he said, "I'd go to Limerick if I thought there was a priest there that could cure him."

"Oh, there is," she said.

So he went on his horse and saddle down to the priest. And he told the priest about his son.

"I can't go up today," the priest said, "but I'll go up in the morning. Where are you living?"

He told him. This priest used to be coming to Moymore church below here. So he did come up the following day. And he came in.

"God bless," he said. "Where is the patient?"

"He's down in that room," they said.

So the priest went down and he closed the door. He was below in the room for about ten minutes talking to him. Then, he came up.

"I have to clear the house now," he said. "I'll have to put you out in that cow house above, the far up cow house near the road. Go in that. And don't come out till I call you. I can't perform the cure while you're in the building. And bear in mind, this cure is only for seven years," he said. "Seven years."

"If 'twas only for a year, itself," says the father, "I appreciate that very much. Thank you very much, Father," says he.

So, he went in, and whatever he was doing below in the room, or whatever way he cured him I don't know, but he called 'em in.

"The cure is done now," he said. "As I already told you, 'tis only for seven years."

"That's grand," says the father.

"How many cows have you?" he asked the father.

I don't know if 'twas five or six, or four, or whatever he had.

"You'll put the very best o' them cows, now, in that cow house above tonight," he said. "If you put the worst of 'em in it, I'll be dead in the morning. You think o' that."

"Oh, God," says the father, "I wouldn't do a thing like that at all. If she was worth a thousand pounds, I'll put her in." So he did. And the cow was stone dead in the morning.

"You'll follow me down, now," says he. "Gimme a chance until I'm below for a half an hour or three-quarters. Follow me down on the horse and saddle and I'll give you blessed Augustines to put on his neck, to wear for the seven years." They're something in the form of scapulars, or something.

So, he brought up the blessed Augustines and he put 'em on his neck.

That man was up working the following day—working! Back to the forge again.

Unfortunately, the seven years fell on a May Eve, when the fairies are out, you see.

So, he said to his father and mother, "I think I'll go up to Seán Pheadair's for a few pints tonight"—that was the pub in Doolin.

"Oh, in the honor o' God," they said, "whatever you do, don't do that."

"Oh, my God," says the mother, "don't do that. Are you aware your seven years are up?" says she. "Don't go out."

Well, if they tied him with a rope they couldn't keep him at home. And 'twas an evil thought, the worst thought he ever thought.

His mother, she didn't sleep one wink o' the night until he came in about two o'clock.

Now, d'you see, when you go up to Doonagore you can't go no higher. You're seven hundred feet over sea level. If you go fifty yards farther than Doonagore quarries you're going down, down, down, down, down, downhill. Or to Doolin downhill. Or to Lisdoonvarna downhill. So, with the drink he took, and the climbing up all the hills, I suppose he lied down at the side o' the road in some dry spot—there was a small lake at one side—lied down and went off to sleep in it, with the drink.

The mother heard him coming in about two or three o'clock in the morning, and she let him alone. She thought he was asleep below in the bed. She stole down, and she put her hand in his bosom, inside his shirt, to his skin. *Tanan 'on diabhal,** wasn't

*Literally, "your soul to the Devil."

the Augustines gone! They were taken out o' his neck. The seven years was up.

She came back to her husband and she said, "He's swept."

That man never rose the following morning out o' that bed. And for days after he didn't rise out of it.

So, his brother—my father—used to go up to Doonagore quarries; there was two great houses up there you'd go on *ragairne*. One of 'em was Darcy's and the other was Davoren's. There was an old man over here, he was old Seán Finn. He's dead for years. He was out in the Bush in Australia, this man, and nothing in the world'd frighten him.

He was here one night saying the rosary with the family on their knees—my father was gone up to Davoren's on *ragairne*—when there was a tin can o' gravel flung against the door from outside. He got up off o' his knees and he went out like a bullet.

"Don't think," says he, "if you have that man in the room taken, you're going to make a mockery o' the rosary. We'll say the rosary in spite o' you." Oh, he was right vexed and cross to 'em. Wasn't he a great man!

After the rosary he asked for my father, where was he.

"He's above on *ragairne* at Davoren's."

"Tell him to mind himself. They're after him, too," says he. He knew the fairies had the man above in the room, you see.

So, when my father came down they told him that.

And d'you know what he had to do to save himself, do you? An unusual thing he had to do. Every time he'd make his water, he'd have to put a cross o' the water on his forehead, a cross o' the urine. They couldn't bring him then, d'you see.

And the man in the bed, they buried him and there was no more about him.

But wait'll you hear what happened to his sister, the sister o' the man that the fairies brought, that was down in that room. She was married above at Doonagore quarries.

Now, her brother was dead a good while by this time and another sister was going up to the sister at the quarries—to some party that was on this Saturday night.

She went out that gate outside there. She turned to her right, and she went over a quarter of a mile to the crossroad. She turned up to her left. 'Twas a mile up exactly from this place. She was only gone up a half a mile o' the road when this woman came out o' the blue and walked by her side, never before seen her.

She said good night to the woman, o' course. No answer. "Good night," again. No answer. "Good night," again. No answer. Oh, she was getting very lonely then, the little girl. Just when they came on top o' the hill above she said, "Good night," again, and no answer.

There was a stream o' water crossing the road above, under the road, a kind of a wide gullet. D'you ever hear they can't cross the water? She was coming to that stream o' water and the woman looked at her and tapped her three times on the shoulder.

That girl went in above to that party and sat down. And the first one that asked her to dance was her boyfriend. No, she refused him. She told him she was sick.

Her brother had to come home with her from that party at twelve o'clock in the night. And she never rose out o' the bed, until she died.

So, her boyfriend, he used go over from Doonagore quarries. There's an old road going over, a bog at both sides of it; 'tis over a mile long. 'Twould bring you out over on a branch that's coming out o' the road that's going past the Cliffs o' Moher. And when you come out on the branch road, if you continue on straight ahead, you was out on the tour road. That's the way he used to go to Saint Brigid's Well. He'd have a few drinks at the weekend.

He went over this night, and 'twas one o'clock when he left the pub. Didn't he hear the music inside at the Cliffs o' Moher, and see the light. Heard the music and seen the light. Sure, when a man has a few drinks, when he's heated up, he'll go anywhere if he hears amusement or light or music and dance, won't he? He went in. I declare to the Almighty God, he saw her dancing within at the Cliffs o' Moher. And she was only dead a month. She was dancing with a man he didn't know at all, a fairy man. There was fairies, you see. Fairies dancing in it. He nearly got a heart attack.

Well, I'm telling you, he wasn't long coming home and never again went to Saint Brigid's Well. He got as sober as a judge. Oh, that's the truest talk.

Lots o' people wouldn't believe them things at all, but, sure, her sister wouldn't go telling a lie, would she? And 'tis her sister told me about her brother, too.

"The fairies done a very cruel turn on us," she said, "to take my brother and sister, to take the two of 'em together."

There isn't a shadow of a doubt about that; 'tis a right true story. A right true story. 'Tis.

But there was one thing baffling me. I'll tell you. My father never told me a word o' them things. No. But when we were young, he did something that gave me a suspicion of it. He got a piece o' that strong cord and he got a lot of old rusty horseshoe nails. Old rusty nails, you see, that came out of horses' shoes, they'd be short. He bended them in and made a ring of 'em and put the cord through 'em, and hung 'em around our necks. Don't you know why he done it? The fairies couldn't touch you then, you see!

The fear o' God was in his heart over what happened to his brother and his sister. He was sure the fairies'd bring us, too. Maybe he was right. Because there's no doubt but the fairies had some set on our family.

Even his father, now, he came into that yard one night with a horse and trap. 'Twould be about twelve o'clock in the night, I suppose. He took the trap from the horse, took off the harness and he was going over around the turn o' the gable o' the house with the horse, and a piece of iron, like a piece of a band of a cart, got tangled in the horse's legs. Oh, a big gash o' light went out of it. He couldn't know for the life of him what 'twas, because there was nothing o' the sort ever around that place. Where did it come out of?

He went out with a lantern—a lantern and a candle they had in them days. 'Twas no good. Searched in the morning. Found nothing.

His father went to Ennis with the horse and trap the

following morning. And that horse broke her leg on the road below around Inagh, without anything coming before her. What do you think o' that? Broke the leg on the road! Hadn't they some set on our family after that, the fairies, hadn't they?! Hadn't they some set on 'em?

It is obvious from the tone of this story that the teller is deeply in sympathy with what he speaks of. His very opening admission, that he prays for the salvation of the fairies, is something I have never come across from anyone else in twenty-eight years of collecting folklore. And the description of the carrying of his uncle which follows, with its demonstration of a "powerful" priest at work, the cured man's carelessness on May Eve, the seeming contempt of the fairies for a family at prayer, how one may protect oneself against them (with urine), all reads graphically and credibly—as does the account of the carrying of his aunt. He is in no doubt that the silent woman who accosts her on her way to the party is one of the Other Crowd; she does not cross the stream of water. And after her three (!) touches it is only a matter of time before the aunt sickens and dies, i.e., is carried.

But her being seen dancing with a fairy man at the Cliffs of Moher a month later—how are we to take this? As the drunken imaginings of a broken-hearted boyfriend? Or as it is here offered, "a right true story." Once again, the reader must be the judge of that.

And his conviction that the whole family was being victimized by the fairies over several generations might seem amusing if it were merely asserted. But when incidents are described which give it some substance . . . !

"I heard of a girl that got clothes long ago near a spring well.
An', Christ, clothes were very scarce, so she put 'em on, an'
they fitted her, an' she wore 'em. But she died a very short
time after. They said 'twas the fairies that done it."

MILTOWN, JUNE 27, 1999

A Rash Intervention Condemns Woman

THERE WAS A MAN not far from here, and his wife was going
in the outhouse one day, in the cabin. And this bowl, now, it
came out o' the blue; 'twas put into her hand.

She brought it in, left it on the dresser. And a neighbor came
in—the same man that was here the night that my uncle was
carried, that went out when the gravel was thrown up against
the door when they were saying the rosary. She told him what
happened.

"Where's the bowl? Where is it?" says he.

She took it out o' the dresser for him.

He brought it out and made forty-five pieces of it against
the wall.

'Twas no length after till the wife died.

And this man above at Doonagore quarries used to come
down on *ragairne* in the nights. 'Twas in the month o' November
or December he came down one night. 'Twas a moonlight
night—oh, you'd see pins fifty yards away. Didn't he see her
standing in the door o' the cabin—and she dead! Seen her

standing, at the door o' the cabin. The cabin was right on from the gable o' the house going up and down, north and west, and he had only this length to the dresser to go, now, to the door o' the house. And he seen her.

But, just as he was taking the knob o' the door, he gave a side-glance, and she was gone.

He went in, and sat down. He didn't say much after going in, at all.

"By God," says Seán Finn to him, "you're in no form tonight, Pádraic. You have no talk."

"Ah," says he, "I'm not feeling that well at all, now."

He never told the story that he saw the man's wife, that he saw her standing in the door. The fairies brought her, d'you see. That was a fairy woman, d'you see, that put the bowl into her hand. And maybe, if he hadn't broke that bowl, she could be living.

From this story it is clear that the action of a man who on one occasion may be commended for his swift action, on another may be a cause of disaster. For as the teller says in his final sentence, if the bowl hadn't been broken the woman might not have been taken——by the fairies.

It seems pointless to look for a motive for the woman's abduction. The Other Crowd wanted her for their own mysterious purposes; that is all. In fact, except that the narrator is so definite that it is the fairies who have carried her, this story could well be read as a ghost story. Which demonstrates once more how difficult it is to distinguish between both of these worlds in the Irish mind.

*"They were very good to you, an' very nice to you, an' harmless
to you, if you were okay. But if you got involved with 'em
in any shape or form, the other thing could happen."*
DRUMLINE, OCTOBER 17, 1992

*Unbeliever Released
from Fort . . . Barely!*

THERE WAS A MAN, Tom Lynch, and he lived behind here.
He used to go on his *cuaird* in the nighttime, and he used to pass
this fort. And there was always a mighty rally of music and song
going on in it.

One night, anyway, he said to the lads in the house where he
was on *cuaird*, "By God, d'you know lads, you should come with
me tonight."

"Why?" they said.

"Well, that fort that's over there," he said, "I've it passed for
the last five or six nights, and there's music and song and dance
and everything. They're having a mighty time there."

"And why don't you go in to 'em?"

So this fellow was in the crowd.

"Listen," says he, "'tis in your nerves it is. You dreamt of it."

"No. 'Tis reality," says the other man.

"By Christ, I'll go with you tonight," he said. So he went with him and they came out straight at the fort, and when they did, this small black man came out and he caught the man by the cape o' the coat.

He said, "You're a disbeliever. You're like Doubting Thomas. You have to see the thing to believe it. Come on in," he said. "We'll show you what's going on here."

Sure, the man got an awful shock.

"I won't bring that man that's with you at all," he said, "because he's a very holy man,"—and he was a very holy man. He used go to communion and everything, and send off money to foreign missions and all that.

"I have nothing to do with him," he said. "But I have to look after you."

That man was held inside that place for a week! And 'tis unknown what he went through. When he came out you could hardly know him. But they released him after a week, and I'm telling you, the man behind here said he had a different story when he came out.

They were dancing and singing in there, he said. And one night there was a whole crowd of 'em round about, and this man was in there with a red cap. And every one of 'em got a bowl o' soup.

So this man in charge of 'em all, the king of 'em, I s'pose, he said to him, "There's a man there, now, and you have to pick out this man. If you aren't able to pick out this man from the crowd that's drinking a bowl o' soup, you'll never be able to leave this place."

God, he put the man in an awful hold.

"I'll do my best," says he.

So then, he got a bit of a tip from one o' the boys that was inside. "D'you know how you'll know him?" he said.

"I don't," says the man. "Sure, 'tis a puzzle."

"'Tisn't," says he. "He's wearing a red cap and he's supping his soup with a noise."

So, he walked over to this man and he says, "There, he's there."

"How'd you know that?" says the king. Oh, he was mad. Mad. I s'pose they were looking forward to keeping him, you see.

He didn't tell 'em, though, that 'twas one o' the lads inside that told him. The lads, they were people that were carried, o' course.

The king said to him then, "Go on. You can go. But you're the lucky man you're not staying here with us. And 'tis all your own fault. The man you was with, he passed here several nights, and we were singing and dancing here, and he knew 'twas going on. But you was a disbeliever. It just goes to show you that you did the Doubting Thomas on it and that's why you was picked up. Go on, now. You're a lucky man."

So, he was let go.

Being a mocker, a disbeliever, where the fairies were concerned could have serious consequences, as the Doubting Thomas in question here discovers. That his lesson was a harsh one is hinted at briefly, but clearly: "When he came out (of the fort) you could hardly know him." That he escaped at all was due more to good fortune than to any desire on the part of the fairies to release him. But we may be sure it served as a salutary example to all other potential scoffers to tread carefully.

"There's no way out if they turn on you.
There's no back door. If you're caught, you're caught."
DRUMLINE, SEPTEMBER 19, 2001

The Shanaglish Weaver

DURING THE FAMINE TIMES, some places got a terrible clearing out. This parish here, Shanaglish, wasn't the worst hit, but 'twas bad enough—about half the people died, or emigrated. And among those that died was the local weaver. That was no small thing in them days, because it wasn't like today, where you can walk into a shop and buy whatever clothes you want, there and then. No. At that time you had to get your wool spun into thread, then have that woven into cloth, and after that, the tailor'd make whatever clothes you wanted out of it. Different times, entirely!

Their weaver died, anyway, and that left 'em in an awful state, because now they had to walk to Gort, five miles away, at a time when they could hardly stand, with the hunger.

It looked bad for 'em, one misfortune down on top of another. Then, about two months after their weaver died this stranger came on the road, a small man with a big pack on his back. They saw him coming and they were afraid of him.

Why wouldn't they be? He might be carrying the cholera or some other disease. Remember, more people died o' cholera than starvation during the Famine. They stopped him—but kept well away from him—and asked him who was he, where was he from, what did he want. He was from up north, he said—someplace they never even heard of. But when he told 'em he was a weaver they wanted to hear no more.

"Just the man we're looking for. You're welcome." And that was that.

A good man at his trade he was, too. It was only when he started work that they saw how poor their own weaver was. The cloth that man used to make shirts, say, 'twould be like the canvas you'd use for the sail of a ship. You'd want thick skin to put up with it! But this new man, he could turn out any kind o' cloth you wanted, thick or thin, soft or hard. And he'd weave little designs into it, too—little patterns, you know—if you asked him.

In no time at all the word went out about him, how good he was. And people started coming to him from miles around. He was working in a stable for a while, but not for too long. The local men, they built a house for him—a small cabin, indeed, mud walls, two rooms and thatched. But 'twas fine for a single man like him.

Things went on like that for six months or so, a queue o' people to his door at all hours of the day. He was making money hand over fist—and giving a good service to the parish, too.

But there was one thing nagging at his mind all that time. You see, the local women were feeding him, but he took it into his mind that he'd rather be independent, able to feed himself.

So he started to make inquiries about renting out a plot o' ground that he could plant spuds in. That should have been very easy, you might say. But no matter where he asked around the parish he always got the same answer: "Sorry. We'd love to oblige you but we can't."

And at last he got so disgusted by all the refusals that he said, "So that's all you think o' me! Here I am for all the past months, making the best o' cloth for you, and this is the thanks I get. Well, if that's the way of it, I'll go someplace I'll be appreciated."

He made to collect his things and go, but they stopped him.

"No! Look, you have it all wrong. It isn't that we don't want to give you the ground for a garden. Not at all! But we haven't it to spare. You can see how small our bits o' farms are."

He had to admit that. But he was still in a temper when one of 'em suggested that he should go and talk to Mick Murphy, the biggest farmer in the parish.

"Try him. He has the best part o' sixty acres. If he can't spare a half acre for you 'tis a poor story entirely."

And he did that, went to Murphy's door and offered a fair price for the rent of a garden for a year—in cash, too. Murphy wasn't so willing at first, but when he saw the gold he changed his mind quick enough. I s'pose that's why he was well off in the first place; he had a sharp eye for money.

"All right," he said, took the money and shook the weaver's hand. "You have a bargain. Come on, and I'll show you your garden."

He took the weaver around the back o' his house, pointed up the field.

"There you are," he said. And what was it that he pointed out—only a fairy fort!

I s'pose he thought he was being very funny entirely. He had the money, and there he was now offering a fort for a garden—a thing he knew well wouldn't be taken by any Irishman in his right senses.

But he was wrong. The weaver didn't blink an eye, only looked at it and nodded.

"That's fine," said he. "I'll go into Gort today and buy a spade and enough seed potatoes. Thanks very much for your kindness, Mr. Murphy."

I can tell you, Murphy was left standing there with his mouth hanging! What kind of a man was this weaver? Set a garden in a fort? The like of it was never heard before.

He went to Gort anyway, just like he said, and o' course the word got out that he was going to dig the fort. People didn't believe it, but they gathered around all the same when he came back from town, and watched him. Sure enough, he had the spade and the seed potatoes. And he made no delay, only went up the field to the fort to get started. They still didn't take him serious. But when they saw him throwing off his coat, spitting on his hands, they knew then he was in earnest.

'Twas then that one of 'em stepped in, held up his hand.

"What kind of a man are you, at all, or where are you from, that you have no fear o' taking the roof off o' the fairies' house? How long d'you expect to live?"

The weaver only laughed, and looked at him like he was some kind of a fool.

"Fairies? Where I'm from there's no fairies. But if you have 'em here I'll tell you this: I'll take the skin off of 'em with this spade if they interfere with me."

'Twas hard to talk sense to a man like that. There was nothing they could do, only let him at it. But they weren't there while he was digging it. They blessed themselves and went off about their business, in case, maybe, the Good People might think they were in on it, too. Would you blame 'em!

He planted his garden anyway, set his spuds, and kept on with his weaving. And nothing happened, even though all the neighbors were expecting the worst from day to day. Time passed. The stalks came up. And remember, now, in them years the first thing people used to look out for was the leaves o' the new plants. 'Cause if they had black spots on 'em there was another year's blight coming, and more hunger.

But there was no spots on any one o' the plants in that fort. They grew up green, lovely and healthy-looking. And you know yourself how high potato stalks grow, don't you? About four feet. Well, these ones grew that much. And then five feet. Then six feet. Seven feet!

The neighbors spent more time there outside the fort look-ing in, more interested in his spuds than their own.

So the summer passed away. The stalks began to wither. And at last it came time to dig the spuds. I can tell you, the morning he turned up with the spade, every one o' the neighbors were there. All he did was salute 'em as if 'twas any ordinary day. And I s'pose he thought 'twas.

But not for long. 'Cause as soon as he started trying to dig he found that he couldn't. No matter how much he leaned on the spade he couldn't turn the sod. 'Twas like there'd be rocks there—but there couldn't be. Hadn't he dug it earlier on, when he was planting the spuds!

They all thought 'twas weak he was getting, or something like that. But no one made any offer to help him, all the same. He kept at it, anyway, until at last he turned up this . . . this thing that looked like a spud, all right, but 'twas about twice as big as one o' them pumpkins the children have at Halloween. They looked at it.

"Holy God, but what's that?" says Murphy.

Whatever it was, 'twas perfect—no blight, no scabs, nothing.

And the next one was the same. And the next. And the next. They couldn't understand it at all. Never saw anything like 'em in their lives.

Now, when you're digging spuds with a spade, you're bound to cut some of 'em. But there's no need to waste 'em. All you do with those ones is use 'em first, before they rot. And he was bound to cut some o' the ones in this garden, they were so big. He was only a small distance down the first ridge when the spade sliced a chunk out o' one o' these huge spuds.

And what do you think . . . it started bleeding! As red as if he cut his own hand.

The crowd outside the fort took one good look, blessed themselves, and left in a hurry. They were certain sure now that that garden was going to come to no good end.

But he didn't seem to care a bit. He took up the piece o' the spud that was cut, looked at it, smelt it, then threw it from him. He thought 'twas some local variety. No more than that.

He cut several more of 'em too, and threw 'em aside the same way, just like they were a thing o' nothing. And when he finished digging for the day he collected up the damaged spuds and brought 'em back to the house for his supper. He was very pleased with himself, and why wouldn't he be, with a good day's work done?

But the following morning, around eleven o' clock, a man from Coole—that's over two miles the other side o' Gort—arrived at the house to collect a piece o' cloth. He knocked. But no answer. He knocked again, and still no reply. So, he was wondering what he'd do. 'Twas more than six miles of a walk home, and if he arrived empty-handed to his wife he'd have a bit of explaining to do. So he knocked again.

Still nothing.

He was wondering what should he do when one o' the neighbors passed by on the road outside.

"What's wrong?" he asked.

"Ah, he told me he'd be here at this time today, but I'm here knocking for the last ten minutes and there's no trace of him."

"That's not like him," said the neighbor. "He's very particular about being here when he says he will."

"Where is he, then?"

"Maybe he's out the back. Did you try there?"

He didn't, he said. So they took a look.

No good.

"Did you try opening the door?" said the neighbor.

"No. When he didn't answer my knock I thought he mustn't be in."

"We'll check, anyway," the neighbor said. "If he went anywhere I'd nearly have noticed him going."

He tried the latch, and when he did, the door swung in. But . . . but . . . talk about a stink that came out against 'em! It nearly knocked 'em. They staggered back, holding their noses.

"Merciful God, what's that?" said the man from Coole.

"I don't know, but 'tis nothing good. I'll get the priest, quick."

He did that—they were near the presbytery—and in five minutes he came, with his bag, prepared for the worst. But when he stepped into the kitchen, he staggered back from the smell.

"Holy God," he said, "is there someone dead?"

And 'twasn't easy to frighten that same man. All during the worst days o' the Famine he was visiting houses where people were dying o' starvation or the cholera, and some o' the things he saw, they'd frighten even the toughest of men—like whole families dead and rotten, or eaten by the rats.

But when he set foot in the weaver's house that morning he knew that 'twas something else entirely was wrong.

He held his handkerchief over his nose and looked around him. No one there. He pushed in the door o' the bedroom and there, stretched on the bed, was the weaver, every bit of him twisted—hands, legs, mouth, and his eyes turned back in his head. He was still alive, though, because as soon as he saw the priest he tried to talk. But all that came out o' him was a kind of a croak, *Agkkhhh!*

"Go for the doctor, quick! Run!" said the priest, and opened his bag. "I'll do what I can, but . . . I don't know will it be enough."

They had to go as far as Gort, and by the time they arrived back with the doctor the priest had done the best he could. The weaver was still alive, anyway.

But the doctor took one quick look at him and said, "I can do little for him. He'll have to be brought in to Gort to the workhouse. They might be able to do something more for him there."

That was done. And when they arrived at the door, the matron looked at their patient, then got the horrible smell.

"What's that?" she said.

"I don't know, any more than you do," said the doctor. "Take him in, wash him, and put him to bed."

They did that, washed him with carbolic soap. But a few minutes after they took him out o' the water and dried him, the smell was as bad as ever.

"We can't put him in with the other patients," said the matron. "He'd stifle 'em."

So they put him under the stairs on a straw mattress, and that's where he was when the surgeon from Galway arrived the next morning. You see, this surgeon used to visit the different workhouses once a week or so—Ballinasloe, Loughrea, Kinvara, and the rest—and the following day 'twas Gort's turn.

But when he looked at the man on the mattress under the stairs all he did was cock his nose. No fear he was going to touch a case that was stinking like that. All he did was to rummage around inside his bag, and took out a jar of ointment.

"Here. Rub this to him three times a day."

That's all he said. No more. I s'pose he didn't care whether the man lived or died. You know yourself how much an Irishman's life was worth in them days—less than a dog's!

He went off about his business, but the matron wasn't going to do the dirty job herself. No fear, when she had nurses to do it!

She called one of 'em, a young country girl, and gave her the ointment.

"Rub that to the lad there under the stairs three times a day for as long as it lasts."

The girl did what she was told, o' course. In the middle o' that day she took him his dinner, whatever it was—not much in the workhouse, you can be sure!—and when he was finished it, she rubbed the ointment to him. But as she was doing it, over his shoulders, arms, chest, she noticed something strange: His skin was peeling off, just like you'd get a bad dose o' sunburn. She went to the matron and told her about it.

"I know nothing about that," was the answer she got. "Just do what you were told."

So she did.

That evening she arrived back with his supper, but he was lying back on the mattress. She called him. No move. So she put her hand under his shoulders, rose him up to feed him. But when she did, every bit of his hair stayed on the pillow. She ran to the matron, told her story.

"I know nothing about that," she said. "Do what you were told to. That's all."

She did. But as she rubbed that ointment on him, every hair on him fell out—arms, chest, any part of him that she touched, even his eyebrows and eyelashes.

The following morning she came back with his breakfast, not knowing what to expect. He was stretched. She helped him up on the pillow, but he couldn't eat. Instead o' that, he started to spit. And what he spat out was teeth, a whole mouthful of 'em, one after the other.

She dropped him and ran to the matron again, but she got the same reception as before. She didn't want to know anything about it.

"Do what the surgeon said! That's all."

The girl had to obey orders, I s'pose, but she was frightened. You can be sure o' that.

And it wasn't over yet, because when dinnertime came she went again with her tray and jar of ointment. And like before, he couldn't get up. She helped him, o' course, but when he tried to hold the spoon she noticed that he had no fingernails on either hand! She was just about to run for help when—I don't know why—she thought to lift up the blanket at the bottom o' the bed. And there she saw that every one o' his toenails had fallen out, too. They were all there together on the mattress!

I don't know whether she told the matron about that or not, but what I do know is that when she went back that evening with his supper, the poor man was dead. Stiff and cold.

The news that he was dead came back to Shanaglish in a few hours. So his neighbors got together and decided that they couldn't let him be buried in the workhouse graveyard, whatever else. To be buried there—like a dog, maybe even without a coffin—was the lowest any man could go. If you were buried there 'twas an admission that you hadn't a single friend left in this world.

So, they got a coffin made, collected him and brought him back here to Shanaglish.

But there was one problem: He had no grave. Because he was a stranger, I s'pose. So, the only place he could be buried was here in this *cillín*.

The grave was dug; the priest was there; everything was ready. But, when the prayers were being said, while the coffin was being let down, one o' the people standing there, he pointed at the coffin and said to the man next to him, "Wasn't he the man that said, that day above in the fort, that he'd take the skin off o' the fairies with the spade if they interfered with him?"

"'Twas him, all right."

There was no more said. The same thing was in every one o' their minds: He thought he'd take the skin off them, but 'twas they took it off o' him—and not just his skin, but teeth, hair, nails, until they took the very life from him.

And how many fairy forts were interfered with in this parish since? Not one. If you don't believe me, do your own inquiring.

If, even after all the examples to the contrary that this book presents, there should still be a lingering feeling that the Irish fairies are cute little creatures with transparent wings and sparkling wands, kindly leaving money under children's pillows for fallen-out teeth, this final story may dispel that feeling. Its message is direct, clear, and all too horrible in its detail: One who knowingly interferes with fairy property must be prepared for the consequences. And such consequences sometimes throw our own carelessly used words painfully back in our faces—a proof that where the Other Crowd are concerned, our opinions are best kept to ourselves.

In this age of wonderful technology, when the impossible is almost within our grasp in so many fields of endeavor, how ironic it is that these foregoing stories, from a technologically far more backward era, should still have that one vital lesson to impart to us, without which all our technology will get us nowhere in the end: respect.

For no matter whether the fairies are seen metaphorically or as real beings inhabiting their own real world, a study of them shows us that those who came before us (and many of that mindset still survive) realized that we are—no matter what we may think to the contrary—very little creatures, here for a short time only ("passing through," as the old people say) and that we have no right to destroy what the next generation will most assuredly need to also see itself through.

If only we could learn that lesson, maybe someday we might be worthy of the wisdom of those who knew that to respect the Good People is basically to respect yourself.

Acknowledgments

ALL OF THE FOLLOWING shared their stories with me. That some of them have since died to this world is merely an interruption; I am certain that they are still telling, but now to an otherworldly audience, large, more comprehending, one to which fairy stories, in particular, must be the essence of everyday life, just as they once were in Ireland.

So, my sincere thanks to (in alphabetical order): Jimmy Armstrong, Martin "Junior" Crehan, Matthew Feheny, Pat Fogarty, Paddy Guthrie, Tom Hickey, Michael Kelliher, Francie Kennelly, Jack Killourhy, Paddy Lawlor, Jack Leahy, Robert Lee, Flann Liddy, John Lynch, Mary McMahon, Tom McMahon, Jim McNamara, Joe Murphy, Patrick Murphy, Michael Noone, Johnny O'Connor, Michael O'Dwyer, P. J. O'Halloran, Siobhán Ní Shúilleabháin, Michael Reidy, Dan Ryan, Paddy Troy, Jack Walsh, Jack Woulfe.

Yet, all of their stories might have remained quietly waiting for God only knows how long on my tape shelves were it not for the interest of Ken and Carolyn Green. Her diligence, especially, has brought this collection together, has shepherded its many parts to the light of day. If only I could be so hard-working, so organized, hardly anything would be impossible!

CAROLYN GREEN thanks Eddie Lenihan, first and foremost, for his willingness to share his treasury of stories, for the delightful process of bringing them to publication, and for carefully opening a window to that otherworld; our agent, Tom Grady, for taking a leap of faith with us; Mitch Horowitz, our editor at Tarcher, for quickly grasping the essence of this book and seeing it through; Mick Bolger for patient hours of decoding Irish words and explaining a bit of the "Irish mind"; Ken Green, husband and partner on every level, for never wavering in his confidence that this project could happen; and Chögyam Trungpa Rinpoche for transmitting a vast vision and teaching respect for the truth beyond cultural and religious boundaries.

About the Authors

Born in 1950, broadcaster, lecturer, folklorist **Eddie Lenihan** is the author of sixteen books, including poetry, railway history, children's stories, and folklore, as well as eleven audiotapes, a double CD, and a video of traditional Irish stories. His highly successful storytelling series *Ten Minute Tales* and *Storyteller* on Irish national television launched him on an international career, and today he visits many countries telling Irish tales to a constantly growing audience.

His *Tales from the Tàin* is due for publication in 2003, *Foreign Irish Tales for Children* in 2004, and *Horrors from the Roads of Ireland* in 2005. He resides in Crusheen, County Clare, Ireland.

A practicing Buddhist since the age of nine, **Carolyn Eve Green** has dedicated herself to preserving traditional wisdom in many forms of media. She has been a writer, director, and editor for theater, video, multimedia, and audio productions including the award-winning children's storytelling audio series *Secrets of the World*. She currently lives in Boulder, Colorado, and is creative director for Windhorse Productions and a director of the Golden Sun Foundation for World Culture.

Printed in the United States
by Baker & Taylor Publisher Services